JACOB'S LADDER: GABE

KATIE ASHLEY

JACOB'S LADDER
LADDER
Gabe

BY KATIE ASHLEY

Cover Photography by Lauren Perry of Perrywinkle Photography

Models: Darik and Cara Chatwin

Cover Design by Hang Le

Interior Design by Lori Jackson

WITH MY WORN, leather-bound journal balanced on my lap, I uncapped my lucky writing pen. Perched in a chair on the back porch of my sister and brother-in-law's farm, I couldn't have asked for a more picturesque place to try to write a song. With its rolling green hills, multicolored leaves adorning the trees, and the rushing waters of the creek in a distance, the scenery around me looked like something out of a Norman Rockwell painting. A gentle breeze rippled through the screens on the back porch while the sun, perched high in the cloudless blue sky, warmed my skin.

Pinching my eyes shut, I focused on the tapestry of vivid images swirling through my mind. Desperately I tried to grasp one of them, hoping against hope it would be the one that would breathe life back into my flat-lining muse, the one that would help pen a top ten single off my next album. Hell, at that point, I'd have pissed my pants with excitement over *any* song, least of all a hit. After all, it wasn't like I hadn't done it before.

Since the inception of my band, Jacob's Ladder, fifteen years ago, I had been the one in charge of songwriting. While I was a mediocre guitarist and a decent drummer, my gift was my ability to weave words into lyrics—well, it had been my gift up until the last few months when I had found myself unable to do something that had once come so easy to me.

When a dark-haired beauty entered my mind, I bit down on my lip in concentration. I searched for words of affection and admiration, the kind of descriptions people wanted to hear when it came to songs about love, the *truly, madly, deeply* type professions that captured the sea of churning emotions they experienced. Instead, my vision turned into an

X-rated one that probably would have inspired a Motley Crue or Guns N' Roses video sans the big hair and '80s spandex.

With a growl of frustration, I threw the notepad and pen to the floor before burying my head in my hands. "I'm fucked. I'm so very, very fucked."

"Correction, brother dearest. *We're* so very, very fucked," my twin, Eli, replied across from me.

"I'm fully aware of that, asshole," I snapped. Sometimes I wondered how I'd managed to share a womb with my annoying-as-hell brother without killing him. He had been a pain in my ass since we exited the womb, thriving on giving me shit since day one. For reasons unknown to me, I still managed to not only to tolerate him, but to somehow love the douche with all my heart. I couldn't have asked for a better brother or best friend.

"Hey man, don't shoot the messenger," he replied with a good-natured wink. With our dark hair, blue eyes, and muscular builds, we were practically mirror images of each other on the physical side, but Eli's reaction was an example of just one of the many personality differences between the two of us. He was always like freaking Little Orphan Annie with *The Sun Will Come Out Tomorrow* bullshit while I was a glass half empty, pit of despair kinda guy. Eli could talk to a celebrity or a homeless man with the same kind of attentiveness and appreciation while I preferred to talk as little as possible to anyone outside of my circle of family and friends.

When we visited the wards of children's hospitals, Eli was the one going full-on Patch Adams and getting the kids dissolving in giggles while I was much more content to search out one or two kids and give them my full attention.

For most of our childhood, I'd wanted to be more like him. Who wouldn't want to light up a room and have people rolling with laughter? It was only after becoming immersed in music that I discovered famous introverts like Jimi Hendrix and Prince. I figured if they had the adulation of millions of fans then it was all right to be me.

Of course, with the mood I was in that day, none of Eli's over-the-top antics or positive thinking mumbo jumbo was going to make me feel better. He'd hit a raw nerve when he'd mentioned the fact that this wasn't about songs for a solo act, but an entire band—one that was made up of my own flesh and blood.

The awareness that it wasn't just my career on the line but my brother's and sister's as well sent a familiar choking panic through me. It was one I had become all too familiar with in the last several weeks. After fifteen years of songwriting, I'd never experienced the quicksand of writer's block I currently found myself entrapped in. I'd penned my first song when I was just ten years old. Inspired by my first crush on a girl I'd met in Peru, it would have hardly sold any albums, but it had started me down the songwriting path.

Since my siblings and I had grown up immersed in music, it wasn't like I'd just gotten the idea out of left field. Our parents were missionaries who raised us off the beaten path until we were teenagers. Without TV or the internet, we'd been forced to amuse ourselves, which had led to learning to play different musical instruments. Even when I'd ditched the guitar to focus on my true love of percussion, I still continued writing songs…until the last few months.

The door of the porch screeched opened, and my baby sister, Abby, cautiously poked her blonde head out. Her blue eyes peered intently at me as she nibbled on her bottom lip. "How's it coming?"

"It's not," I grumbled.

"Maybe you need a break?" she suggested. Before I could argue that nothing short of a lobotomy was going to help me, Abby disappeared back into the house. When she returned, she came out with a pitcher of lemonade and some fresh pound cake.

Eli snorted. "Feeling domestic?"

Abby narrowed her blue eyes at him. "Yes, as a matter of fact, I am, smartass. Whenever we're off the road, I try to hone my Martha Stewart skills."

"Hey, I'm not knocking it. You know I love your cooking—reminds me of Mom's."

Eli's compliment smoothed Abby's somewhat ruffled feathers. At twenty-five, my baby sister was a pint-sized powerhouse of talent. She wasn't just the lead singer and guitarist of our band, Jacob's Ladder;

she was also the wife of Runaway Train rock star, Jake Slater. She was also an extremely hands-on mother to four-and-a-half-year-old twins, Jackson and Julia, AKA Jax and Jules, who she insisted come along on the road with us in the tricked-out, kid-friendly tour bus she and Jake owned. I'd seen her backstage with a kid on each hip, singing lullabies before she handed them off to the nanny for bedtime. With everything on her plate, I couldn't imagine how she managed to keep her shit together, least of all be a wife and mom. I was so very proud that she was my sister.

Abby sat the lemonade and the slices of cake down on the table in front of me and Eli. "Come on, take a break. Get some sugar in you to get the juices flowing."

With a ragged sigh, I handed Abby my now empty glass of vodka to pour some lemonade. "I might as well. It's not like I'm getting a damn thing done."

Abby's face shrouded with worry. "It's really bad, isn't it?"

"Honestly, it's never been this bad. Ever."

"Do you think it's the pressure from the label that's blocking you?"

"It shouldn't be. It's not like I haven't had them on my back before."

"I don't mind having a little talk with them and telling them to get off our back."

Eli and I chuckled. "Easy, killer," I warned.

"No offense, little sis, but I hardly think we would choose you if we were going to turn the dogs on the suits at the label. You're way more Chihuahua than pit bull," Eli said.

Abby swept her hands to her hips. "I can be intimidating when I want to be."

"Riiight," Eli and I replied in unison.

Rolling her eyes, Abby huffed, "Whatever." When she started to pour my lemonade, she sniffed and then recoiled slightly. "Do I smell vodka?"

"Yes, *Mother*, you do."

"It's barely noon, Gabe."

"I needed a little pick-me-up this morning."

4

"More than a pick-me-up, you need to take a shower," Eli quipped.

"Bite me."

"Did you even sleep last night?" Abby questioned softly as she handed me back my glass.

"Christ, by the way you two talk, I must look like I could get a job on as a walker on *The Walking Dead*."

Abby shook her head, sending her blonde ponytail swishing back and forth. The sight of her swinging hair reminded me of when she was a kid. *What are you playing, Gabe? Will you teach me how to play it?* When she peered up at me with her big blue eyes, I could never tell her no. She was spoiled endlessly by all of us, but I always had a special place in Abby's heart.

Although she had initially started college to become a nurse, there was never any doubt as to the musical talent Abby possessed. She was belting out tunes with an impressive vocal range before she started school. "I never said you looked bad."

"You alluded to it."

Eli grinned. "I stand by my shower comment. You stink, not to mention you look like some of the fans we see at those all-weekend rock fests."

As I shot Eli the bird, Abby said, "I'm seriously concerned about how you slept."

"Fine. I slept here and there." Whatever sleep I'd gotten hadn't been very restful. Although I'd been set up in the very lavish converted barn, I'd ended up sleeping in the hammock out in the yard. For some reason, I thought it would be romantic to sleep out under the stars, thus enabling me to pen a love song. I'd done the same thing back at home on my apartment balcony, but the only thing I'd achieved by the end of both nights was a host of mosquito bites.

Dropping down in the seat beside me, Abby sighed. "I just wish I could do something to help."

"You want to write with me?"

Abby wrinkled her nose. "I've only written songs with Jake. I'm not quite sure how I'd write love songs with my brother."

I laughed. "Well, I sure as hell didn't mean for us to write a duet."

"What about Micah? Do you think he could help?"

Abby was referring to our older brother. Along with Eli and me, Micah had been one of the founding members of Jacob's Ladder. Six years ago, he'd left the band to get married and go to seminary. Now he was working as a youth pastor at a church out in Seattle and had two kids of his own.

I shook my head. "He's busy with his own life now. Besides, the last time I wrote songs with Micah, the band had a different direction."

"That's true. Back before I came on the scene," Abby mused.

Once upon a time, my brothers and I had been Christian rockers. Shocking, huh? When Micah left the band, our new label was interested in us taking a different direction and delving more into our country sound. We'd always been far more Chris Stapleton and Florida Georgia Line type praise music than Creed. They also wanted us to have a female lead singer like Lady Antebellum, and we didn't have to look too far when it came to recruiting. After auditioning for the label, Abby left nursing school and officially became a member of Jacob's Ladder. The rest was history.

"We could always buy our music," Eli suggested.

"Hell fucking no," I practically growled before Abby had a chance to reply.

"Chill out, Gabe. It's not like I was suggesting we sacrifice a virgin on stage. Lots of bands purchase their songs."

"It's not who we are. We've always been about the music and the lyrics." It was more about the fact that it wasn't who *I* was. For as long as I could remember, part of my identity had been wrapped up in songwriting. It wasn't even the fact that I'd won two CMAs for songwriter of the year. It was that it was the one area where I would always outshine Eli; it was a talent with which he couldn't compete.

Eli gave me a knowing look. "That's true, but at the end of the day, it's not worth giving yourself a nervous breakdown over."

"Or becoming an alcoholic," Abby chimed in.

I rolled my eyes. "I had one drink, for fuck's sake. If I were an alcoholic, I would have drained the entire bottle."

The sound of a vehicle tearing down the gravel road thankfully interrupted our conversation, and I didn't have to look to see who it was. I knew it was the one and only Jake Slater, lead singer of Runaway Train and my brother-in-law. Besides, I knew it wasn't a stranger since only those who knew the code for the security gate would get down the road to Jake and Abby's farm, and as far as I knew, they weren't expecting any more guests for the weekend.

After he'd become a mega star, Jake had been forced to secure the hundred-acre property that had been in his family for over a century. While he and Abby had a place in Atlanta, their true home was the sprawling colonial farmhouse where Jake had grown up. Besides the nostalgia of his childhood, it was special to Jake because it had been a favorite of his late mother, Susan, who had passed away of cancer right after Jake and Abby started dating. Besides my brothers, I'd never known a man who was as close to his mother as Jake.

Although most celebrities would probably hire a security guard to sit in a tower to patrol the property, Jake merely enlisted a security company to watch over it from afar. The main reason he did that was all the locals in the small town of Ball Ground, Georgia, loved and respected him and his family enough to watch out for any crazies who might come by to say hello. He also wanted to keep things as normal as possible, especially after the twins came along. He and Abby were both insistent that they wouldn't grow up in a vacuum.

The Jeep carrying Jake and his twins careened around to the back of the house. As soon as he threw the gear into park, my dark-haired nephew and niece came barreling out of the back. "Mama! Mama!" they cried.

Abby's face lit up as she practically sprinted down the length of the porch to meet them. After she opened the door for them, the twins leapt at Abby and she began smothering their faces in kisses. "Oh, my babies! I missed you guys!"

"They were barely gone twenty-four hours," I muttered through a mouthful of cake. While Abby either ignored my comment or didn't hear me, Eli kicked me under the table. Of the two of us, Eli was the kid-friendly one—or I guess I should say niece-and-nephew-friendly one. He loved entertaining the twins as well as the kids of the other

Runaway Train members. Before shows, he looked like the fucking Pied Piper with them all running behind them.

"What? I was just making an observation."

"You were being a dickhead."

With a smirk, I replied, "It's something I do well."

Eli snickered. "That's true."

Jake had taken the twins camping on the far side of his property to give me the quiet I needed for songwriting. In my state of mind, the last thing I needed was Jax and Jules disturbing me. It was common knowledge among my family that I wasn't a kid person. Don't get me wrong, I loved Jax and Jules with all my heart and would kill anyone who laid a hand on them, but I just wasn't one who really knew how to relate to kids. While Eli was ready to settle down and have a family of his own, I wasn't sure that life was for me. Sure, I thought about finding that special girl to spend the rest of my life with—in fact, now that I was thirty, I was growing to like the idea of settling as well. I just didn't know if kids were going to be a part of that future, and that fact made it seem extremely hard to find a wife.

Some people would think my aversion to children came from having a terrible father, but nothing could have been farther from the truth. There wasn't a better father than my dad. While he might've been selfless when it came to his ministry, he was even more selfless as a father. He had ensured that my siblings and I had a wonderful childhood. Others might have resented the fact that we lived off the grid and didn't have the cool modern gadgets or devices, but I appreciated the hell out of my raising. It was an endless adventure that molded my outlook on life, and I certainly wouldn't have been in a successful band without my childhood.

Not only did my dad give me the perfect model of a father, I'd also seen the men of Runaway Train, who we toured with, almost effortlessly take to parenthood. I just didn't know if I had it in me. In my mind, I couldn't seamlessly merge the two worlds. I was bound to screw up, and in the end, screw up my kids.

Maybe it was the perfectionist in me, or maybe it was the part of me that always felt inferior. While my siblings all had amazing voices and played multiple instruments flawlessly, my only talent was in songwriting. I didn't have Eli's outgoing personality or Abby's sweetness or Micah's spiritual and emotional strength.

Abby brought me out of my thoughts when she asked, "Did you catch anything?"

The twins bobbed their heads enthusiastically. "My fish was this big!" Jax exclaimed, his small hands widening to indicate a huge catch.

"Not quite, bud, but it was pretty big," Jake countered before bestowing a kiss on Abby's lips.

"It's still big enough for us to eat, right, Daddy?" Jules asked.

Jake grinned. "Of course it is. All the fish we caught are. I'm going to start cleaning them right now."

"I'm sure TMZ would pay big money to see a video of rock star Jake Slater cleaning fish scales," Eli teased.

With a laugh, Jake replied, "Before you get any ideas, they won't give you jack for any video that doesn't involve me and Abby in a compromising position."

Abby's eyes bulged. "Jake!"

"Like the twins know what *compromising* means, Angel," Jake replied.

I fought my gag reflex as Jake called Abby by his pet name for her, one he'd given her right after they met. She'd taken it so far as to name their Golden Retriever Angel as well.

Huffing out a frustrated breath, Abby said, "I don't know why I even bother. With everything they see and hear on the road, my babies are going to corrupt their classmates next year at kindergarten."

"There's nothing wrong with corrupting others. I think I did a fine job of it with you." He playfully smacked Abby on the ass while giving her a look that made an older brother want to throat punch him.

Abby's outrage waned, and instead of giving him a piece of her mind, she winked at him. "Go get the fish."

Jake saluted Abby. "Yes ma'am."

As Jake headed back to the Jeep, Abby steered the twins over to our table. "Are you hungry? I made your favorite kind of pound cake."

While Jax dove at the dessert, Jules hopped up into my lap, threw her arms around my neck, and placed a kiss on my cheek. "Hiya Uncle Gabe."

"Hi Jules," I replied as I squeezed her tight. She was a tiny thing like her mom, but she had a personality that surpassed her size.

Her curious blue eyes peered up at me. "Didya write some songs last night?"

"No, I didn't."

Her tiny brows furrowed. "Daddy said that's what you came up here for, and that's why you couldn't play with us."

Inwardly, I groaned. I mean, Jesus, could it get any worse than catching shit for my writer's block from a four-year-old? "It was."

Jax leaned over to whisper rather loudly in Jules's ear. "Shh, Daddy said not to talk about that in front of Gabe, remember?"

Jules clamped her hand over her mouth. "Oh no, I forgot."

I glanced past the twins to eyeball Jake, who had just walked up on the porch balancing a cooler brimming with fish on his shoulder. "I see my writer's block was a matter of discussion among you guys," I said tersely.

He winced as he set the cooler down. "Sorry. I was only trying to help."

Deep down, I knew he was. The man had not only offered up his guesthouse for me, he'd also shuffled his kids away for a night. Still, in spite of being a celebrity, I was a private person. I didn't like anyone knowing my business. It was bad enough that Eli, Abby, and Jake had to know about my writing issues, but now the twins did as well.

"I'm sowwy I mentioned you can't write songs," Jules whispered.

Inwardly, I was unraveling, but I couldn't let Jules see that. I couldn't have her thinking less of me. I basked in the fact that she thought I was ten feet tall. "Thanks, Julesy-pie."

Swallowing hard, I fought the anxiety that slithered its away up my body. It was the same kind of feeling I got when enveloped by a crowd of fans. I could see now that trying to escape to Jake's farm was just a bust. "I think I'm going to head back to Atlanta."

Jules tightened her grip around my neck. "Don't leave yet, Uncle Gabe. I haven't gotten to play my drum set for you yet."

In true annoying uncle form, Eli and I had gone in together to get a mini drum set for Jax and Jules for their birthday. After two seconds of listening to them bang loudly, Jake had threatened to kick our asses for getting them such a gift. While we'd had a good laugh, Eli and I really did have good intentions. It was never too early to get the twins started on the musical path. Considering how talented both their parents were, it was a given that they would be as well.

"I really want to hear you play, Julesy-Poo, but I've got to write these songs. If I don't, your mama and Uncle Eli and I won't have anything to put on the album."

Jules's lips turned down in a pout. To show how I'd made her sad, she crawled out of my lap and went over to her mother. "Maybe going home isn't such a good idea," Abby said.

"It's not like I'm getting anything done here."

"You could head south to Savannah and stay at Rhys and Allison's house, or head over to their condo on Tybee Island. I know they wouldn't mind."

Rhys McGowan was the bassist for Runaway Train. He'd grown up in Savannah, and now he owned a house in the historic district as well as a condo on Tybee Island. After a long engagement, he'd just married Jake's little sister, Allison, a few months ago. They were spending some of Runaway Train's downtime in between album recording and touring by heading over to Scotland, where Rhys's grandparents were from.

"That's a nice idea, little sis, but I'm not a fan of crowds at the moment."

"I've got a better idea," Jake said.

With a questioning smirk, I asked, "And what's that?"

"Heads up." Before I could question what the hell he was talking about, he tossed me his keys. "Better than wasting all that time on the road to Savannah, take my Jeep and go off-roading in the mountains. It's still packed with camping gear and food. Then you won't have to worry about running into anybody."

"Except some toothless hillbilly playing the banjo who might think you have a purty mouth," Eli joked.

Jake laughed. "For your information, there are very few *Deliverance*-esque people in the mountains."

"For Gabe's sake, I hope you're right. I'm not sure I want to see the type of songs he might write after being tied up and told to squeal like a pig."

"You're impossible," I muttered as I ran my fingers over the key fob. Maybe Jake was right. Maybe I needed to get off by myself, just me and my notebook with no distractions whatsoever, not even my family. "You're sure you're okay with me running off with your Jeep?"

"I think I'll be fine. You've seen my garage—I think I've got enough vehicles to pick from."

I laughed. One building on Jake's property was a tricked-out garage where he had several cars and trucks, and then there was also the Volvo SUV and the Escalade he and Abby used to get the twins around. After grabbing my notebook and pen, I popped out of my chair. "I guess I'll see you guys later."

"Make sure you text us and let us know you're okay," Abby said.

"As long as I have a signal, I will."

She frowned at me. "Don't make me worry about you, Gabe."

I smiled. "I'll try hard not to." I wrapped one of my arms around her. "Thanks for having me last night and for trying to help."

"Any time," Abby murmured.

Eli rose out of his chair to come over to us. "I hope you break through, brother."

"So do I."

"Just remember what an amazing talent you have."

I grinned. "I think that's one of the nicest and most serious things you've ever said to me."

With a laugh, Eli replied, "I know. I shock myself sometimes."

After hugging the twins and giving Jake one of those typical bro hugs, I headed off the porch and to Jake's vehicle. I'd need to make a quick pit stop at the barn to grab my things, and then I'd be off. To where, I had no idea. The only thing that mattered was if I would find the words when I got there.

2

"FUCK!" I shouted as I banged my fist against the hood of the Jeep. The acrid smell of burning rubber still hung in the air and stung my nostrils, the aftermath of me stomping on the accelerator in an attempt to free the Jeep from being imprisoned in mud. While the trip up 515 into the North Georgia mountains had been smooth sailing, I now found myself in a brand new hell: thoroughly and completely stuck somewhere in the middle of nowhere.

Just like in the movies, everything had been going great until I made one wrong turn. When the gravel road turned into a stream, I figured I could ford it. I was in a four-wheel drive Jeep for fuck's sake. Yeah…it *so* hadn't worked out like I'd planned. Not only were the back wheels encased in the sloshy Georgia clay, I was standing in water up to my knees.

With a growl, I dug my phone out of my pocket. Glancing at the screen, I thanked God that somehow I still had cell service. "Siri, what's the nearest wrecker service near me?" I demanded.

"Hart and Daughter Wrecker Service is ten miles away."

"Then Hart and Daughter it is." After I dialed the number, it rang three times before a perky sounding woman answered it.

"Hello, Hart and Daughter. How may I help you?"

"Uh, yeah, my name's Gabe, and I seem to have gotten my Jeep stuck while doing some off-roading. Can you guys come get me out?"

"Certainly, sir. I'll just need your location."

"Somewhere in backwoods bumblefuck," I grumbled.

The woman had the audacity to laugh at me. "You must be from the city."

"If I said I am, would that make a difference?"

13

"It's just most people who are from around here know the road names, or at least they know points of interest close by."

"Okay, fine. I turned off Briarwood Road then followed it until it turned into gravel and then dirt. A path to the right looked good so I took it. That's when it all turned to shit."

After hearing scribbling in the background, the woman said, "Got it. I think someone will be able to find you with those descriptions. Just let me get some information. What's your name?"

"Gabe Renard."

There was a pause on the line. "Did you say Renard?"

"I did."

The woman giggled. "You wouldn't happen to be *the* Gabe Renard of Jacob's Ladder, would you?"

At that moment, I had two choices. I could tell her no and keep some semblance of anonymity, or I could say yes and hopefully parlay my celebrity status into getting faster service. I decided to go with option B. "Yes. As a matter of fact, I am."

A high-pitched shriek pierced my eardrum, and the shock almost caused me to fumble my phone. When I brought it back to my ear, I heard, "OMG, OMG, OMG, OH MY GOD! I can't believe it! We never have any celebrities around here. Then, the first time we have one, it's one I absolutely love."

"I'm glad to hear that."

"It's funny because I thought your voice sounded familiar."

"I take it you're a fan of my band."

Her response came in the form of another high-pitched shriek. "Oh my God, YES, I'm a fan. I've been to each and every one of your concerts in Atlanta. I even went to one in Chattanooga."

"That's amazing. Thanks for the support. Maybe I can sign something for you when the technician gets out here."

"You would really do that?"

"Hell yeah. Anything for a true fan."

I heard some rustling of papers before the woman's voice became slightly muffled. "Listen, there are actually two towing calls ahead of you, but I'm going to radio Ray to come to you first."

Jackpot. "Thank you so much…I'm sorry, but I don't think I got your name."

"It's Candice, but everyone calls me Candy."

"Thank you, Candy."

At the sound of her name coming from my lips, Candy dissolved into a fit of giggles. After a few deep breaths, she managed to compose herself. "Okay, now, you just sit tight, *Gabe*, and Ray should be there in about ten to twenty minutes."

"I will. I can't thank you enough for all your help," I replied in my sincerest voice.

"Oh, trust me, it was my pleasure."

"Bye, Candy," I drawled.

After another fit of giggles, she replied, "Bye, Gabe."

I shook my head as I hung up the phone. Even after years of being famous, it never ceased to amaze me the reactions fans had. When it came down to it, I was a person just like anyone else, but to them, the fact that I played in a successful band elevated my status slightly above them.

While I waited on Ray, I hopped back onto Jeep's front seat, thanking God again, this time for the leather seats so my soaking jeans wouldn't ruin the upholstery. After opening the dashboard, I took out my notebook. I figured I might as well try to make the most of the time I had. Sure, the Jeep might be stuck, but part of my plan was still intact. After all, I was in the middle of nowhere with no distractions. Nibbling on the pen cap, I closed my eyes and searched for the right words.

Seconds passed. Then minutes. *Fuck.* Nothing was coming. Not words, not images—absolutely nothing. With a frustrated grunt, I hurled my pen onto the dashboard. Once again, a sense of dread cloaked me. I swallowed hard before taking in a few deep breaths. The last thing I needed was to go into full-on panic attack mode in the middle of nowhere. Lifting my head, I gazed up at the sky. "I could really use some help right now."

At the sound of a vehicle coming down the road, I tossed my note-book back into the glove compartment. I threw open the door and jumped back down into the muddy water then watched as the black and red wrecker moved closer to the stream. After the engine was cut, the driver's side door opened.

When a chunky high-heeled boot slid out, I slowly trailed my hand down my face. Another boot dangled out the open door before the driver jumped down, and I muttered, "Holy shit." The stereotype of a potbellied, trucker hat-wearing guy named Ray was not what I saw in front of me. The owner of the sexy boots wore skin-tight blue jeans, a white tank top, and an open flannel shirt. One would adequately describe her body as *bangin'*, and if I focused any longer on the way her perky tits strained against her tank top, I was going to get a boner right here in the boonies.

I forced my gaze back to her face. Her long dark hair was pulled into a ponytail, and her dark eyes locked on mine. I couldn't help being further surprised by the somewhat amused glint burning in them.

"Looks like you got yourself into mess, city boy," the woman said with a teasing lilt in her voice.

AFTER HUFFING OUT A FRUSTRATED BREATH, I dipped my paintbrush into the container of bright yellow paint. Usually when I sat at the table in our formal dining room, I stared out at a sea of culinary delights. Today, however, I merely saw red Solo cups filled with vibrantly colored paints, Styrofoam balls, and a black poster board sitting on top of the plastic drape protecting the table. Basically, it was everything you could possibly need to construct a model of the solar system.

Normally, I didn't enjoy spending my Sunday afternoons painting the planets. After a full week of managing my family's collision business, I wanted nothing more than to drink a glass of wine while catching up on the *Real Housewives* I'd DVR-ed. But, as it tends to be with motherhood, my life wasn't truly my own, and Sundays inevitably became project time.

"Remind me again when this is due?" I asked as I put the final yellow touches on the largest sized ball we'd deemed the sun.

My nine-year-old son, Lincoln, AKA Linc, glanced up at me sheepishly. "Um, Tuesday."

I shot him my best *ticked off mom* look. "And why have you only started working on it today?"

"I guess 'cause I forgot."

"Please tell me we're not going to have to go back to me really checking your agenda every night instead of me just signing it so you don't get in trouble with your teacher?"

With a scowl, Linc replied, "No. I'll do better, I promise."

My older sister, Kennedy, shook her dark head of hair at me before turning to Linc. "Don't let your mom give you grief. When we were growing up, she was notorious for waiting until the last minute to do her homework and projects. It used to drive Papa crazy."

I stilled my paintbrush to glare at her. "Thank you so much for undermining my parenting."

She grinned. "You're welcome."

As I sat the sun down to dry, I said, "You know, you really shouldn't feel like you have to help. I'm sure you have a ton of other things you could be doing."

"Nope, I'm good. Just waiting until it's time to head to the shop to get started on tomorrow's prep."

Kennedy was co-owner of Harts and Flowers, a combination bakery and florist that used a cutesy play on our last name. The other half of the business was owned by our younger sister, Eleanor Rose— or Ellie, as we called her—who did the floral arrangements.

From our names, one might assume our parents had a thing for the presidents. The love of historical figures really falls to my dad. It had started when his parents gave him the moniker of Abraham Lincoln Hart. He was known as Abe for the better part of his life, and most people in town also called him Honest Abe for the way he ran our family's collision business.

Our mother hadn't really cared too much for the business of naming us, so she had deferred to my father. The truth was Mommie Dearest hadn't really cared too much for *anything* regarding her three daughters. She'd blown town with a traveling musician when I was just four years old, leaving my father to raise us girls all on his own.

He'd then moved us into the sprawling 1890s home on Main Street, where my sisters and I still lived. The house actually belonged to my great-aunt Sadie. It had been in the Hart family for several generations, and as the only daughter, it had been left to my Aunt Sadie since she never married. Like Andy Taylor having his Aunt Bea move in with him to care for him and Opie, Aunt Sadie helped fill the maternal role we needed since Dad's parents had moved to Florida before we were born. While Dad had eventually remarried and moved out ten years ago, Aunt Sadie's sprightly ninety-year-old self still resided in the house, and she had the room across the hall from me.

Although my sisters and I were in our late twenties and had our own careers, we still lived at home. Some people liked to joke that we were cursed to be old maids like Aunt Sadie, but I liked to point out that in a small town, there weren't a lot of men to choose from. With its population of just under five thousand, Hayesville could certainly be considered a very small town.

Truthfully, I really didn't have time for a relationship. Between running Hart and Daughter and being a single mom, my plate was full. Part of me wished a decent man might come along, one who would make me want to make time for him. At the moment, there was no one on the horizon who fit that bill, so I just focused all my energy on Linc. That was one of the reasons why I was spending my Sunday painting the solar system.

"Just out of curiosity, besides your science project, is there anything else going on at school you've forgotten to tell me about?" I asked.

Linc tilted his head in thought before his dark eyes widened. "Oh yeah, it's Donuts with Dad on Wednesday."

"Who do you want to come? Me or Papa?"

After giving me a *you just asked me the stupidest question in the world* look, Linc replied, "Papa."

"I'll let him know."

It went without saying that I didn't need to ask Linc's father if he was going to come. I had no idea where he was. The last time I'd laid eyes on Ryan Perkins was when he came to the hospital after I gave birth to Linc. He'd taken one look at him before turning on his heels and getting the hell out of Dodge. It was probably a good thing he ran because my dad was ready to shoot him for knocking up his seventeen-year-old daughter.

Although Ryan had grown up in Hayesville, he'd had his eyes set on Nashville and being a country star. To a teenage girl, there was nothing hotter than having a boyfriend in a band—at least, that was the way I'd felt when Ryan first asked me out. Most of the guys at Hayesville High were intimidated by the fact that my mad soccer skills had found me a place as kicker on the all-male high school football team, but Ryan thought the idea of me kicking guys' asses on the field was hot. It was on our six-month anniversary that I got the second blue line on the pregnancy test.

Thankfully, Linc looked nothing like his blond-haired, blue-eyed sperm donor. He had the same dark hair and brown eyes my sisters and I had, and he was basically a mini-me of my dad. Over the years, Dad had gotten used to playing the dual roles of father and grandfather to Linc. He'd had a lot of practice considering he'd been mother and father to me and my sisters.

"Which one should I work on now?" I asked.

"Uranus."

"What color do I paint Uranus?"

Kennedy closed her eyes. "I'm seeing your anus as a giant, black hole."

While Linc doubled over with laughter as only a nine-year-old boy can, I shot my sister a look. "Wow, you're so mature."

"I'm just trying to lighten the mood."

"Try a different way."

"Fine," she grumbled.

When my phone rang, I put down the Styrofoam ball and my paint-brush to glance at the ID. "Crap, it's the shop," I muttered. I quickly used the wipes to remove the leftover paint on my hands. Rising out of my chair, I grabbed the phone and started into the kitchen. "Hello?"

"Hey Rae, it's Candy."

"Hey girl. What's up?"

"We have a VIP that needs a tow ASAP."

I snorted. "Did Ronnie Tillman get his boat stuck again?" Our mayor was known for throwing back a few too many beers at the lake on the weekend and somehow always managing to get his pontoon stuck in the shoreline.

"No, no. It's not anyone from here. It's Gabe Renard."

"Who?"

"Oh my God, how can you not know Gabe Renard? He's the drummer of Jacob's Ladder."

"Are they kinda country rock?"

"Yes!"

"Yeah, I think I've heard a song or two of theirs."

"We need to get you out of the house more and to one of their concerts. They're amazing. Gabe is hell of a drummer."

I laughed. "I'll make a note to go see them, but what's the deal with Gabe?"

"He's stuck off Vanderbilt road. Billy has two tows ahead of Gabe, one way out in LaFayette, and I can't get Wayne to answer his phone. He's probably hungover from painting the town last night."

"I see. Since all the usual weekend workers were occupied, you were kind enough to offer him my services on my day off?"

"I couldn't let someone like him wait. Honey, I never let a man as fine as he is wait."

I laughed. "Spare me."

"Come on, Rae-Rae, it won't take you that long to tow him. Then you can have the bragging rights that you not only met Gabe Renard, but you saved him." Candy gasped. "He might even ask you for a date!"

"A famous rocker ask me out? Ha! I think you've been huffing too many fumes from your essential oil diffuser."

"You never know. Stranger things have happened. You're a hot ticket, too."

"Thanks for the vote of confidence." After putting Candy on speakerphone, I did a quick Google search of Gabe Renard. *Hmm, not bad... okay, fine—he's incredibly good-looking.* I especially liked the pictures of him shirtless at his drum set, dripping with sweat. Yeah, sweaty men got me hot. Sue me.

"If I go tow him, I'm charging him double the weekend fee, so make sure you note that on the paperwork."

Candy screeched. "You go get him, girl!"

I laughed. "Whatever. Send over the billing when you send the location and I'll have him do an electronic sign."

"I will." Before I could hang up, Candy said, "I want to hear every single detail about him just as soon as you leave."

"I'm not exactly sure how tantalizing a tow is, but I'll be sure to fill you in."

"And he's supposed to sign something for me as well."

"I'll try to remind him."

"You better. Don't make me drive out there and get him to sign my boobs."

Oh good lord. I was both horrified by her suggestion and by the mental image it conjured. "Um, goodbye, Candy."

"Bye, Rae."

I couldn't help eyeing the phone before I hung it up. I had known Candy pretty much my entire life, and I had never heard her quite so giggly. She would have rivaled one of the high school girls at a Bieber concert—not that I actually listened to Bieber.

Don't get me wrong, I got her enthusiasm to a certain point. We rarely saw anyone remotely famous around here, so it was understandable that Candy would be star-struck. I just couldn't help having a preconceived notion that this Gabe guy was going to act like an uptight jerk because of being famous.

Walking back into the dining room, I said, "Kennedy, are you going to be around for a little while?"

"Just until six. Then I need to go get tomorrow's breads started."

"Can you keep an eye on Linc for me while I go do an emergency tow?"

"You're doing a tow on a Sunday? Who is it, the governor?" Kennedy asked incredulously.

I laughed as I got my keys. "Not quite." Pointing at Linc, I said, "Listen to Aunt Kennedy. When you finish your box, you can watch TV. Not until then, understand?"

Linc didn't look up from painting Saturn's rings. "Yes, Mom."

Turning my pointer finger to my sister, I said, "And don't you be going behind my back and letting him watch television instead of doing his work."

Kennedy rolled her eyes. "You're such a killjoy."

"It's called being a parent," I called over my shoulder as I started for the door.

At Linc's laughter, I knew Kennedy must be making some sort of face or gesture at me. I decided to be the bigger person and ignore it. She might've been a year older than me, but it always seemed like I was the older sister. Since we were only fourteen months apart, it sometimes felt like we were twins. Where I was the somewhat mature and responsible one, Kennedy was the wild child. Regardless of how crazy she could be or how much she got on my nerves, I loved having her for a sister. I even loved sharing a house with her. Both Kennedy and Ellie had been my lifelines while raising Linc.

After pounding down the back steps, I slid into my Honda Passport. I drove past the residential area of Main Street and down into the business section. I'd lived in Haysville all my life. I'd had big plans of escaping for college at the University of Tennessee at Chattanooga on a soccer scholarship, but those plans had changed when I got pregnant with Linc. Instead of going out of state, I'd gone to the community college in the next town. When I graduated with honors in business management, it was a nice way to thumb my nose at all the naysayers who said I would never graduate high school, let alone college.

It was then I went to work for my dad. Although I could have earned more money other places, it was the best fit for me and for Linc since I could bring him to work with me. At first, I only handled the billing and payroll. Slowly, over the years, Dad immersed me more in the physical side of the business. While I wasn't out welding on new bumpers, I did know how to price parts and services as well as handling some minor repairs. After two years of me working for him, he had all the signs redone and the wreckers and trucks repainted to pronounce that it was no longer Hart Wreckers, but Hart and Daughter.

It wasn't exactly an easy transition for the people in town, and to be honest, it wasn't for me either. Sure, we were just a small-time operation, but having that sort of affirmation from my dad? The gesture touched my heart more than anything else ever would. Even after some of my missteps, Dad believed in me, and it was the best feeling in the world to have his support—well, next to the feeling of being Linc's mom.

After making the second turn off Main Street, I coasted down the road that dead-ended at Hart and Daughter Collision. Once I punched in the numerical code on the keypad, the barbwire fence slid open and I drove inside the lot. Usually at this time of day, the place was teeming with both workers and customers. Not only did we have an immense collision center, the property also included ten acres of land, and some of those acres were used as a junkyard. Thankfully, they were the ones on the back side of the property, so it wasn't such an eyesore.

Once I parked my car, I hopped out and started over to one of the empty wreckers. At the sound of a friendly woof, I turned around to see Demo—short for Demolition—running toward me. Demo had shown up in the demolition yard about two years ago, and we had decided to let him stay. In true junkyard dog form, he was a wiry pit bull with a nick in his left ear and part of his tail lopped off. "Hey boy, I'm just picking up one of the wreckers."

After scratching his ears, I patted his head and then hopped on up in the wrecker. Once I put the location Candy had given me into my navigation app, I started off to rescue the lost star.

JUST AS I was about to call Candy to check if I had the right location, I finally located Gabe's Jeep. "How in the hell did you manage to get yourself way out here," I muttered under my breath. Considering that the Jeep's tires were completely immersed in the water, there was no way in hell he would have ever been able to get it out on his own.

After easing the tow truck to a stop just before the road during into a stream, I threw open the door and hopped down. Shielding my eyes from the sun, I surveyed the damage before letting out a low whistle. "Looks like you got yourself in a real mess, city boy," I called out as Gabe approached me. As I got a better look at him, I sucked in a breath. Although I wasn't sure how it was possible, he was better looking in person. Even with his disheveled hair and whiskered face, he melted my thong. *Get a grip, Rae. You're here to do a tow, not have an afternoon delight.*

"Did Candy tell you I was from the city?"

"No, but she wouldn't have had to tell me. Anyone from around here would know you don't take Cutler's Ridge after a rainstorm."

After glancing around, Gabe asked, "Is that where I'm at?"

I nodded. "The road's really only passable in ATVs when it's been consistently dry for a few days."

"I'll keep that in mind."

I opened one of the boxes on the wrecker and pulled out a pair of waders. "Excuse me for a moment. The call came in so fast I didn't have a chance to change."

"Wait a second, you're seriously Ray?" he demanded incredulously.

"Um, yeah, that's me."

Gabe scratched his head. "Huh, I was expecting some guy named Ray."

"I'm R-a-e, not R-a-y. It's short for Reagan. But, don't worry—it's not the first time someone has confused my name and my gender."

"Let me get this straight: *you're* going to get my Jeep out."

Tilting my head, I smiled sweetly up at him. "Let me guess, you don't think little ol' me can get your big bad Jeep out of the mud."

Just like it wasn't the first time someone had confused my name and gender, it wasn't the first time some sexist man didn't think I was capable of doing my job. After years as the lone female in a male-dominated business, I was used to having my credentials questioned. While I'd grown accustomed to it, it still stung a little. It also pissed me off.

"I'm sorry for being surprised, but for a minute there, I thought you'd been sent as a joke or something."

I swept my hands to hips that were encased in the waders. "Just why in the hell would someone do that?"

Gabe shrugged. "I don't know. It wouldn't be the first time someone did something weird to meet me."

"While this might hurt your overinflated ego, I'm not a fan. I'm a businesswoman who is doing your ass a favor by coming out here on her day off."

My declaration sent Gabe's head snapping back. He stared at me for a moment before a slow smile spread across his face. "First, let me extend my sincere apologies for underestimating you, as well as for my assumption that you might be an overzealous fan."

"Thank you."

He extended his hand to me. "Let me start things over by formally introducing myself. I'm Gabe Renard."

"I'm Rae Hart."

"As in Hart and Daughter?"

"Exactly."

Gabe shook my head. "I would say it's nice to meet you, but under the current circumstances, I'm not so sure."

I smiled. "It's nice to meet you, too. Although I'm not a fan, I have heard of your band and your music."

"You have? I hope you like it."

"I'm not a huge fan of country, but from what I've heard of your music, I liked your songs."

Gabe laughed. "I'm glad to hear it."

"Tell me something—what are you doing all the way out here by yourself?" I brushed away a strand of loose hair that had escaped my ponytail. "I mean, it's pretty evident you're not the usual mudding type of guy."

"I came out here to write."

"You're a songwriter?"

Gabe nodded. "The only one for our band."

"Were you able to write anything?"

"Nope, but I guess I shouldn't be too surprised."

"What do you mean?"

"I've had the worst writer's block of my life the last couple of months. My band's album is due in a couple of weeks, and I don't have jack shit for us to record."

"You came out here to write and got stuck in more ways than one? No offense, but you have really crappy luck."

He laughed. "For the most part, that's the truth, but in my defense, it's not my Jeep. It belongs to my brother-in-law. I've never driven it so don't know how to maneuver it well."

"That doesn't surprise me at all. You don't impress me as the Jeep or off-roading type."

"Just what type of guy am I?"

I tilted my head at him. "A sporty little convertible."

Gabe laughed. "Good guess. I have a Mercedes AMG SL63 convertible roadster."

"That's a sweet ride."

"You know cars?"

Rolling my eyes, I replied, "Knowing cars is my business."

"I don't think I've ever met a female mechanic."

"Well you're not meeting one today either. I run the business side.

I'm only out here today because Candy pressured me into taking an emergency tow since our other workers were busy on other jobs."

Gabe's brows furrowed. "While I'm grateful you came out so quickly, but are you sure you're the best one for the job?"

I rolled my eyes. "Just when I think you can't possibly say anything more sexist, there you go." When Gabe opened his mouth to argue, I held up my hand. "I pulled my first tow when I was ten years old. I might not be a certified mechanic, but I can guarantee I know just as much from learning on the job training with my dad."

"I'm sorry."

"You should be."

A grin curved Gabe's lips. "I don't think I've ever met someone quite like you."

"Sadly, I've met more than my fair share of sexist, narrow-minded men. Now if you don't mind, I think I need to get to work."

"Of course."

After grabbing a tow strap out of the back of the truck, I attached it to the wrecker's hitch before pulling it over to attach it to the Jeep's hitch. At Gabe's confusion, I asked, "What?"

"You're not going to use the big hook thing?" Gabe asked.

I laughed. "I think you mean the boom."

"I guess so."

"If the tow strap doesn't work, I'll go to the boom. I don't want to put any more pressure than I have to on the hitch."

"Thank you for that. Jake will kill me if I bring his Jeep home all banged up."

Once the straps were in place, I motioned to Gabe. "Okay, can you shift the gear to neutral?"

"Yeah, sure." Gabe sloshed through the water to climb into the Jeep. "Done," he called as he craned his head out the window.

Nodding, I got back inside the cab of the tow truck, threw the gear into drive, and eased my foot down on the accelerator. At first, the Jeep didn't budge, but after switching to a lower gear, it started inching slowly out of the mud. Thankfully, it hadn't been too submerged, or it might've taken even more effort. Once I had it completely out of the water, I hit the brake and then shifted the wrecker into park.

After grabbing my iPad on the seat beside me, I jumped back down. I placed it on the back of the wrecker before I went to undo the tow straps. When I finished, I deposited the soaking strap on the truck bed before taking off my waders. I then collected the iPad and walked back over to Gabe. "Okay, you're free and ready to go just as soon as you sign the paperwork."

Gabe jerked his hand through his hair. "Ms. Hart—"

"Rae," I corrected.

He nodded. "Rae, I…uh…I just wanted to apologize for my earlier comments. I certainly never meant to disrespect you, and I really do appreciate the fact that you came out here so quickly. I'm sure it was an inconvenience on your day off."

"Normally, I would say you might regret those words when you see how much it is for the emergency towing fee, which your insurance doesn't cover, but I have a feeling you can easily cover it."

Gabe grinned. "Yeah, I think I'm good." I unlocked the screen and opened the program. "Just sign here." I handed Gabe the Hart and Daughter pen that had a stylus on the end.

After he signed in a flourish, Gabe said, "Listen, after the way I acted, I'd really like to do something to make it up to you. Why don't you let me buy you dinner to say thanks for all your help?"

And there it was: the offer for dinner, which I would have wagered good money was really just a lead-in for sex. While I wasn't too accustomed to that happening with men here in my hometown, it had been standard practice when I was in the Legends Football League, or *Lingerie Football*, as some people like to disdainfully call it because of the uniforms—or maybe I should say the *lack* of uniforms. I'd played for the Atlanta Steam for three years when Linc was just out of diapers. During those years, I'd received countless invitations for dinner, AKA sex. I'd only taken one man up on the offer, and that was because he was a starter for the Falcons. It wasn't one of my better decisions, not to mention the not-so-fabulous sex.

Turning my attention back to Gabe, I said curtly, "Our standard towing cost plus the emergency weekend tow fee will more than compensate me."

"Come on, I'd really like to see more of you." Gabe's gaze slid from my eyes down to my breasts. "Maybe all of you."

Ugh. What a creep. I couldn't believe he was seriously standing there spouting that bullshit. Crossing my arms, I gave a low whistle. "Wow, do you seriously score women with those pickup lines?"

With a smirk, Gabe replied, "Women usually don't make me work so hard to take them out."

"Of course not. They usually throw themselves at you, right?"

"Yes." He waggled his brows. "Along with their underwear."

"They must not be on as tight of a budget as I am—I don't have the money to waste my underwear by throwing them at some rocker with an overinflated ego."

Gabe stared at me for a moment before bursting out in laughter. "Damn, you have a sassy mouth. I like that in the women I date."

Tilting my head, I asked, "Do you actually date, or do you just screw?"

"Well, I prefer the screwing, but I do like dating when it serves my purpose."

"*Your* purpose?" I rolled my eyes. "It would be all about you."

"Come on, Rae. Let me buy you dinner and get to know you better."

"As in the biblical sense?"

"Sure, why not?" A wicked smirk curved his lips. "I bet you do wonders with that sassy mouth of yours."

"Because that's not who I am. Call me old-fashioned, but I don't jump into bed with random douchebags—even famous ones."

"You could always make an exception in my case."

"I know this is probably a shock to your ego, but not every woman in the world has a lady boner for you." Okay, so maybe I was lying with that one. He had certainly gotten my nether regions up and running, but that was before he opened his mouth. I'm pretty sure my once-on-fire vagina had withered to cold ashes now.

"I promise I'll make it good for you.

"Oh, how that statement repulses me rather than turns me on."

Gabe threw up his hands. "Fine. It's your loss, babe, not mine."

"Trust me, if you were the last man on earth and the survival of mankind relied on us copulating, I still wouldn't fuck you.

On that note, I turned on my boot heels and marched back to the wrecker.

HOLY. Shit. I had just been rejected—no, let's rephrase that: I'd been *annihilated.*

Trust me, if you were the last man on earth and the survival of mankind relied on us copulating, I still wouldn't fuck you.

Rae's words echoed in my ears as I watched her hips sashay somewhat provocatively back to the wrecker. I was glad she had her back to me, because I must've looked pretty fucking pathetic standing there in all my rejected glory. As hard as I tried, I couldn't recall the last time I'd been rejected.

It had to have been back in middle school when Shelley Dupree wouldn't go to the end-of-the-year dance with me. In her words, she didn't want to go with "the fat Renard". Sure, I was a bit heftier back then. After three years of my parents working in different parts of Mexico, I had come to love the cuisine. Would I have called myself fat? Probably not. Up until Shelley's rejection, my weight hadn't been much of an issue since it served me well on the football field. As I grew older and my height evened out with my weight, it was no longer an issue.

When I hit high school, I had my pick of any girl I wanted. After all, I played football and was in a band. That was like bottled sex to girls, but back then, I was a lot more pious and faithful than I was lately. While I wasn't sporting a purity ring like the Jonas Brothers, I didn't lose my virginity until I was seventeen, and that was in a long-term relationship.

Then when Jacob's Ladder saw a little success, my appeal with women skyrocketed. Not only did our music turn more secular, you could say I succumbed to the temptations of the world. While I still considered myself someone of immense faith and belief, I wasn't on the straight and narrow path.

As Rae screeched off in the wrecker, it kicked up a mud storm that splatted all over the hood of the Jeep. "Fuck!" I shouted when a blob smacked me in the face. Tearing my shirt over my head, I wiped my cheek. Apparently when I'd thought this day couldn't get any worse, the universe had decided to say, *Hold my beer!*

I stomped around the car and threw open the door. I was sure I looked just like Jax and Jules when they threw a tantrum. After pressing the ignition button, I shifted the gear and the Jeep lurched forward. As I started careening back down the dirt roads to get the hell out of Bumblefuck, my thumbs absentmindedly began tapping out a beat on the steering wheel.

Momentarily taking my eyes off the road, I glanced down at my hands. Without a second thought, I began humming the melody my thumbs were playing. While humming a few bars, words began to form in my mind.

"You pried me from the walls of my prison," I sang out.

The moment the line escaped my lips, I slammed on the brakes. "Holy shit!" After cutting the wheel hard to the right, I pulled off the road into a clearing. I threw open the glove box and grabbed out my notebook. My hand fumbled inside to try to retrieve my pen, but as hard as I searched, I couldn't find it. "No, no, no! Not now!"

My wild gaze spun around the inside of the Jeep. Just as I was ready to prick my finger and write in blood so as to not lose my muse, something shiny flashed from my cup holder. "Fuck yes," I muttered.

Holding the pen up to the light, I read the words embossed on the side: *Hart and Daughter Wreckers.* I rolled my eyes as I realized Rae was going to be saving me for the second time that day. Furiously, I began scribbling the line down, and then, like a dam had broken, the words started rushing at me so fast I feared I might not be able to write fast enough.

The first streaks of amber sunlight sliced across the blackened sky, waking me from a deep sleep. Blinking my eyes, I surveyed my surroundings. Sometime during the night, I'd passed out in the back of the Jeep. Based on the position I'd slept in, I was sure I was going to have a hell of a crick in my neck.

With a groan, I rose into a sitting position. As I ground the sleep from my eyes with my fist, my elbow brushed against my notebook, knocking it onto the seat. Then it hit me: I'd spent most of the night writing. The words had come so fast and furiously that my hand had cramped trying to keep up.

Glancing through my notebook, I slowly shook my head back and forth. "I'll be damned," I muttered.

Somehow I'd managed to crawl out of my pit of writer's block to pen a song. After I read over the lyrics, I smacked the pages with an enthusiastic fist bump. They weren't just words taking up the lines of the paper; they were good words—fucking incredible words.

I couldn't help wondering what had made the difference. Was it staying out all night under the stars? No—I'd tried that already both from my balcony in the city and at Jake's farm. It hadn't helped.

I realized what the difference was: a petite brunette with a tight ass, perky tits, and a smart mouth...a woman who hadn't given two shits about my celebrity status and had put me in my place.

Rae was the difference.

She had been the key to unlocking my writer's block. Something about just being in her presence had inspired me more than any other woman, and I couldn't help thinking the more I was around her, the more I'd be able to write. I might even be able to get the entire album done in just a couple of days.

Fuck. I had to see her again as soon as possible.

Of course, there was the glaring issue that she despised me. Yeah, she hadn't just turned me down; my advances had utterly crashed and burned. But, maybe if I explained my situation to her, she would change her mind. What woman wouldn't want to be a man's muse? That was all kinds of romantic.

Glancing in the rear-view mirror, I recoiled at my reflection. Not only was my hair a mess, I was starting to resemble the Wolfman with my lack of shaving. I lifted my arm to sniff under my arms. Eli might've been exaggerating about me stinking the previous day, but I certainly did now after wading through the mud and sleeping in the car.

There was no way I could see Rae like this. If I was going to ask her to hang out with me, I needed to look presentable, sexy, desirable —not like a swamp-man, as I did now. Surely if she spent more than five minutes with me, she'd want me. Yeah, I could start slow, lure her in, let her see what she was missing because she'd written me off.

Although I had a change of clothes with me, I found myself with a lack of running water. When I checked the time on my phone, I saw it was barely seven a.m. I had plenty of time to find a hotel or motel to get presentable in before Rae got to work. While I worked on improving my physical self, I would also need to work on how to get Rae to accept my compromise. Then she'd have no choice but to like me...right?

Rae

6

AS STRONG ARMS enveloped me within their grasp, a warm mouth closed over mine. Stubble brushed against my cheek as his tongue thrust inside my mouth. Our tongues tangled together with the same desperation as our arms and legs. With his cock buried deep inside me, I raised my hips to meet his frantic thrusts. The most intense pleasure I'd ever experienced ricocheted through me.

"Yes, Gabe!" I cried.

And just as I orgasmed, I came awake with a start. As my gaze swung around my empty bedroom, both relief and mortification pulsed through me. First, I was thankful to see that Gabe Renard wasn't actually in my bed, and second, I was embarrassed as hell that I had just experienced an orgasm merely off his image.

The truth was, I often took a while to come with physical stimulation, but I seemed to be doing just fine without it this morning. Both my hands were above the covers and nowhere near my center. I was sure Gabe would find it amusing as hell that just me dreaming of his hands and mouth on my body had the ability to make me come. As cocky as he was, I knew he would have never doubted his ability with a woman.

"Dammit," I huffed as I kicked off the sheets. How could I have possibly just had a sex dream about someone I detested? Even if he was physically sex on a stick, Gabe was a complete asshole and egomaniac. He was exactly the kind of man I loathed to come in contact with both personally and professionally, the kind who thought a woman's true purpose was to be a life support system for a pussy.

The blaring of my alarm clock on the nightstand drew me out of my thoughts. Rising out of bed, I threw my arms over my head and stretched. After pulling my hair into a messy bun, I threw my robe on over my nightgown. When I opened my bedroom door, the deliciously decadent scent of espresso entered my nostrils. I padded down the hallway and into the kitchen, where Kennedy stood at the stove and Ellie sat at the counter, manning the espresso maker. Since we all needed caffeine running through our veins to not only survive but not throat punch someone, we'd all chipped in to buy the rather expensive appliance.

"Morning," I called as I walked over to the cabinet to get a coffee mug.

With spatula in hand, Kennedy glanced at me over her shoulder. "Morning."

"Were you running this morning?" Ellie asked, her dark hair swept up in a ponytail.

"No. Why?"

"Your face is all red, and you're sweaty."

My skin burned like a raging wildfire under her inspection. "Oh... must be a reaction from the nightmare that woke me up." I wasn't totally lying—any form of a sexual scenario with me and Gabe Renard was a nightmare, regardless of what my traitorous body wanted to think.

With a gasp, Ellie's hand flew to her mouth and her brown eyes widened.

"What?" I demanded at her reaction.

"Were you..." She waggled her brown brows.

Kennedy whirled around at the stove. "Seriously, Ellie, if you're going to talk about it, at least say the word: masturbating. Rae was *masturbating*."

"I was not!" I huffed.

She jabbed the spatula at me as her dark eyes narrowed on mine. "Then why did I hear moans coming from your bedroom?"

Ducking my head, I focused on pouring some espresso. "Because I was having a scary nightmare." Once I had filled my cup, I finally met Kennedy's intense stare. "Look, I don't want to talk about it, okay?"

"What's with you?"

"Nothing."

Kennedy shook her head as she flipped the omelet in the skillet onto a plate. "I call bullshit, little sis. You're never one to shy away from sex talk." After she passed the plate to me, she lowered her voice to ask, "You didn't sneak a man in here last night, did you?"

"No, I most certainly did not. You know how I feel about that with Linc." Since the time he was old enough to understand what was going on, I'd always feared Linc finding a strange man in my bed. Because of that, I'd always had sex at the guy's place or let Linc go spend the night with my dad and Stella.

Shrugging, Kennedy said, "You could always lock the door and sneak the guy out the window."

"Thank you. I'll remember that if the need ever arises."

Ellie eyed me thoughtfully as she chewed on a piece of bacon. "If a man wasn't in your room, then you must've been masturbating."

I sighed. "Fine. If you must know, I was having a sex dream." Shuddering, I added, "A very intense sex dream."

"Ha! I knew it was something sexual," Ellie replied as she gave me a triumphant look.

After handing me the omelet, Kennedy chewed her lip in thought. "Why are you so embarrassed about a sex dream?

"Because of who starred in it."

Wrinkling her nose, Ellie said, "Ew, it wasn't Vernon, wasn't it?"

I started choking on my omelet. After I threw back some coffee, I replied, "God no!" Vernon Neighbors was a sixty-year-old front-end specialist at Hart and Daughter Wreckers. With his greasy hair and wiry frame, he was no woman's fantasy lover.

"Ah, but he's a *front-end specialist*," Kennedy joked, waggling her brows.

"For the record, Vernon will never be allowed anywhere near my front end." When Kennedy opened her mouth, I shook my head. "That goes for my rear end as well."

While Kennedy laughed, Ellie slid into a chair across from me at the table. "Don't hold out on us—tell us who the mystery fucker was."

"Gabe Renard."

"Like *the* Gabe Renard, the drummer for Jacob's Ladder?" Ellie questioned.

"I'm pretty sure he's the only Gabe Renard I know."

"What brought that one on? Were you listening to some of their music before you went to bed or something?"

As Kennedy brought her plate over the table, she replied, "Nope. She answered the tow call when he got his Jeep stuck out on Cutler's Ridge yesterday."

Forget the old adage of saucers—Ellie's eyes widened to the size of dinner plates at this revelation. "You actually met Gabe Renard?"

"Yeah, I did."

"I cannot believe you told Kennedy but didn't tell me!"

Since I hadn't been able believe what had transpired between me and Gabe, I'd gone straight home to tell Kennedy about it, not even taking the time to drop the wrecker off. It was still parked outside in the driveway. "Just how was I to do that when you were gone all day?"

Huffing, Ellie replied, "Ever heard of a phone call or text? You two could have at least FaceTimed me."

I shook my head. "It wasn't the kind of story I wanted to tell over the phone or a text, least of all on FaceTime."

"What happened?"

After drawing in a deep breath, I filled Ellie in on my rendezvous with Gabe. She sat in such rapt attention, I wasn't sure she even stopped to blink. Once I finished, she slowly shook her head back and forth. "I cannot believe you turned him down."

Clanking her fork noisily on her plate, Kennedy huffed, "I swear, sometimes I think you would give a serial killer a chance if he was hot enough."

"Gabe Renard is not a serial killer," Ellie countered.

"No, but he's an arrogant dickhead," Kennedy shot back.

"That's an understatement," I murmured.

"Weren't you at least tempted to go out with him?" Ellie asked.

With a sigh, I ran my hands over my face. "Of course I was. I'm not blind—I saw perfectly well with my own eyes how good-looking he is."

Ellie nodded. "Not to mention rich and famous."

"Thanks for reminding me." The last thing I wanted was to ever be seen with Gabe. While being famous certainly had its perks, it also had a downside. I never wanted my face splashed across the internet, not to mention print magazines. Nasty memes created about my boobs or my ass, derogatory posts about me being a single mom—hell no. There was no way I would expose Linc to that.

I shook my head. "But at the end of the day, I do have my pride. He only wanted a one-night stand from me."

"You don't know that."

Kennedy groaned. "Stop being such a romantic. Do you actually think someone like Gabe Renard is looking for a relationship?"

"You never know. He tours with the guys in Runaway Train, and they're all married."

"Considering his twin brother is single also, I'd say the Renard brothers are commitment-phobes," Kennedy said.

Ellie frowned. "I just wish you'd given him a chance."

"The last time I gave a musician a chance, I got knocked up at seventeen." Eyeing the clock on the stove, I winced. "I don't have time to talk about this anymore. If I don't light a fire under Linc, he's going to be late for school."

"Just answer one thing for me before you go," Ellie said.

"What?"

With a wicked grin, she asked, "How good was Gabe in your dream?"

"Multiple Os."

"Oh yeah, my favorite kind of Os."

"What's an O?" Linc suddenly asked from the doorway.

As Ellie and I shrieked and jumped in our chairs at his appearance, Kennedy spewed out the espresso she'd just drank. When I finally recovered enough to find my voice, I said, "Nothing you need to know about. Hurry up and sit down for your breakfast."

Before he could question me any further, I popped out of my chair to give it to Linc. I then made a mad dash out of the kitchen to both grab a shower and escape my mortification.

It was nothing short of miraculous that in forty-five minutes, I got Linc and myself out the door, but some how I managed to do it. "Why didn't you take the wrecker back last night?" Linc asked as we headed down the porch steps.

Because I needed to haul ass home to talk to your aunt about this hot, arrogant rocker guy asking me out. "I knew I needed to get back home to make sure you finished your project," I replied. Inwardly, I patted myself on the back for coming up with a quick, clever reply.

Linc grumbled something under his breath as he hoisted himself up into the cab of the wrecker. We made a quick trip down Main Street and over to Hart and Daughter. When I pulled around back, I wasn't too surprised to see my father's pickup already in the lot.

Two years ago, he'd been in a serious car accident which caused him to suffered a traumatic brain injury as well as a shattered pelvis. He spent months in rehab relearning basic skills, as well as how to walk again. Since he would never be one hundred percent again, he had turned the entirety of Hart and Daughter Wreckers over to me. Nowadays, he came to the shop to lend his expertise, but mostly it was to hang out and shoot the shit with some of the other retired men. He also considered it an important part of his continued rehabilitation to walk Lincoln to school every day.

I grabbed my purse and then headed in the back door while Linc stayed outside. Most of the guys arrived somewhere between seven and eight, even though we didn't officially open until nine. Scanning the group for my dad, I finally spotted him in front of a BMW that needed a new front fender.

Leaning in, I gave him a smacking kiss on the cheek. "Morning, Daddy."

"Morning, sweetheart. I went ahead and put on a pot of coffee for you."

"My hero," I teased as I crossed the room for more caffeine.

"Linc outside?"

Taking one of the plastic cups, I poured myself some joe. "Yep, ready and waiting. I'm sure he's out there giving Demo some love."

"Speaking of waiting, there's a man here to see you. I went ahead and told him to have a seat in your office."

Furrowing my brows, I blew rivulets into the steaming coffee. "Don't tell me it's Flannigan's trying to sell us used parts again."

Dad shook his head. "His name is Gabe."

The cup slipped through my fingers and sloshed onto the floor. "D-Did you say Gabe?"

With his brows disappearing into his forehead, Dad asked, "Are you okay, sweetheart?"

"I'm fine."

"You look like you've seen a ghost."

I couldn't exactly explain to my father that while Gabe wasn't a ghost, he certainly haunted my sex dreams. After taking a few seconds to get ahold of myself, I grabbed a wad of napkins and started mopping up the coffee. When I glanced up from cleaning, Dad was staring quizzically at me. "He's just an old acquaintance I'm not looking forward to seeing," I lied.

"Need me to come in with you for backup?"

Smiling, I gave Dad a pat on the back. "I think I can handle it. Besides, you need to get Linc to school."

"If you're sure."

"I am."

"Hey Abe, can you come over here and give me your opinion on this sealant?" one of the men called.

Dad glanced at his watch before replying, "Yeah, but you better make it quick. I gotta get Linc to school by 8:15." He smiled at me. "Don't worry, I'll get him there on time."

"I wasn't doubting you."

After watching Dad hustle across the room, I drew in a deep breath and threw my shoulders back before flinging open my office door. Sitting in one of my ratty office chairs that I always meant to replace was Gabe.

"What in the hell are you doing here?" I demanded.

He flashed his sexy-as-hell grin. "And good morning to you, too."

"Forget the bullshit pleasantries and cut to the chase."

"Won't you sit down?" he asked.

"In case you missed it, this is *my* office, and I'll sit down when I damn well please."

"Man, who pissed in your Cheerios this morning?"

"Excuse me?"

"I just meant it seems as though you woke up on the wrong side of the bed."

"I woke up just fine, thank you very much. It's my present company that's pissing me off."

Gabe held up his hands. "Look, I'm truly sorry if I offended you yesterday."

"I'm thinking you're sorry I bruised your inflated ego, not that you offended me," I countered.

"I really need to talk to you. Can you please give me just five minutes?"

"Unless there's something else wrong with your Jeep, we have nothing to talk about."

"My Jeep is fine."

I jerked my thumb at the door. "Then have a lovely day."

"Are you always this infuriating, or is the universe just really fucking with me?"

"If anyone is infuriating, it's you. I'm pretty sure I made myself abundantly clear last night when I told you I didn't want to sleep with you."

"I'm not here to ask you to sleep with me again."

"You're not?" I asked. I hoped my surprise masked the slight disappointment I felt that he wasn't there to ask me out again.

Shaking his head, Gabe said, "I have a different proposition for you."

"Why do I not like the sound of this?"

Gabe huffed out a frustrated breath. "Would you please just sit down for a minute?"

"Fine." Slowly, I walked around the side of my desk before plopping down in my chair.

After sitting for a few seconds in stony silence, Gabe said, "Your dad's a cool guy."

"Yes, he is."

"He was kind enough to keep me company when I first got here, not to mention hospitable. He told me all the places where I could eat in town."

"That's my dad, always kind to the stranger—and the undeserving."

A smirk curved his lips. "Talk about not looking the type."

"What does that mean?"

"I would have never pegged you for being a football player."

Inwardly, I groaned at the thought of Gabe seeing Dad's pride wall in the far corner of the shop. There were pictures of all the accomplishments of his daughters, as well as Linc. There were also framed prints of the newspaper articles about when I joined the football team. "Your dad told me all about how you went from playing soccer to being the kicker. I don't think I've ever met a female football player."

"I'm sure you would prefer the thoughts of me in a cheerleader skirt, right?"

"Actually your arena football uniform was far racier than a cheerleading one," he replied with a wink.

Ugh. Like I really wanted to be reminded of the days I'd played in the league by someone like Gabe. In my defense, it was a good way to stay in shape, and the extra money helped out. That said, I seriously needed to take those pictures down and burn them. If it wasn't Gabe leering at them, it was one of the other men in town. Raising my brows, I said, "Why don't you nix the bullshit and get to the point?"

"Fine. Do you remember yesterday when I told you about how I've been having so much trouble songwriting?"

"Yeah."

"Well, last night, I was able to write not one, but three songs."

"While I applaud you, I'm not sure what this has to do with me."

"It has *everything* to with you. *You* inspired them."

The conviction of his tone had me sitting up straighter in my chair. I blinked at him in disbelief as I tried processing the enormity of what he had just said to me. "Let me get this straight: you believe *I* helped inspire the songs you wrote?"

"Without a doubt in my mind."

The only reply I could manage was, "Wow."

I'm sure you've heard artists use the term *muse* before."

"I have."

"After the hell I've been through with writer's block the last few months, there's not a doubt in my mind that you are my muse, Rae."

Holy shit. A rich and handsome musician was sitting before me professing that I was his creative muse. Things like that just didn't happen—at least they never had for me. My ex had never called me his muse or told me I was inspiring. The only thing I'd inspired in him was the ability to blow out of town and never look back.

"I would be lying if I said I wasn't totally flattered by what you're saying."

Gabe leaned forward in his chair. "I didn't come here to flatter you. I came to here to ask you to continue feeding my muse."

"Just exactly how would I do that?"

"By spending time with me."

I widened my eyes at him. "You can't be serious."

"Trust me, I wouldn't be throwing myself on the mercy of a woman who rejected me if I wasn't."

Sitting back in my chair, I surveyed Gabe. Gone was the cocky and arrogant man who had hit on me the day before. In his place seemed to sit a much more sincere and down-to-earth person. I wondered if his truer self was more like my first impression, and now he was merely putting on an act to get in my good graces. After all, he knew full well what I thought of the previous day's man.

"You think by hanging out with me, you could write even more songs?"

"I know it sounds crazy, but there's something about just being in your presence that inspires me."

Nibbling on my bottom lip, I replied, "I don't know. I mean, I'd like to help, but I do have a very busy life. I'm not quite sure how I would fit time in to be your muse."

"I'm willing to compensate you for your time."

My eyes bulged. "Like a hooker?"

Gabe scowled. "Of course not. I'm not paying to fuck you, just to hang out with you."

"I'm sorry, but something about a man paying for my time screams prostitute."

"Look, I'm just trying to make this beneficial for you."

Crossing my arms over my chest, I remarked, "It sounds pretty desperate."

Lightning-quick anger flashed in Gabe's eyes. "Trust me, nothing short of extreme desperation would ever have me begging any woman, least of all *you*." *Ouch.*

While there had been a part of me that had softened to Gabe's plight, his last statement caused it to shrivel up and die. "For being an alleged songwriter, you certainly don't know how to say the right words to benefit your case."

Gabe grimaced as he raked a hand through his hair. "Okay, so maybe that didn't come out like I meant it to."

"I'm pretty sure you said exactly what you truly feel. Because of your lack of respect for women, there is no amount of money you could offer that would induce me to spend time with you." Rising out of my chair, I motioned to the door. "Now I'd like you to leave."

A barrage of emotions came over Gabe's face—anger, fear, sadness, panic—before he finally settled on frustration. While I expected a much harsher response, he merely replied, "Thank you for hearing me out." He then rose to his feet and calmly walked out of my office.

Once he was gone, I collapsed back into my chair. I brought my hands to my head, which was swimming from my encounter with Gabe. *What the hell just happened?* Had I done the right thing in turning him away? Had I let my past with Ryan sabotage me in the present? "Yeah, keep blaming yourself, Rae. I'm pretty sure Gabe is the one at fault here," I muttered to myself.

"...there's not a doubt in my mind that you are my muse, Rae." Gabe's voice echoed through my mind. He had been able to write a song for the first time in months. I told him off and left him to fend for himself in the backwoods, and somehow because of all of that, he'd written a song.

A song.

After what had just occurred, there was no way I was going to be able to concentrate on my work, at least not until I headed over to Harts and Flowers and unburdened myself to Kennedy and Ellie. Grabbing my keys, I headed for the door.

Gabe

7

FOR THE SECOND time in less than twenty-four hours, Reagan Hart had annihilated me. Of course, I had no one but myself to blame. I had been a glutton for punishment by attempting to see her a second time.

When I started out of Rae's office and into the service center, I bumped into someone. "Ow," they cried. Realizing none of the men around would say *ow*, I glanced behind me. A kid was rubbing his head where I must have beaned him with my elbow.

"I'm sorry."

"It's okay."

As I resumed stalking out of the service center, the boy called "Hey Mr. Renard!"

I whirled around. "What do you want, Opie?"

His dark brows knitted together. "Uh, my name's not Opie."

"I didn't think it was."

"Then why did you call me that?"

"It's called sarcasm, kid." When he continued to give me a blank look, I added, "'Cause you're a small-town kid like Opie off *The Andy Griffith Show*."

"The show in black and white that my Papa watches?"

"That's the one."

Opie extended his hand, which I reluctantly shook. "My name's Linc. Well, it's really Lincoln, but everybody calls me Linc."

"Good to know."

Even though I picked up my pace, he fell in step beside me. "Do you really want to hang out with Rae?"

"I must be crazy as hell, but yeah, I do."

"But she turned you down flat."

"How do you know that?"

He gave me a sheepish grin. "I was standing outside her office while you guys were talking."

"So you're not only nosy, you're also a creeper."

"I didn't mean to listen. I was waiting for my grandpa."

"Is there a point to you telling me you're a snoop?"

Linc nodded. "I was thinking you need a middle man to get on Rae's good side."

After the last twenty-four hours of rejection and runaround, my patience was wearing extremely thin. "Kid, I don't have time for games."

"It's not a game, I swear."

"Then what?"

Linc cocked his head. "If I could get Rae to hang out with you, would you do something for me?"

"You're serious?"

"Yes sir."

Crossing my arms over my chest, I said, "And what mystical power do you have over Rae that would make her want to hang out with me?

Linc grinned triumphantly. "I'm her son."

Holy shit. Rae had a kid? I'd never even stopped to think that she might be a mom, but it went without saying that she was definitely a MILF. Now that I knew Linc was Rae's son, I could see the resemblance. "How old are you?"

"I turn ten next month."

"She doesn't look old enough to be your mom," I remarked, more to myself than to Linc.

"She was seventeen when I was born."

"That explains it." So Rae had been a teen mom before MTV had made it cool.

Scratching my chin, I narrowed my eyes at Linc. "If you know your mom doesn't want to hang out with me, why are you willing to help?"

"I want a favor."

"What kind of favor?"

"You see, my mom has this thing about musicians."

I snorted. "Yeah, I kinda got that."

"I've begged her for a guitar, but she keeps telling me no." Jerking his chin at me, he said, "That's where you come in."

"You want me to get you a guitar?" Of all the things the kid could have asked me for—concert tickets, money, expensive gadgets—I couldn't help being slightly surprised that he'd asked for a guitar.

Linc nodded. "It doesn't have to be one of yours or one that costs a lot of money. I just need one to learn on. You see, my friend's older brother has been teaching me chords and stuff, but I don't have a guitar to practice on at home."

"Let me get this straight: you want me to go against your mother's wishes and give you a guitar so you can smooth things over for me to hang out with her?"

"Exactly."

"Damn, kid. That sounds a little devious to me."

Linc's expression saddened. "Didn't you ever want something so bad you were willing to do anything to get it?"

"Well, yeah, of course I have."

"Then can't you see my point?"

"Yeah, but it's—"

"I make all As at school, even in math which I'm no good at. I always clean my room and make my bed. I never get into any trouble at school or at home."

"That's quite a sell job you're doing there. I had no idea I was in the presence of such perfection," I mused.

He grimaced. "Okay, sometimes I get in trouble because I forget things, like when my homework is due."

"Ah, so you aren't perfect."

"You see, my mom's afraid if I start playing guitar and get in a band, I'm going to turn into a shit like my dad."

Bingo. I was about to get some insight on Rae's ex-files. "Your dad's a musician?

Linc nodded. "At least he was when he and my mom were together." He shrugged. "I don't know what he is now 'cause I've never met him."

No wonder Rae hated rockers—she'd been knocked up and abandoned by one when she was just a kid. That would certainly be enough to turn you off to them, as well as leading you to reject any offers to be one's muse.

"Please, Mr. Renard."

"Give me a minute to think." When it came down to it, getting the kid a guitar wasn't the issue—I had three back at my apartment in Atlanta. It was the problem of going behind his mom's back. If Rae hated me now, she would be out for my blood when she found out I'd given her son a guitar. There would be no way in hell she would want to be anywhere near me, which would totally screw up my songwriting.

Maybe it would be possible to blow town before she knew what I'd done. I could stay in Bumblefuck for the next week or two, get enough songs for the album, and then get the hell out of dodge. Once Rae realized what I'd done, I'd be safely back in Atlanta.

"Okay, here are my conditions: you get me the hookup with your mom, then after a week or so when I'm done writing songs, I'll get you a guitar."

Linc mulled over my words. "How do I know I can trust you to deliver on the guitar? No offense, but I just don't think your word is enough."

Jesus, the kid drove a hard bargain. "Would you like me to sign something?"

"Like a contract?"

"Yes."

"I think that would be in both our best interests." His brows crinkled. "I'd like to have it notarized, but I'm afraid Candy would want to know what it was."

"My signature and my word are my bond. I won't back out."

"Okay, until I can write up the contract, why don't we shake on it?"

With a roll of my eyes, I replied, "Fine." I threw my hand out, and Linc shook it.

"So how we do this?" I asked.

"I think a sneak attack is the best way to start."

"Okay. I'm listening."

"On Mondays we always eat dinner at The Hitching Post on Main Street, so you could just happen to be there when we get there. Then I could ask you to sit with us because I recognized you from Jacob's Ladder." Just when I started to agree with him, Linc frowned. "Wait, I don't know if it's a good idea that we play up your rocker status. What do you think?"

I blinked at him. I was starting to think Linc was nine going on thirty. "Hmm, you're probably right."

"We don't get a lot of strangers around here. Maybe I could ask you to sit with us because you're sitting by yourself and look lonely?"

"Oh yeah, let's ditch the rocker angle and go for me looking sad and pathetic," I muttered.

Linc laughed. "I'm just trying to come up with the best plan."

"I say we stay with rocker. Moms are usually pretty weird about their kids talking to or hanging out with strangers."

"Oh yeah, she's always telling me that. Plus, it makes more sense that I want you to sit with us as a musician since she knows how much I want to play guitar."

"Works for me. What time should I be there?"

"Mom usually closes up the shop at six then we head on over there."

Nodding, I replied, "I'll be there."

8

"HEY MOM, aren't you ready to go?" Linc asked.

I glanced from my computer over to him. "I'm sorry, sweets, but I'm running behind today. I might have to stay until seven to catch up. You want to call Papa to come get you?"

The devastated look on Linc's face made me feel like Mother of the Year. The reason I was running behind on paperwork was because I'd spent over an hour at Harts and Flowers, hashing and rehashing Gabe's visit with Kennedy and Ellie. By the time I had gotten back to the shop, I was needed out on the floor to oversee some insurance adjusters, and I'd even eaten lunch sitting at my desk with my head buried in my computer.

"But we always go to dinner together on Monday nights," Linc protested.

Not only did he have the most pitiful tone in the world, he also somehow managed to stick his bottom lip out. "You really want to go out to eat with me instead of seeing what goodies Stella cooked?"

"Yessss."

My gaze trailed back over to the computer screen. It wouldn't kill anybody if I did cut out early; the paperwork would still be there in there morning. I hit save on the file I had open and turned off the computer then held up my hands in defeat. "Fine. You know I can never say no when you pick me over Papa."

A guilty look flashed in Linc's eyes before he quickly replaced it with pure happiness and rushed over to tug on my sleeve. "Come on, Mom. I'm starving."

"Okay, okay, keep your stomach at bay. I have to close up." I grabbed my purse out of the desk drawer and then rose out of my chair. Usually when I got ready to leave, Linc would be running around the shop or outside playing with Demo. Today, though, he never left my side. I had a shadow as I checked to ensure all the equipment was off and the doors were locked. I started to think he was going to come in the bathroom with me, but thankfully, he waited outside the door.

Once Hart and Daughter was thoroughly closed up, Linc and I headed over to the car. As I pulled out onto Main Street, I noticed a clanging noise. Just when I started to think I had a mechanical issue, I realized it was the zipper on Linc's backpack hitting the underside of the dashboard as he bounced his knees. It was something he did when he was anxious—a little nervous habit. I wondered if something had happened at school. Maybe Mrs. Lockhart had hated his solar system project. Inwardly, I groaned when I thought maybe he was upset about Donuts with Dad. Was he really okay with my dad going with him, or was he starting to wish he had a father? Even though I was dying to press him about what he might be nervous about, I decided I would wait until we sat down to eat.

I eased the SUV up to the curb outside of The Hitching Post. It was one of the three restaurants in town, and since it was on Main Street and close to the house, we usually ate there at least twice a week. I'd barely put the car in park when Linc bounded out of the door. "Linc, be careful! Watch for cars!" I shouted.

Ignoring me, he was already around the front of the vehicle, and he managed to open my door for me before I had the chance.

"Wow, what's brought on the chivalry tonight?"

"Nothing. I'm just hungry."

"Whatever, buddy," I replied as I reached out to ruffle his hair.

After I hopped out, my gaze caught a dark-haired figure standing inside the restaurant. Whipping my sunglasses off, I squinted at the man. At the realization of who it was, I gasped.

Oh no. It wasn't possible that Gabe Renard was waiting to be seated at the very restaurant we were going to eat at. The last thing on earth I wanted was to see him again, especially not with Linc since I didn't know how Gabe would react.

When Linc's hand reached for the door, I swatted it away. "What would you say if we skipped out on The Hitching Post and drove over to Preston for some Chinese?"

"But we always eat here on Monday nights."

I shrugged. "So? We can mix things up and get your favorite Chinese."

Linc stared at me like I'd grown horns. "But I want a burger tonight, not Chinese."

Inwardly, I groaned. "Okay. I just thought I'd suggest it."

Without another word, Linc pushed on inside. When the bell tinkled over our heads, Gabe turned around, and my breath hitched as I waited to see his reaction. Surprise flooded me when he gave me a genuine smile—the kind of smile you reserve for people you like, not ones who had turned you down for both a date and to be your musical muse.

"Oh wow! It's Gabe Renard!" Linc shouted before pointing at Gabe.

Jerking Linc's hand down, I said, "It's not polite to point."

Linc stared up at me, wide-eyed. "But he's famous! Papa said some famous rocker named Gabe was in town, but I had no idea it was Gabe Renard."

"It's nice to meet you," Gabe said, throwing out his hand.

Linc stared at it in awe for a moment before shaking Gabe's hand. "I can't believe I just touched Gabe Renard's hand. None of my friends are going to believe this."

"Why don't we take a selfie together? Then you have photographic evidence."

Linc's eyes bulged. "You'd really do that?"

"Sure. I'd be happy to."

Thrusting his phone at me, Linc said, "Will you take it, Mom?"

"Uh, sure," I replied. As I brought the phone up, Gabe threw his arm around Linc. I tried to hide my utter shock at Gabe's behavior as I snapped a few pictures of the two. "Okay, there's your photographic evidence."

"It would be rude of me not to say thank you again for getting my Jeep unstuck yesterday," Gabe said.

Waving my hand, I countered, "It was nothing."

"Oh, but it wasn't. It meant a lot to me." I knew Gabe was no longer talking about the tow.

"Are you here by yourself?" Linc asked.

"Yep."

My son turned to me. "Can Mr. Renard eat dinner with us?"

"I'm sure Mr. Renard doesn't want to eat with us, sweetie." I narrowed my eyes at Gabe. "Do you?"

"As a matter of fact, I would love the company. Besides, I never like to let my fans down." He winked at me. "Where are we sitting?"

I fought the urge to reach over and smack the smug look right off of Gabe's face. Instead, I took a few deep breaths and tried to keep my temper at bay. "Linc, why don't you go wash your hands while Mr. Renard and I get a table?" I suggested.

"Okay. I'll be right back."

As soon as Linc was out of sight, I turned back to Gabe. "What are you doing here?" I hissed.

With a shrug, Gabe replied, "The same thing you are—grabbing some dinner."

"I mean, what are you doing still in town?"

"I booked a room at the Grandview for a few days. I thought I might stick around and see if I could rekindle the writing vibes, even without you."

Slowly, I shook my head. "You're going to stay in Hayesville?"

"Yep. Mrs. Paulson was kind enough to rent out the entire third floor to me so I wouldn't be disturbed."

Of course Mrs. Paulson had. As Aunt Sadie would say, Rejune Paulson had come out of the womb man-crazy. She might've been in her fifties, but she would have been more than happy to make Gabe one of her cougar cubs. I wrinkled my nose at the thought.

"But you're a big city boy...there's nothing for someone like you to do here."

"If you mean the town doesn't have distractions, you're correct, and that is exactly what I need."

I stared at Gabe for a few moments before huffing in frustration. "You're impossible."

"Right now, I'm hungry, so what do you say we get a table?"

"Fine," I grumbled.

The owner of The Hitching Post, Kenneth Maxwell, sat propped up on a stool at the register. He doubled as both the cashier and host. "How many?"

"Three."

"Follow me."

I couldn't hide my surprise when Gabe motioned for me to go ahead of him. "And here I thought you didn't have a remotely chivalrous bone in your body," I remarked.

"I'm full of surprises."

"I'd say it was more you were full of shit."

Gabe threw back his head and laughed. Just as Kenneth pointed out our table, Linc arrived back from the bathroom. When I started to pull out my chair, Gabe once again shocked the hell out of me by stepping in front of me to do it himself. "I believe that makes me two and oh when it comes to chivalry points," he mused.

I rolled my eyes before allowing him to push me up to the table. When I reached out to take a menu from Kenneth, he was staring open-mouthed at Gabe. "Yes, he's a famous country rocker. I'm sure he'll sign something for you after dinner."

Kenneth head jerked back at my response. "I didn't realize that. I was just surprised to see anyone under sixty pulling a chair out for a woman." He then turned his interested gaze over to Gabe. "Are you really famous, or is she just pulling my leg?"

Gabe laughed. "She's telling the truth. I'm the drummer for the band Jacob's Ladder."

"Well, I'll be damned. I think the last time we had anyone famous in town was years ago when they were filming that movie about the circus with the guy who played the sparkly vampire."

"Sparkly vampire?" Gabe questioned.

"Robert Pattinson. They filmed some scenes for *Water for Elephants* at a farm not too far from here."

With a grin, Gabe replied, "I see. He did play a sparkly vampire in the *Twilight* series. He's a pretty cool guy though."

I sucked in a breath. "You know Robert Pattinson?"

"I met him at a party a few years ago right after the last *Twilight* movie came out—*Breaking*…whatever it was."

"*Breaking Dawn*," I replied breathlessly.

"Yeah, that's the one."

Linc snickered. "Mom thinks he's hot."

"I do not," I protested as I felt warmth flooding my cheeks.

"Yes, you do. You and Aunt Ellie are always talking about how you'd have his babies when there's a *Twilight* weekend on Freeform."

Refusing to look at Gabe, I turned to Kenneth. "Linc and I will have sweet tea."

After bobbing his head, Kenneth looked over at Gabe. "And you?"

"I'll have the same."

"Three sweet teas it is. I'll let May know. She'll be your waitress tonight."

"Thanks, Kenneth."

After staring down at my menu for a few seconds, I could feel Gabe's eyes on me. Finally, I dared myself to look up at him. "What?"

"Robert Pattinson?" he asked with a smirk.

"Shut up. I should be able to have my celebrity crushes without any judgement."

Gabe held up his hands. "No judgment, just surprise. It makes sense now why you turned me down." With a wink, he added, "I must not be your type."

"Trust me, whether or not you're my type had nothing to do with me turning you down."

May returned with our drinks. "Rae, can I get you and Linc your usual?"

I looked at Linc for confirmation before replying, "Sure."

"What about you?" she asked Gabe. At that moment, she got a good look at him then proceeded to freak out. "Oh my God, you're Gabe Renard. You're in Jacob's Ladder." Her usually porcelain face flushed to a tomato red.

Gabe flashed her a genuine smile. "I am. It's nice to meet you."

"I've listened to you guys for years. I even have some of your CDs from when Micah was still in the band."

"That is a long time."

With her free hand, May fanned her face. "Whatever you want to eat is on the house—my treat."

"I can't let you do that."

She giggled. "I insist. Then I can tell everyone I bought Gabe Renard dinner!"

"While I'm still not agreeing, I'll take the chicken and dumplings, macaroni and cheese, and the fried okra."

With a trembling hand, May wrote down Gabe's selections. "I'll be right back."

"Looks like if you play your cards just right, May might take you home with her tonight," I mused.

He grinned. "She's not my type."

"Because she's old?" Linc questioned while wrinkling his nose.

Shaking his head, Gabe replied, "Because she's tall and blonde." His gaze came to me. "I like petite brunettes."

I rolled my eyes in reply to his come-on. "Linc, do you have any homework you could be working on?"

"Nope. I got it all done at the shop."

"You're absolutely sure? We're not going to get home and you realize you were supposed to do another project like the solar system one?"

Linc laughed. "No, Mom. I promise."

"Good."

Gabe broke apart one of the cornbread muffins in his hand. "Tell me, Linc, do you play any sports?"

"Soccer."

Gabe glanced from Linc to me. "Not football like your mom?"

"I'm really not comfortable with him playing until he's a little older," I said.

"He's got plenty of time. I didn't start playing until I was about twelve."

"Was it because your mom was a scaredy-cat and thought you'd get hurt?" Linc asked while shooting a look at me.

Before I could respond, Gabe shook his head. "No. It was more about the fact that we were living overseas at the time."

"Was your dad in the military?" I asked.

"No. My parents were missionaries."

I stilled my fork midway to my mouth. "*You're* the son of missionaries?"

"What does that seem so shocking to you?"

"I guess I never stopped to imagine it." I gave him a pointed look. "Maybe it was because of your behavior when we first met."

"How did he act?" Linc asked.

"Uh..." While Gabe smirked at me, I quickly answered, "Not very Christian."

May interrupted us by bringing our food. "Let me know if you guys need anything else."

"Thanks," Gabe replied as he picked up his fork. When we were once again alone, Gabe stared intently at me. "As I said this morning, I am truly sorry for the way I acted yesterday."

I cocked my brows at him. "And this morning?"

With a scowl, Gabe added, "Yes, this morning as well."

"Whatever," I muttered before taking a sugary sweet sip of tea.

"You are going to forgive him, aren't you Mom?" Linc asked.

As Gabe leaned forward expectantly in his seat, I slowly set my glass down. "You know, Linc, that's really between me and Mr. Renard."

"But they always say in Sunday school that we're to accept sincere apologies and love our neighbor."

For the first time in my life, I regretted that my son paid attention in church. I obviously couldn't tell him that part of me not forgiving Gabe stemmed from the fact that he was a sex fiend who wanted to get in my pants. He also wasn't old enough grasp the enormity of a man being a sexist pig either. "Fine. In light of what you said, I forgive him."

Gabe smiled. "I'm glad to hear that."

"Let it be noted for the record that it was only under duress," I hissed at Gabe.

"I'll take it in spite of that."

Even as we began devouring the Southern goodness on our plates, the conversation never died down. Like an obsessed member of the paparazzi, Linc wanted to know every facet of what it was like to be in a band, and Gabe was kind to humor Linc's incessant questions about what it was like to get a record deal and to go out on tour.

Of course, as I watched Linc's eyes light up as he heard about the antics of life on the road, I couldn't fight the uneasy feeling that came over me. It was the same feeling I got whenever Linc talked about music and wanting to play the guitar. My heart had been broken too many times because of music. I'd ultimately lost my mother and my boyfriend because of music, and I would be damned if I lost my son as well.

With his plate empty, Gabe leaned back in his chair and rubbed his belly. "Damn, that was good. I can't remember the last time I had really good Southern food. I guess it was the last time I was at my mom and dad's in Texas."

"They really do have the best food in town. I guess that would be obvious since we eat here at least once a week," I said as I wiped my mouth with my napkin.

"Yeah, Linc told me you did." The moment the words left his lips, a panicked look took over Gabe's face. At the same time, Linc gasped next to me.

Glancing between the two of them, I asked, "Wait, when did you say that?"

Linc swallowed hard. "Uh…back when Gabe was asking what was good."

Although I didn't remember Linc mentioning our dining habits to Gabe, I merely nodded. After clearing his throat, Gabe asked, "So who's up for dessert?"

"Yes, pie!" Linc exclaimed as I said, "No, I think we're good." Of course, my son wanted to get dessert, which would equate to having to spend even more time with Gabe. Truthfully, it wasn't that bad spending time with Gabe. I certainly liked the side I was seeing of him tonight more than the one I had the previous day or that morning, even if Linc's eyes were a little too star-struck for my liking.

"Come on, Mom, we always have pie." Linc waggled his brows at me. "I'll even get the lemon and let you have some."

I laughed at his antics. "You sure know how to sweeten the pot, don't you?" With a sigh, I added, "Fine. You can have a piece of pie, but don't get lemon just because of me. I can get my own." I'd barely raised my hand off the table to wave May over when she came charging forward.

"Is there something I can get you?" she asked, ignoring me and staring straight at Gabe.

While I rolled my eyes at her actions, Gabe merely smiled politely. "Yes, we'd like dessert."

"Yes, yes, of course. What kind would you like?" Once she scribbled down our orders for two slices of chocolate pie and one of lemon, May scurried off to the kitchen.

"You handled her pretty well," I remarked.

"After all these years, I'm kinda used to it."

"Are fans always that way?" While I wanted to ask if women were always that way around him, I decided it was best to stick to fans in general—I didn't have any doubt in my mind what women were like with Gabe Renard. It was part of why he'd seemed so horrified yesterday when I'd told him no.

"Most of the time, yes. While I try to just handle it politely, my brother Eli goes way over the top. He starts conversations, asks about their families, what they do for a living." With a smile, Gabe shook his head. "He was born to be a politician. He's all about the shaking hands and kissing babies."

I laughed. "He sounds pretty cool."

"He is. He and my sister are so much alike—all sunshine and roses. Me, I'm more Oscar the Grouch when it comes down to it."

Tilting my head at him, I teased, "You? Never."

Gabe grinned. "Whatever."

May returned with our pies. When Gabe practically inhaled his,

Linc and I stared at him in shock. "That was amazing. I think I'll get another slice."

Loud chatter interrupted us. At the sight of my Aunt Sadie's silver bouffant peeking out from under her wide-brimmed red hat, I fought the urge to dive under the table and hide. I'd forgotten she and the other silver-haired ladies loved to come by The Hitching Post for desert after their Red Hat Society meetings. There was no way in hell she wasn't going to come over and demand to know what I was doing with Gabe. She might've been an old maid, but she was bound and determined that her nieces would tie the knot.

When she met my gaze, her blue eyes widened. After saying something to the other women, she made a beeline to our table—well, as much of a beeline as a ninety-two-year-old woman can.

"Well, well, look who it is—my darling niece and nephew," Aunt Sadie said. Her gaze bobbed from us over to Gabe. "And I don't believe I've met your handsome companion."

"This is Gabe Renard. He's just passing through from Atlanta," I replied.

Aunt Sadie smiled her usual cat-ate-the-canary smile. "Why, I'm aware that he's not from here, sweetheart. I know everyone in this town, and I've certainly never had the pleasure of meeting him before."

Although Aunt Sadie had never married, she certainly had never lacked for male attention. After her fiancé had been killed in World War II, she'd vowed never to marry. While she might not have ever donned the white dress and veil, she was not going to die a virgin. She was probably one of the first liberated women of her day in Hayesville.

When Aunt Sadie dangled her hand in front of Gabe's face, he politely shook it. "It's very nice meeting you as well. In my short stay in town, I've met several of Rae's family members."

"I'm sure the pleasure is all mine."

"Would you like to join us for dessert?" Gabe asked.

"I would love to."

"But what about your friends? Surely it would be rude to leave them," I piped up.

Aunt Sadie waved her hand. "They certainly won't mind me jumping ship to have dessert with my niece and her handsome friend."

My mouth gaped open when Gabe rose out of his chair to pull out the chair next to him for Sadie. Was he seriously that thoughtful and considerate? It was too hard to believe the same egotistical jerk-wad from the previous day and that morning was acting like he was a gentleman out of a Jane Austen novel. It was like he had pulled a Dr. Jekyll and Mr. Hyde.

"If you don't close your mouth, Reagan, you might catch a fly," Aunt Sadie chided as she took a seat.

After clamping my lips together, I made the mistake of looking at Gabe, who had the audacity to wink at me like he knew exactly what I was thinking about him.

God, he was such an egomaniac, and man, I hoped he didn't make a reappearance in my dreams that night. Well, maybe it wouldn't be *so* bad…

SITTING around the table with Rae, Sadie, and Linc felt just like being at home, which was strange considering they were practically strangers to me. More than anything, they were completely genuine around me. They weren't spending time with me because I was Gabe Renard of Jacob's Ladder. To all of them except for Linc, I was nothing special, just an average Joe. After so many years in the business, it was refreshing as hell to be able to feel so free.

When a melody entered my head, I froze mid-sentence. Pinching my eyes shut, I searched for the right lyrics to go with it. As they started to come, I started tapping my foot in time with the melody.

"Are you all right?" Rae asked.

I snapped my eyes open. "Uh, yeah, I'm fine." Glancing around the restaurant, I looked for the restroom sign. When I saw it at the back of the dining room, I popped out of my seat. "I'll be right back."

The heated stares from the others at the table bore into my back as I made my getaway. I was sure they were all wondering what the hell my problem was. Knowing Rae's disdain for me and rockers in general, she probably thought I was escaping to the bathroom for a drug fix.

When I hurried into the bathroom, I thankfully found it empty. Since I'd left my journal in the Jeep, I would have to improvise as far as what to write on. As my gaze spun around the room, I held out hope for paper towels rather than a dryer. I could write so much better on paper towels than I could toilet paper. *Jackpot.* Ripping off a long section, I then locked myself in a stall and pulled the Hart and Daughter pen out of my pocket. After knocking out three songs with it the other day, I'd decided to replace my once lucky pen.

I balanced the paper towel across my knee and started furiously scribbling down the chords I heard in my head. When I'd gotten the main melody down, I started adding in the lyrics that flowed through me. Reading back over my work, I smiled. This one was certainly lighthearted and brighter in tone than the other three I'd written.

"Gabe?" Linc questioned outside the stall.

I jerked my head up. "Yeah?"

"Are you okay?"

"Yeah, I'm fine. Why?"

"Mom wanted me to check on you since it's been almost thirty minutes."

Holy shit. It felt like I had just sat down. I'd been so lost in the songwriting zone that I had no idea how much time had passed. Even though I could have continued writing, I couldn't leave Rae and Linc hanging. I gently folded up the paper towel and stuffed it into my pocket, along with my pen.

When I came out of the stall, I met Linc's concerned face. "Do you want me to see if Mom has some tummy medicine?"

I laughed. "While I appreciate the offer, it's not necessary. I wasn't in here with the shits. I was writing a song."

Linc's face lit up. "You were?"

"Yep."

"So you weren't lying when you said just hanging out with my mom helped you with your songs."

"Nope. It's the God's honest truth." I went over to the sink to start washing my hands. Glancing back at him in the mirror, I said, "Besides the win of me starting another song, I think tonight went pretty well. How about you?"

Linc nodded enthusiastically. "Mom made it all the way through dinner and dessert without going off on you. Sometimes she even seemed to like talking to you."

With a grin, I replied, "I thought as much."

"So, what happens now?"

"There's no doubt about it—I *have* to see her again tomorrow."

"What excuse are you going to use this time? She knows you're in town, so you can't really just bump into her like you did tonight."

"Good point." Tilting my head in thought, I dried my hands. "I need—no, I *want* to do something nice for her."

"Like flowers?"

"Nah, that's a go-to kind of gift, the kind every guy uses when he wants to do something nice for a girl. I want to do something unique, something that would make her day."

"You could bring her breakfast."

"That's not exactly the angle I was going for, but since you're her son and know her pretty well, I'll hear you out."

"She loves French toast, and even though my Aunt Kennedy owns a bakery, she refuses to make French toast."

"Why?"

Lowering his voice, Linc said, "It's because of this guy she dated a long time ago when she was taking cooking classes in France."

"Ah, I see."

"Anyway, Mom hardly ever gets her favorite breakfast because the restaurants around here only serve pancakes and waffles, not French toast."

"If there's none around here, where the hell am I going to find it to bring it to her?"

"Her favorite one is forty-five minutes from here."

Groaning, I rolled my eyes to the ceiling. "Let me get this straight: I'm supposed to spend an hour and a half on the road just to get French toast."

"Yep."

"Maybe I could hire your aunt to make some."

Linc shook his head. "Trust me, she won't do it."

"Maybe not for free, but money talks."

"But don't you see? It's the fact that you're going out of your way to get her the food she really likes that counts. It's something you can do from your heart, not your wallet."

I stared wide-eyed at Linc. "Damn, kid. How could you know that?" I swore he was some sort of wise old soul in a kid's body. He was absolutely right—Rae wasn't impressed with my fame or money, so she certainly wouldn't appreciate me throwing money at her sister.

She was more likely to be impressed that I did something for myself—that I didn't ask my assistant to deliver it to me. "Once again, you're completely right. You're going to be a total ladies' man when you get older."

Linc's cheeks flushed. "Maybe."

"Trust me, most men don't possess the level of understanding about women that you do, and you're only nine. There must be something to be said for being raised in an all-female household."

"Aunt Kennedy says I'm surrounded by estrogen, whatever that is."

With a laugh, I replied, "You don't need to worry about that right now." I rubbed my hands together. "Okay, what's the name of the place with the fantastic French toast? To make it back in time before your mom leaves for work, I might have to throw some money at them to open early."

After Linc gave me the name of what I could only imagine was some backwoods version of iHop, I motioned to the door. "Okay, let's get out of here before everyone else thinks I crapped out my intestines."

Linc snickered. "That's pretty sick."

"Yeah, it is."

When we started out of the bathroom, Rae was pacing in the hall-way. At the sight of us, a relieved expression replaced her concerned one. "Thank God. I was just about to go in after you two, and I really, really didn't want to have to do that."

I grinned. "I'm sorry. I should have sent Linc back to the table to let you know I was all right, but when he found out I had been writing a song, we started talking about it."

Linc gave me a look that said, *Nice save.*

Rae's dark eyes widened. "You were writing a song? In the bathroom?"

"Yep. On paper towels."

"That's…"

"Insane?" I finished for her.

She shook her head. "Amazing," she murmured. For the first time since she'd met me, she appeared actually impressed by me. "I can't imagine doing anything creative, least of all in a bathroom."

"When the words and the music come, I have to go with it. I'm sorry I ran out on you like that."

"You don't need to apologize."

"I'm sure Sadie must think I'm a psycho with the runs."

Both Rae and Linc laughed. "Speaking of Sadie, we better get back to the table. If we all disappear, she'll think it's some kind of conspiracy to get away from her."

"I'll go tell her everything is okay," Linc suggested before hurrying around the corner. Once again, I had to give the kid some props. He knew exactly when to try to give us some alone time.

After nibbling on her lip, Rae said, "So you really weren't lying to me when you said I influenced your songs?"

"Why would I have lied?"

With a matter-of-fact look, she replied, "To get me in bed."

"I thought I made it clear to you this morning that I wasn't interested in sleeping with you. I just want to platonically hang out with you to get my songs written." At Rae's quick intake of breath, I realized I'd once again fucked up by saying the wrong thing. *Not interested in sleeping with her? Yeah, keep telling yourself that. You'd fuck her up against the bathroom wall right now if she gave you the chance.*

"Excuse me for being overly cautious and not completely trusting you," she snapped.

There it was: the simmering rage beneath the surface, directed at me and only me. *Yeah, you deserved that one, asshole.*

I held my hands up in front of me. "It's okay, I get it. After the way I acted yesterday, it makes sense that you would be wary of anything I have to say."

"That's right."

"But after spending a little time with me and seeing me in the process, don't you believe me now?"

Rae's dark eyes held mine for a long moment. "Yes, I do."

Inwardly, I did a fist bump. "Does that mean you'll reconsider hanging out with me?"

"I don't know…maybe."

"I promise I won't interfere with your life or with Linc's. When you have some downtime, you can just hit me up."

"You mean you don't want to follow me around all day?"

I laughed. "Would that be so horrible?"

"It certainly wouldn't be ideal."

"I'll take whatever you can give me, Rae."

She slowly nodded her head. "Okay. I guess I can *try* to make time to hang out with you."

"Can you *try* not to make it sound like it's absolute torture being in my presence?"

A small smile curved her lips. "It's a hard job, but I'll give it a shot."

"Good. Why don't I come by for breakfast in the morning?"

Rae's smile faded slightly. "Oh, I don't know. The mornings are kinda hectic with my sisters and me trying to get to work and getting Linc to school."

"Just sit me at the table. I promise you won't even know I'm there."

With a roll of her eyes, Rae said, "Considering I'll have to make sure I'm decent, I'm pretty sure I'll know you're there."

"Please don't feel you have to be decent on my account." I waggled my brows at her.

She groaned. "I walked right into that one, didn't I?"

I laughed. "Yep. You did."

"Fine. You can come by in the morning, but just be warned that while my younger sister will be drooling over you, my older sister will be out for your balls."

"Damn. Do I even want to know why your sister has an axe to grind with me?"

"Let's just say I filled her in on what happened between us the other day."

"I see. I'll be sure to steer clear of her, especially if she's carrying a knife."

Rae laughed, and I could help noticing how good it sounded. I certainly hadn't heard it much; I supposed I hadn't given her very many reasons to laugh.

"Since she owns a bakery, that wouldn't be out of the norm."

"Wait, is it the one down the street from the Grandview?"

With a nod, Rae replied, "Yep. Harts and Flowers. The longer you're in town, the more you'll find that all the stores and businesses are either on or right off Main Street."

"That's good to know. I'll have to stop in there." Grinning, I added, "After I try to smooth things over with her tomorrow."

"Good luck with that one."

At that moment, the wide brim of Aunt Sadie's red hat came around the corner, and she eyed the two of us suspiciously. "Are you trying to cut out on the check, Mr. Rich and Famous?" she demanded.

I laughed. "No ma'am, I'm not."

"May begged to buy his dinner," Rae piped up in my defense.

"If you're not trying to run out on the check, what other nefarious things are the two of you doing back here?"

Rae sighed. "We're not doing anything, Aunt Sadie."

"Unfortunately," I quipped with a wink.

While an *Aha!* look flashed in Aunt Sadie's eyes, Rae appeared ready to kick me in the balls. "I thought Linc told you what was going on with Gabe and his songwriting," Rae said.

"He did, but what am I supposed to think when the two of you don't come back immediately?"

"Maybe that we're talking?"

"Mmhmm," she harrumphed.

"You're impossible," Rae replied as she brushed past her aunt.

Aunt Sadie whirled around, suprisingly agile for an old lady. "I'm just looking out for you. I don't want the gossip tongues in town wagging about how you were found in a compromising position with a strange man."

"It would be a nice change from 'Poor Rae, she's never going to find a husband working in a man's job like she does' or 'Men don't like strong women who act like they don't need a man.'"

"That's bullshit," I muttered.

Rae's brows shot up. "Excuse me?"

"The part about men not liking strong women."

"I'm sorry to disagree with you, but it's often been the case for me," Rae replied.

"Then you're obviously surrounded by a bunch of little boys in this town, rather than men," I countered.

Rae's stony expression melted before my eyes. As she stared almost incredulously at me, it was like she was seeing me for the first time—or maybe she was seeing the real me for the first time and not the opinion of me she'd formed in her mind. "Thank you," she murmured.

"You don't have to thank me for calling it as I see it."

"Regardless, I'm grateful that you're able to see it that way. I wish more men could be like you."

"You might be rethinking that statement as you get to know me better," I countered.

With a grin, Rae said, "I might. We'll just have to see." She jerked her chin toward the front of the restaurant. "Come on, let's get out of here."

"While mine is covered, I would like to buy yours and Linc's dinners." I winked at Aunt Sadie. "And your pie."

"You really don't need to do that," Rae protested.

"But I want to, for your trouble."

She laughed. "The trouble of hanging out with you?"

"Exactly."

"Okay then, I'll let you get dinner—but just this time."

"That seems fair to me." As we started back to the table, I asked, "What time should I come by tomorrow morning?"

"We usually get up between six and six thirty."

Linc made a face. "That's when you get up. I don't get up until around seven."

"That's because you're young and can look super cute in five minutes. It takes me and your aunts way longer."

With a laugh, I said, "How about I see you at seven?"

"That sounds good."

"See you tomorrow, Rae."

"Bye, Gabe."

Something in the way she said my name took me by surprise, and I couldn't help glancing back at her. God, she really was gorgeous. It was no wonder she'd become my muse, and if I was right, she was softening toward me. My plan was starting to work.

NORMALLY WHEN THE alarm clock went off in the mornings, I blew through three or four snooze alarms. On this day, however, the instant I heard the shrill decibels going off, I threw back the covers and practically sprinted from the bed. There was no way in hell I was going to let Gabe Renard catch me not dressed, least of all not looking my absolute best.

As I showered at record speed, I couldn't help slightly regretting telling Gabe to come by the house. Although I was being silly, there was a small part of me that didn't want him seeing where I lived. It wasn't so much about keeping things somewhat impersonal, but more about me worrying what he might think of the house. I was sure when he was off the road, he lived in some palatial mansion with a butler and a housekeeper while I lived at home with my two sisters, my son, and my geriatric aunt. It was hardly glamorous, not to mention most men found it rather unattractive.

After I got out of the shower, I pushed those thoughts out of my head and focused on my appearance. Most mornings I just dried my hair before sweeping it back into a ponytail. Today, I put extra gel and product into it. I also left it down and flowing over my shoulders. As for my makeup, I went so far as to put on lip liner, which I only used for special occasions. When I pursed my fuller lips at the mirror, I knew I'd made the right choice.

When I went into the kitchen, I expected to find both Kennedy and Ellie in their bathrobes with their usual bed hair. After breaking the news to them the night before that Gabe was coming to hang out with me before work, I should have known they would pull out all the stops. Both were already outfitted in their work attire with perfectly coiffed hair and gorgeous faces.

A pang of jealously shot through my chest at their appearances. Although I hated myself for it, I couldn't help thinking Gabe might find one of them hotter than me. Even worse, what if him writing songs in my presence was just a fluke and suddenly he was able to make music with Kennedy or Ellie?

Great. Gabe wasn't even there yet, and he was already bringing out the worst in me. First, it was completely uncharacteristic of me to feel threatened by my sisters. I always wanted the best for them in life, especially when it came to love, and I knew they felt the same about me. Although it would be hard when one of us found someone and moved out, we ultimately wanted each other to be happy.

Second, I couldn't believe I even cared if Gabe was attracted to them. I mean, it wasn't like I wanted him for myself. I wasn't remotely interested in pursuing anything with Gabe other than a relationship built on a professional basis, i.e. his songwriting.

But something had happened the previous night at dinner. Children were always a good judge of character, and Linc had a finely tuned radar for fakeness. He hadn't just been star-struck by Gabe; he'd found someone who genuinely took an interest in him.

As for me, I hated to admit it, but I'd been charmed as well by the fact that Gabe seemed interested in the mundane aspects of my life.

Inwardly, I rolled my eyes at how delusional I sounded. Of course there was a small part of me that was interested in Gabe. He was insanely good-looking, and although he could be a little cocky for my liking, it was certainly warranted considering his profession. Handsome and deserving of praise were two traits alone that were often hard to come by in Hayesville. There was also the fact that he seemed genuinely attracted to me. The odds were forever not in my favor that I found a man I wanted to date who in turn wanted to date me as well.

"You guys look great," I remarked as I went over to get my usual morning espresso.

"You don't look so bad yourself, sis. I'm especially digging the uncharacteristically low-cut shirt you're wearing, not to mention the tight jeans in place of your usual khakis," Kennedy said.

"I don't know what you're talking about."

Kennedy snorted. "What I'm talking about is the fact that you haven't worn a low-cut shirt to work since they caught Wes jerking off in the shop bathroom."

"No one could prove that was about my shirt," I countered.

"Considering he'd been standing over you at your desk for the ten minutes beforehand, I'd say it was most definitely your cleavage that sent him over the edge."

With a roll of my eyes, I said, "Like you're one to talk. When's the last time you wore makeup to work?"

Kennedy dropped her gaze back down to the pan of blueberry scones cooling on the stovetop. "The ovens are hot, and I end up sweating it off."

"Riiiight," I muttered.

Sweeping a hand to her hip, Ellie said, "For your information, I'm dressed with my makeup on because Aunt Sadie always said to put your best foot and face forward when company was coming."

I laughed. "Thank you, Emily Post." Glancing around the kitchen, I said, "Speaking of Aunt Sadie, I'm surprised she's not out here already."

"She was gone before we got up this morning. She has that AARP trip to Harrah's in Cherokee," Ellie replied.

"Ah, I should have known the only thing that would keep her from aggravating me about Gabe would be gambling."

"True on that one," Kennedy said.

Just as I threw a glance at the clock, the doorbell rang, causing my sisters and me to all jump out of our skins. "Oh shit, he's here!" I screeched. After momentarily wringing our hands, all three of us then proceeded to fluff our hair and smooth our clothes.

As I checked my appearance in the stainless steel refrigerator for probably the millionth time, Kennedy nudged me. "Go on. Let him in."

"I'm going, I'm going," I snapped back. Of course, it was at that moment that I found my feet seemed to be frozen to the black and white checkered floor. After my mind screamed at them to pick their sorry asses up, I started out of the kitchen and down the hallway.

When I threw open the front door, I found Gabe smiling at me.

"You know, you really should have asked who it was before you just opened the door. It could have been a pervert."

"Oh, but it *is* a pervert," I teased.

Gabe rolled his eyes. "You know what I mean."

"Thanks for the tip. While that might be standard practice in Atlanta, it's not really an issue here. I think the last real crime we had was when someone painted a giant dick on the side of the mayor's face on one of his campaign signs."

With a laugh, Gabe said, "Seriously?"

"Yep. People obviously have way too much time on their hands around here."

"At least they have a sense of humor about it. I would assume the mayor really is a dick if they did that?"

"Yeah, he is for the most part." I furrowed my brows at the bag in his hand. "What's that?"

"Breakfast."

"You didn't have to bring yourself something to eat. We would have fixed you something."

"It's not for me. It's for you."

My traitorous heart melted at gesture. "You brought me breakfast?"

Gabe grinned. "Not just any breakfast, your *favorite* breakfast."

I sucked in a breath so fast I wheezed. "Whoa, hold the phone—you brought me French toast?"

"And not just any French toast. It's French toast from Rafferty's."

"You're joking."

"Do I look like I'm joking?"

"But they're like forty-five minutes away."

"It was actually a nice drive."

Oh. My. God. This so wasn't happening. Gabe Renard had not just spent an hour and a half on the road to bring me my favorite breakfast. It was like a scene out of a cheesy Hallmark movie, and so help me God, I loved every minute of it. Of course, then it hit me: how in the world did he know what my favorite breakfast was, least of all where it came from? "Wait, how did you know about the French toast?"

Gabe grinned. "A little birdy told me."

My mind flashed back to the night before. "Ah, one named Lincoln."

"Yep. That's right."

"I don't know what to say."

"I sure as hell hope you say you're starving because I don't want this to go to waste."

I smiled. "There's no way I would ever let French toast from Rafferty's go untouched. I would probably have to be in the hospital in a body cast or something. Even then, I'd demand for someone to feed it to me."

Gabe laughed. "I'd be happy to feed it to you today if you'd like."

With a roll of my eyes, I replied, "That won't be necessary. Next you'll suggest I have breakfast in bed and you'll join me."

"Actually, that sounds quite nice. Will you be dressed in some form of lingerie while you have your breakfast?"

I smacked his arm playfully. "Keep this up and you won't be enjoying any of my presence today."

He winked at me. "Okay, okay, I'll rein it in."

"For you, I think that's easier said than done."

We stood there for a moment before Gabe asked, "Uh, are you going to invite me in?"

Slapping my hand to my forehead, I said, "Oh my God, I'm such an idiot. Yes, please come in."

As he stepped into the foyer, Gabe tilted his head to take in the interior of the house.

"I love your place."

"You do?" I questioned incredulously.

He nodded. "It reminds me of the house we moved into when we came back to the States."

"How long were you guys out of the country?"

"I was two when my dad got his first assignment, and then I was almost thirteen when we moved back."

"That's amazing. I can't imagine what it must be like to live in a different town, least of all in a different country. Hayesville is all I've ever known." I motioned around the foyer.

"This house is really all I've ever known—we moved in when I was three."

"Do you live with your dad?"

His question sent heat to my cheeks. "No. He lives about five minutes from here."

"You mean it's only you and Linc in this big place?"

"No, my two sisters have the upstairs." I gave him a tight smile. "And the house belongs to Aunt Sadie. She's in the room across from me."

Gabe nodded. "It must be nice having your family here to support you and Linc." At what must've been my slightly horrified expression, Gabe quickly added, "I don't mean financially. I mean, it must be nice to have them here *emotionally*."

I exhaled the breath I'd been holding. "Yes, it is…although there are times when I wouldn't mind having a place for just Linc and me."

"I know what you mean. My brother and I are in such close quarters on the bus when we're touring. There are days when I want to strangle him."

With a laugh, I replied, "Oh yeah, I have many days like that."

When Gabe and I walked into the kitchen, I saw that Linc had joined Kennedy and Ellie at the table. At the sight of Gabe, he bounded out of his chair. "Hey Gabe, good to see you again."

"It's good to see you again, too, buddy," Gabe replied with a smile.

Motioning to the others, I said, "I'd like to introduce you to my sisters, Kennedy and Ellie."

Gabe extended his hand to Ellie first. "It's nice to meet you."

With her face flushing bright red, Ellie emitted a nervous giggle. "It's a pleasure meeting you."

When Gabe turned to Kennedy, a smirk spread across his lips. "You're not packing any sharp utensils at the moment, are you?"

Kennedy's brows furrowed. "No. Why?"

"Rae said you might harbor a little ill will toward me."

"Ill will?"

"Like 'cut my balls off' kinda ill will."

While Kennedy laughed at Gabe's summation, I smacked his arm playfully. "You weren't supposed to mention that."

"I figured it was the best way to break the ice."

Kennedy nodded. "You figured right. It is true that I wasn't initially a big fan of yours, but I'm willing to get to know you better."

"That's a relief."

"Would you like to fix a plate, Gabe? There's plenty to eat."

Glancing over Kennedy's shoulder, Gabe eyed the goodies lining the counter. I usually didn't see so much breakfast food except on the weekends or if we had company, but once again, I shouldn't have been too surprised that Kennedy went all out to impress Gabe.

"It looks and smells delicious. While I brought breakfast for Rae and myself, I'd love to try some of yours as well."

I grinned at Gabe. By offering to taste Kennedy's food, he was knocking it out of the park when it came to getting on her good side.

Kennedy pulled her shoulders back. "If it's from any of the restaurants here in town, I guarantee mine is better."

Before Gabe could reply, I said, "Actually, he went to Rafferty's."

Both Kennedy and Ellie's eyes widened to the size of the antique dinner plates on the counter. "You got her breakfast from Rafferty's?" Ellie asked.

"Yes, I did."

Kennedy swallowed hard. "Like her favorite French toast from Rafferty's?"

When Gabe nodded, Kennedy swore under her breath. Glancing between Kennedy and Gabe, Ellie quickly said, "That was so sweet of you."

Gabe turned to smile at me. "It was the least I could do considering Rae's been kind enough to give up her time by allowing me to hang out with her."

Shaking my head, I replied, "You really didn't need to do anything else. After all, you bought Linc's and my dinner last night. That was plenty."

"But this was more about a gesture of my appreciation."

Oh, it was a gesture all right—an epic one. Sure, the old adage said the way to a man's heart was through his stomach, but I was certainly feeling it that morning as well.

After handing the Rafferty's bag to me, Gabe piled a plate full of blueberry scones, croissants, and sweet rolls. "I have a feeling I'm not going to get any songwriting done today because I'm going to be in a food coma."

With a triumphant grin, Kennedy said, "I hope it gives you the fuel you need to write."

"Thank you. I'm really grateful to both you and Ellie for your hospitality."

Gabe's statement rendered all of us speechless, and I was sure Ellie and Kennedy were both thinking the same thing I was: how was it possible for this eloquent and gracious Gabe Renard to be the same asshat from the other day?

"You're very welcome," Ellie squeaked as Kennedy and I nodded.

When Gabe started over to the table, Kennedy reached out and stopped him. "Actually, why don't you guys take your breakfast out on the veranda?"

"Is this because you don't want to see my French toast?" I questioned under my breath.

With a roll of her eyes, Kennedy replied, "No. This is more about you and Gabe having time to yourselves—you know, to feed his muse."

"I really appreciate that," Gabe said.

When we started out the side door, Ellie said, "You guys take your time. Kennedy and I will drop Linc off with Dad."

"Really?"

Ellie smiled. "Yes, really."

"Okay, thanks." Pointing at Linc, I said, "Make sure you have your homework and your lunch."

He rolled his eyes but smiled in spite of himself. "I will, Mom."

"I love you, sweetheart."

"I love you, too." Linc waved at Gabe. "Bye, Gabe."

"Bye," Gabe replied.

When we walked out the side door onto the veranda, I gasped. Sometime during the morning, one or both of my sisters had set up the glass-top table for us. While I'd imagined eating out of the takeout containers, there were real china plates and crystal goblets, and a pitcher of orange juice sat on the white linen tablecloth, along with a carafe of coffee.

"This is impressive," Gabe remarked.

"I wish I could take the credit, but my sisters must have done it."

"You'll have to thank them for me."

"I will."

As he gazed at the heaping plate in front of him, Gabe asked, "Do you guys eat like this every morning?"

I laughed as I poured a glass of orange juice. "While she does cook every morning, that"—I motioned to his plate—"is strictly for your benefit."

"I'm going to have to stop by her store. These scones look amazing."

"They are. Everything Kennedy makes is amazing. She has a natural talent for it, plus she spent a summer in Paris back in the day, taking classes at Le Cordon Bleu."

"That's impressive. She never wanted to leave here and try her hand in the big city?"

"She did. She lived in Chattanooga for a few years but really didn't like it, so she came back home."

Gabe smiled. "You Hart women are small-town girls through and through."

I took the box of French toast out of the Rafferty's bag. "Pretty much. I really want to travel more. We do a yearly beach trip to the gulf, but I want to see other places and other cultures." I motioned to the French toast in front of me. "Taste French toast in Paris, or maybe crepes."

"Paris is a gorgeous city. Great architecture." He winked at me. "And lots of sinful diversions."

"I'll pass on those." When I took my first bite, I pinched my eyes shut and moaned in ecstasy.

"That good, huh?" Gabe questioned, amusement vibrating in his voice.

"Practically orgasmic."

"Now I'm regretting that I didn't get any for myself."

"Do you want to try a bite?"

"Sure."

After spearing a piece on my fork, I started to hand it over to Gabe when he leaned in and opened his mouth. Ah, so we were going to play it that way. Fine. I could do that. I could totally feed him some of my French toast. It wasn't like it screamed foreplay or anything.

When I brought the fork to his lips, Gabe took the tines between his teeth and slid off delicious morsel. As he chewed, I found myself unable to look away, still holding the fork frozen in mid-air. When his tongue darted out to swipe off the excess powdered sugar and syrup, heat burned between my legs.

"That is pretty fucking amazing French toast," he replied.

"Yeah," I so eloquently muttered.

Gabe grinned. "You better hurry up and eat it before it gets cold."

"But I'm warm now." At the realization of what I'd just said, I jerked my hand back. Oh, I was warm all right. My face felt like an inferno because I couldn't believe what I had said. "I mean, it's still so warm. The French toast is so warm."

"I'm glad."

"How did you manage that?"

"They gave me a heated sleeve."

"Ah, I see." Since it was past time for a conversation change, I quickly said, "Tell me something, do you always write songs in odd places?"

"Sometimes. It really just depends on where I'm at when the mood hits." He grinned. "I will say that last night was the first time I ever wrote in a public restroom."

"Any porta-johns?"

"No, smartass," Gabe muttered through a mouthful of bacon.

"Do any of your siblings write songs?"

"My oldest brother, Micah, did, but that was back when we were doing more praise music."

"Wait, you were in a Christian praise band?"

"If I said yes, would that be so shocking?"

"Duh. Of course it would. After all, you're the guy who said he wanted to see more of me while ogling my boobs."

"Then you can just be shocked because that's what Jacob's Ladder originally was—a Christian band with crossover potential."

"Ah, now the biblical reference in the band's name makes sense. Of course, it would have made even more sense if it was just you and your twin brother, like Jacob and Esau," I remarked.

Gabe's brows popped behind his coffee mug. After he took a sip, he said, "So you know the biblical story?"

"Contrary to the opinion of some people around here, I'm not a total heathen, and I do know my Bible."

"I'm very impressed."

I laughed. "Very few men are ever impressed by that."

Staring intently at me, Gabe replied, "Well I'm not all men."

No, you sure as hell aren't. Most men couldn't make me wet from eating a piece of French toast off my own fork. I cleared my throat. "Speaking of twins, tell me about your brother." When his expression slightly darkened, I said, "Oh, is there some hidden sibling rivalry there? Who is the Jacob, AKA your father's favorite?"

"Wow, you really aren't letting up with the biblical ties, are you? Next you'll be asking which one of us is the Esau, AKA the hairy one."

I giggled. "I can't help it. Aunt Sadie really went all out with the Bible study when we were kids." Cocking my head at him, I couldn't help asking, "I bet you're both Esaus, but you get manscaped to look metrosexual."

Gabe snorted. "There is no manscaping going on with me."

"Bullshit. Your eyebrows are most definitely too symmetrical to not be plucked or waxed."

"I don't consider having my eyebrows done manscaping."

Pointing my finger at him triumphantly, I cried, "Aha, I'm right."

"No, you're not, at least not about me."

"And how is that so?"

"While I might have my eyebrows done, my chest, dick, and balls are completely untouched by grooming utensils."

"Interesting."

"Eli got used to waxing his chest when he was doing musical theater in high school and still does from time to time. He also has one of those electric clippers to trim back his dick and ball hair."

"Um, ew, I didn't need to know that."

"You asked if we were Esaus."

"Yeah, well, I didn't expect such an in-depth answer about your brother. I mean, you totally just violated his privacy."

Gabe snorted. "Eli doesn't have a sense of privacy. If he were sitting here, he would have told you himself—maybe even shown you."

"He's pretty extroverted, huh?"

"Oh yeah. *Extremely* extroverted."

After hearing Gabe's description of his brother, I thought about how different the two of them sounded personality-wise. "Is it hard for you having such an outgoing twin?" I questioned softly.

At first, I didn't think Gabe was going to respond. When he finally did, I got the very curt reply of, "You could say that."

I pondered his response while spearing my last piece of French toast. "Would you like to elaborate on that?"

Gabe shot me a look. "With all your questions, I'm starting to feel like I'm doing press for the band."

"I'm sorry if I seem intrusive. I'm just trying to get to know you better." After chewing thoughtfully, I asked, "Isn't that what you do when you hang out with someone?"

"My version of hanging out is watching a movie or playing Xbox."

"And you never talk to the person you're with?"

"Talk during a movie? Oh hell no. That's a deal-breaker for sure."

"What if it's a movie you've seen before?"

Gabe shook his head. "The only reason you should be talking in a movie is if you're repeating a favorite line."

"I'll keep that in mind."

We went back to eating in silence. Finally, Gabe sighed. "Okay, yes, at the risk of sounding like a jealous prick, it's both a blessing and a curse to have a brother like Eli. I've always felt like I was a little bit in his shadow. I'm not the oldest or the youngest, so it's always felt like I'm in some weird middle child limbo."

"You're the Jan Brady," I mused.

Gabe grinned. "Yes, you could say that, except it's Eli, Eli, Eli, instead of Marcia, Marcia, Marcia."

"I get it. I'm the Jan Brady too, except I'm the second of three dark-haired girls, rather than blondes. In my case, Kennedy and I seemed to get our roles reversed. For some strange reason, I was always the mother hen to her and Ellie, and Kennedy was the one doing anything and everything to stand out."

"That is interesting." Gabe swiped his mouth with his napkin. "As for standing out, I think that's why songwriting appealed to me so much. It was something Eli had no talent for. Sure, he can play more instruments than me, he can sing better than me, and he can entertain people better than me, but he can't write songs."

As I processed Gabe's words, a thought came to my mind. "Is that one of the reasons your writer's block hit you so hard? It wasn't just about getting the songs for the album, it was about failing in front of your family—more specifically, in front of Eli."

Shifting in his chair, Gabe widened his blue eyes at me. "Holy shit, you really get me, don't you?"

With a shrug, I replied, "Aunt Sadie would tell you I'm a natural empath. Somehow I'm able to read people."

Leaning forward across the table, Gabe asked, "If that's true, why weren't you able to see that I'm a decent person the first day we met?"

I threw my head back and laughed. "Maybe because you were scrambling my Spidey senses with your douchery."

Gabe grinned. "I could buy that."

"But usually I have to spend time with someone. I'm not a human whisperer where I can just walk past someone in a crowd and immediately know what their problems are."

"If that were true, you would have known I was a nutcase out in the backwoods."

"Now that I've gotten to know you a little better, I really hate to hear you run yourself down so much. In case you missed it, you really are somebody special."

"I am?"

I waved my hand at him. "Oh come on, don't go fishing for compliments."

"No, I'd really like to hear something positive from the woman who, up until last night, hated my guts."

Laughing, I said, "Okay, fine. For starters, you're rich, and you're famous."

"I'd argue that I'm a B-list celebrity at best, maybe even pushing C, and although I do really well, I'm not that rich."

"Oh boo-hoo, let me cry you a river."

Gabe chuckled. "Okay, so maybe my last statement made me sound like a douchebag."

"Pretty much."

He frowned slightly. "I don't know why, but sometimes things just come out wrong. Like, I see them the way I want to in my head, but then something happens between my mind and my mouth. Just now, I was trying to emphasize my normalcy, that I'm not really all that rich and famous."

"It's interesting that a songwriter seems to have trouble putting thoughts and emotions into words."

"I guess it's like musicians who are a mess in real life but can wow an audience when they're onstage."

"That's one way to look at it."

"I know I feel the most at peace with myself when I'm on stage, and when I'm writing a song." He gave me a wry grin. "At least I did until I started going through hellish writer's block."

"But you're finding the words again, aren't you?"

"I am—thank God." He jerked his chin at me. "And thank you."

"Although I still don't understand it, I will say you're welcome."

As Gabe poured another cup of coffee from the carafe, he quirked his brows at me.

"What about you? Do you ever feel threatened by your sisters?"

His question made me think about how I'd felt toward Kennedy and Ellie that morning, and I felt ashamed all over again. "Of course I have. You saw my sisters—they're beautiful."

The corners of Gabe's lips quirked up in a smile. "So is their sister, if not even more beautiful."

Although I didn't exactly understand why, his compliment had me ducking my head and feeling somewhat shy. "Thank you."

"You've only ever felt jealous of their looks?"

Glancing back up at him, I replied, "Of course not. They're just as gorgeous on the inside. They managed to start and run a successful business before they were twenty-five."

"Don't sell yourself short. You're doing pretty well at Hart and Daughter."

"But that business wasn't mine. My father was the one who built it up for me to take over."

"You also made a professional sports team."

I laughed at Gabe's reference to me being on the Atlanta Steam. "Since neither of my sisters enjoyed playing sports, I don't think there was anything to envy there—not to mention how Kennedy thinks the uniforms are completely sexist."

"But you were MVP three years running. I saw the plaques myself."

"Once again, I don't think they lost any sleep over it."

"I certainly would have." He waggled his brows. "At least over fantasizing about you in your uniform."

"Spare me," I replied with a grin.

Leaning back in his chair, Gabe took a long sip of coffee. "Sometimes I find myself envious of Micah and Abby, of the fact that they've found someone who loves and accepts them for who they are."

"Wow," I murmured.

Gabe winked at me. "Didn't think Mr. Manwhore over here could be that deep, huh?"

I grinned. "You got me there. Now you're the one who is able to see through me." I leaned forward in my chair to pour another cup of coffee. "Since both Kennedy and Ellie are single, I can't really envy that aspect of their life."

"That's like me and Eli, although he does seem to do better with the ladies."

"I find that hard to believe."

"Why's that?"

"Um, because you two look exactly alike. If I saw the two of you together, I would be interested in both of you, not just him."

A wicked gleam burned in Gabe's eyes. "You would, huh? Like a ménage thing?"

Groaning, I replied, "Um, no, not a ménage situation. I'm not into two dudes period, least of all two brothers." I shuddered. "There's some kinda incest there."

Gabe laughed. "I would agree with you on that one. There's no way in hell I'm going to be doing the deed and have my nut sack touch Eli or his touch me."

Wrinkling my nose, I said, "Ew!"

"Sorry, just have to call it like I see it. But, going back to your original statement, trust me, you would want to date Eli over me."

"And why is that?"

"Once you met Eli, he'd be making you laugh. Women love a man who makes them laugh."

"You have a point there."

"I rest my case." And dammit, I really hated that I'd just given her that option. Of course, she would choose Eli over me any day. Looks *aren't* everything.

"But you act like you're some loser who lacks any redeeming personality. After getting to know you more last night, I know that isn't the case at all."

Gabe grinned. "Thank you. Now before you continue your campaign to build up my failing self-esteem, I'm going to need more of Kennedy's scones."

I laughed. "Okay. We can take a scone break."

After Gabe rose out of his chair, he asked, "Would you like anything from the kitchen?"

It was quite a change being waited on by a man, least of all a man who was used to having people wait on him. "I appreciate it, but no, I'm stuffed from all the French toast."

"There are two more orders in there."

I gasped. "Seriously?" Before Gabe could respond, I dove into the Rafferty's bag. "Oh my God, there's more."

"I thought you might enjoy having some the rest of the week."

Ha, the week? They won't last twenty-four hours. "I will." I grinned at him. "If I don't reheat it today."

"Whatever you want to do. I'll be right back."

"And I'll be right here." Because, God help me, I couldn't pull myself away.

11

Gabe

ALTHOUGH I KNEW it was probably past time for Rae to go to work, I didn't say anything; I was enjoying her company too much. After I picked up another scone, I grabbed the coffee pot from the kitchen and went back outside.

When I got to the table, Rae was smiling down at her phone. "Good news?"

She glanced up at me. "Just Linc letting me know he got to school all right, and that he got a 100 on the vocab test we studied for last night."

"Hmm, I'm thinking Linc is pretty spoiled to already have a phone before he's ten years old."

"You sound like my dad," Rae mused as she took the coffee pot from me and poured it into the carafe. "I just like to always be able to get in touch with him. I figure it's worth the money for my piece of mind."

"And now you sound like my sister, except she has special go-phones for everyone who takes care of the twins. That way she doesn't have to worry about not getting in touch with them."

"Yep. That's a mother for you." She grinned. "We're crazy as hell, but we're lovable too."

"I agree with that."

"Speaking of Linc, I can't thank you enough for humoring him last night with all his questions about being a professional musician."

"You don't need to thank me. I really enjoyed hanging out with him."

Rae's brows creased. "You did?"

"It was nice talking to someone who seemed so genuinely inter-

95

ested. Most of the time when people ask me about the business, they're either being polite or they have an angle."

"Oh Linc's certainly interested, much more than I'd prefer."

"Because his dad was a musician?"

Jumping in her seat, Rae's knife and fork clattered to the floor. "How do you know that?"

Oh shit. Once again, I'd forgotten the information that had been given to me through Linc. In this case, I was going to use that fact to my advantage. After all, Rae knew Linc and I had had some alone time the previous night. "Linc told me."

"Oh," she murmured. With a rueful smile, she added, "It's at this moment that I wish Kennedy and Ellie had thought of mimosas."

"I'm sorry. We can change the subject if you'd like."

Rae gave an emphatic shake of her head. "No, it's okay. I mean, it's not like Linc's father was something truly shameful like a serial killer —although to me, being a dead-beat dad ranks pretty high up there with people who are shameful."

"Linc said he hasn't seen his dad since he was a baby."

"That's right. Although Ryan pretty much bailed on our relationship when I got pregnant, I held out hope that he would at least step up and be a father to Linc. I should have realized he was too self-absorbed and selfish to be a parent."

"I know Linc hasn't ever talked to his father, but what about you? Do you talk to Ryan?"

Rae's lip curled in disgust. "He's never even bothered to pick up the phone. His parents tried to get him to call a few times, showed him pictures I gave them of Linc, but he still never called. They moved to Tennessee a few years ago, and they haven't seen Linc since."

Damn. Just when I thought the situation couldn't be worse, it was. Rae had really gone through some shit with Ryan and his family. "Sounds like he comes from a pretty shitty family."

"They're good people, really, just enablers. They keep thinking he's going to make it big on the music scene and pay them back all the money they've loaned him over the years."

"I take it Ryan isn't that successful?"

"He's a wannabe. From some of my friends who have been to see him, he mainly plays in dives in and around Nashville." She ran her finger over a crease in the tablecloth. "I've spent most of Linc's life fearing that some of Ryan's DNA would somehow manage to outweigh how I raised him. I've tried to head any of that off by keeping him away from music."

Fucking hell. It was one thing to hear Linc's side of the story on why his mother didn't want him to have a guitar; it was quite another to hear Rae's side. Maybe it was the palpable fear in her voice when she spoke that drove home the seriousness of the situation. Clearing my throat, I asked, "What do you mean you've kept him away from music?"

"Well, for starters, I put Linc in soccer and tee-ball when he could barely walk because I wanted to foster a love of sports in him."

Although I already knew the answer to the question, I still asked, "And it worked?"

"For a while. I even coached his soccer team—it's the reason I gave up arena football. Our schedules were overlapping." She shook her head. "But then he came home one day in second grade with one of those annoying as hell recorders. I almost lost my shit."

Trying to ease some of the tension in the air, I laughed. "Yeah, Eli and I tortured our parents with those back in the day."

"It wasn't just the irritating noise that got to me, it was that he wanted to play an instrument *so much.* All of a sudden this intense love for music had blossomed within him. All he could talk about was notes and beats."

"I'm going to take a wild guess and say Linc's love of music didn't die out after his class moved on from the recorder."

"No, it didn't. In fact, it got worse. He became hell-bent on learning the guitar. He begged me for one last Christmas."

"But you said no."

She nodded. "Well, I said *Santa* said he wasn't old enough. Then he started pestering me to do chores around the house and the shop to earn the money to buy it himself, but I just can't let him have a guitar."

Going out on a limb, I asked, "Would it really be so bad to give the kid a guitar?"

Rae narrowed her eyes at me. "To me, yes. It's a crapshoot when it comes to genetics. Although he hasn't exhibited much of Ryan's tendencies so far, I'm determined not to let a guitar be the gateway drug to losing him."

Well, fuck me. Rae was in full mama bear mode about this. There was no way in hell I could possibly win this argument. "So you've basically forbidden music?"

With a groan, she shook her head. "God, it sounds horrible when you say it like that. It makes me feel like the preacher in *Footloose*."

I chuckled. "I'd hardly say you were that extreme." Leaning forward, I added, "You do let him listen to music, don't you?"

She huffed out an indignant breath. "Of course I do. I even let him get *Guitar Hero* for Christmas two years ago."

"Aren't you Saint Rae?" I replied teasingly.

"For me, that was huge."

"I get that, but maybe you could consider it as baby steps working up to getting Linc a real guitar."

"It might've been a consolation prize, but it's not a starting point."

"Playing devil's advocate here, it can be very beneficial for kids to be involved with music. It's been proven to help their focus in school and improve grades."

"While all that might be true, I just can't take the chance." At what must've been my skeptical look, she asked, "Don't you see? In my life, everything negative has come from involvement with a musician. My mother ran off with one, and I got knocked up and abandoned by one." Tears pooled in her eyes. In an agonized voice, she said, "I don't want to lose my son."

There was nothing that could have prepared me for Rae losing her shit in front of me. Gone was the tough-as-nails sassy-pants. The woman before me was stripped to the bone and as vulnerable as I could ever imagine. It was both oddly beautiful and frightening.

As for me, I froze—like, I became a perfectly sculptured statue. I wasn't one of those men who couldn't handle female emotions. I was actually known among our backup singers and female road crew for being a shoulder to cry on. The fact that I was a good listener made me very accustomed to seeing tears.

It was the fact that they were Rae's tears that floored me. Rae was one of those women who I imagined was made of steel. She would never be caught blubbering into her popcorn during a sad movie. She was the kind of woman who made fun of the women who did that.

More than anything in that moment, Rae needed comforting. While she would never verbally ask, I could read it in her eyes. I slid my chair around the table to where it bumped against her. Since I wasn't sure how she would feel about me putting my arms around her, I reached out for her hand instead. "There is no way in hell you're going to lose Linc."

Swiping the tears from her cheeks, she countered, "You don't know that."

She certainly had me there. I didn't know how I could possibly argue with that, so I switched tactics. "You're right, I don't, but here's something I do know: not all musicians are bad. They're not all home-wreckers or dead-beat fathers. The ones I know and surround myself with are devoted to their wives and children. They're not only hard-working, they also give freely of their time to charities and helping others. I know that because I see it firsthand."

"Really?"

I nodded. "Here's something else I know: Linc is a fucking amazing kid. Trust me, I'm not usually a kid person, but he won me over the first day I met him. There's no way a kid that amazing is going to turn into a shit."

When Rae smiled at me through her tears, I exhaled a relieved breath. Although she always looked beautiful when she smiled, she looked fucking gorgeous right then.

"Thank you. It means a lot to hear you say that."

"I wouldn't have said it if I didn't mean it. I don't believe in bull-shitting people."

She smiled at me once again. "I know you don't." After squeezing my hand, she said, "I really do appreciate everything you said."

"Does that mean you'll give some more thought to Linc having a guitar?"

Her expression darkened a little. "I wish I could say yes, but no, I don't think so. There's no way I can ever see myself changing my mind."

Great. I was so utterly and completely fucked. When Rae found out about what I'd done with Linc and the guitar, she would kill me—she would *annihilate* me. "While it's understandable for you to feel the way that you do, I hope you can understand it's not a love of music that makes someone terrible—it's who they are as a person. Maybe I can prove that to you, and then maybe you'll reconsider your stance—you know, for Linc's sake." *And mine.*

"I guess we'll just have to see." We sat there for a few moments, her hand in mine, our gazes locked on each other. I had to admit, it was really nice. It reminded me of the stolen moments I'd seen between Jake and Abby or AJ and Mia. There was an ease and a peace with Rae that I'd never expected I'd feel, and it felt amazing.

I could have stayed like that with her for the rest of the day, but all too soon, Rae shook her head like she was shaking herself out of a dream. Then she pulled her hand away. "I don't even want to look at my phone to see what time it is. I'm surprised Dad or one of the guys hasn't called me."

"Yeah, you better get to work. I'm sorry for keeping you so long."

"It's okay. I really enjoyed it."

"Me too." Gazing around the table, I said, "Can I help you clean up?"

Rae shook her head. "We'll leave it for Linc to do as part of his chores."

"And does he get compensated for these chores?"

Wagging a finger at me, Rae replied, "Don't think I don't know where you're going with that, and no, I'm not giving money to a guitar fund."

I held up my hands. "I was just asking."

She gave me a knowing look. "Uh-huh." As we started back into the house, she glanced back at me over her shoulder. "When did you want to see me again?" Widening her eyes, she quickly said, "I mean, do you think you need to see me again? You know, for your writing, not like for a date or something because that is *so* not what we're doing."

She was damn cute being so flustered. Of course, if I told her that, she'd probably punch me. Rae wasn't the kind of woman who wanted to be *cute*.

"Like I said before, I'll take as much of your time as you'll give me." That was the truth. The more I got to know her, the more I wanted to spend time with her.

"Since you're new in town, I guess the hospitable thing for me to do would be to invite you to dinner with us. Tuesdays we eat with my dad and stepmom."

"Are you sure they won't mind you bringing me along?"

"Of course not. Stella always cooks enough for a small army."

"Then I would love to come."

"We usually eat around 6:30, so you could pick me and Linc up around 6:15."

I cocked my brows at her. "You mean you actually want me to pick you up?"

"Why is that surprising?"

"I just figured you were a little too independent to allow a man to pick you up."

Rae laughed. "Maybe I'm making an exception for you."

"Ah, I like it. I'll see you then."

"Bye, Gabe."

I waved. "Bye."

As I walked back to the Jeep, I marveled at just how fucked I was. I was fucked in the fact that I was starting to feel way more than I should for Rae, but I was even more fucked in the fact that she was going to kill me for promising Linc a guitar.

My mind spun with solutions to the quagmire I currently found myself in. The easiest solution would be to just back out of my deal with Linc, tell him that after careful consideration, I now sided with his mother and didn't think he should have one. Of course, he would probably retaliate by telling Rae I stiffed him on a guitar, which would in turn piss her off.

Oh yeah, I was thoroughly fucked. My tirade was interrupted by my phone ringing. It was Eli.

"Hey man, are you alive?" he questioned.

"Yes, I am."

"Are you just saying that because the *Deliverance* people who kidnapped you are forcing you to say that? Cough once into the phone if you're not okay."

Rolling my eyes, I laughed in spite of myself. "I have not been abducted by any *Deliverance* people. I am here in Hayesville of my own volition."

"Yes, it's your volition that's questionable. I mean, you said yourself they don't even have a Starbucks. What could you possibly still be doing there?"

"Actually, I'm here writing."

Eli sucked in a breath. "Holy shit. You are?"

When I'd called him the day before, I hadn't told him anything about Rae or songwriting. Since everything had still been up in the air with her, I'd just told him I was just staying in Hayesville to get away. "Yeah, man. I've gotten two songs done already."

"I'm so fucking proud of you."

"Thanks. I'm not gonna lie, it sure feels good to be putting words on paper. They're good words, too, and you know I wouldn't just say that."

"I sure do. You are your own worst critic. When were you planning on sharing them with me and Abs?"

"Are you still at Jake and Abby's?"

"No. I came back to Atlanta the day you left."

"As soon as I get back to the hotel, I'll Google Hangout with you guys and play what I have." At the familiar tingle running up my spine, I said, "Strike that. I think I'm feeling something new coming on."

"Seriously?"

"Yeah. I'm not too surprised considering I was just with—" I abruptly cut myself off. For reasons I didn't understand, I didn't feel ready to tell Eli about Rae.

"You were just with who?"

"Nobody. Forget it."

"Look, if you've fallen in love with some hillbilly woman named Earlene, it's okay. You don't have to be ashamed."

I laughed. "Considering I've only been gone for forty-eight hours, I'm not quite sure how I could have fallen in love with a hillbilly."

"You never know—they move fast."

"How the hell would you know? Past experience?"

"Just an observation."

"Whatever." A knock came on the Jeep's window, causing my phone to fly out of my hand and onto the passenger seat. When I glanced over, Rae was grinning at me. After I rolled down the window, I said, "Hey."

"Hey. Listen, I was thinking instead of coming over here, you should just come to the shop to pick me and Linc up. Dad lives closer to the shop than here."

"Okay. I'll see you at the shop."

She smiled. "Okay." Jerking her chin, she added, "Now get the hell out of here so I can go to work."

"I'm on it."

After she waved and headed back to her car, I leaned over and picked up my phone. I knew there wasn't a chance in hell that Eli had hung up. The minute he heard a female voice, he would be hanging on to every word he possibly could. "Hey. I'm back."

"Was that Earlene?" he asked teasingly as I cranked the Jeep up.

"No, smartass. Her name is Rae."

"Sounds like you guys are having dinner tonight."

"We are, at her father's house," I replied as I backed out of Rae's driveway.

"Mmhmm."

I laughed. "Like that's all you have to say. I mean, don't hurt yourself holding back."

"It's just that you said it would be impossible to have fallen in love with a hillbilly girl in two days, yet here you are having dinner with a woman. Not only that, you're having dinner with her family. Do we need Selma to prepare a press release on your impending nuptials?"

"Har fucking har."

"Hey, you told me not to hold back. I mean, you're already eating dinner with her parents—what am I supposed to think?"

"It's not like that with Rae."

"Then enlighten me."

I sucked in a deep breath before unloading the soap opera of what had transpired.

"Holy shit," Eli remarked when I finished.

"Yeah. Pretty much."

"I can't believe you found your muse in the backwoods."

"It surprised the hell out of me as well, but I'm not going to question it."

"I wouldn't either." After pausing for a moment, Eli asked, "So she's beautiful, huh?"

"Gorgeous, but not like the fake women I usually go after. She's real."

"She's real or her tits are real?"

Groaning, I replied, "Once again, it's not like that with her."

"It's not like that because she won't let it be like that," Eli countered, amusement vibrating in his voice. It was times like these I lamented having a twin brother who knew exactly how my brain worked.

"Yeah, it's true that she shot me down, but I'm glad she did."

"Seriously?"

"If we had fucked, who knows what would have happened to my songwriting mojo? I might still be blocked."

"That's one way to look at it, and a very mature way, I might add."

I snickered. "I'm not sure I would trust your judgment on what's mature."

Eli laughed. "Whatever. So you really think you have another song brewing?"

"Yep. I'm pulling into the hotel now. Just as soon as I can get to my pen and journal, I'm at it again. Once I get to a stopping point, I'll text you about doing a Google Hangout with Abby."

"Sounds good. I'll call her and let her know what's going on."

"Thanks, man. I probably need to text Jake and tell him I'll be commandeering his Jeep for a little while longer."

"I don't think he'll mind, especially if you're finally getting the words you need. When do you think you'll be back?"

"I'm not leaving here until I have enough to fill the album—or until my mojo runs out."

"I'll be interested to see what you come up with, but more than the songs, I'm interested to see how things pan out with Rae."

"You mean you'll be interested to see if we finally bang."

"Actually, I was thinking more long-term than that." *Really, Eli?*

"Like a relationship?"

"Bingo."

"Get real, bro."

"You're the one who needs to get real, not me."

"It's not happening."

"We'll see."

Scowling at the phone, I replied, "If you don't have anything else to do but give me shit about Rae, I'll let you go. Unlike someone else I know, I have work to do."

Eli chuckled. "Whatever, man. Call me when you're done penning our next CMA winner."

"I don't know about that, but I'll let you know when the next song is done.

"You do that—oh, and tell Rae hello for me."

"I will."

"And thanks for putting up with my knuckleheaded brother."

I laughed. "Goodbye, Eli."

"Bye, Gabe."

I'D JUST SET down the last bag of groceries when the doorbell rang. Instantly, a giddy yet anxious feeling swept over me because I knew it was Gabe. After breakfast the previous morning, he'd come with us to Dad and Stella's. When I'd first asked him, I hadn't thought he would really do it. I mean, it was one thing to hang out with me and Linc, but my dad and sisters as well?

He seemed to have a great time, though, and I don't even know how long we spent talking around Dad's dining room table. After Gabe brought Linc and me home, we sat on the couch in front of the fire talking until Linc passed out around nine, and then Gabe ended up leaving sometime after eleven.

It had never felt so easy talking to a man, which surprised me given his life was so completely different than mine. There was no awkwardness between us. I never felt like I had to be something I wasn't because Gabe appeared to appreciate me exactly as I was. He was also one of the few men I'd ever been around who was as actively interested in hearing about my life as he was about telling me about his. In fact, he seemed to shy away from talking a lot about life on the road and in the band, focusing more on talking about his family and his friends.

After the late night, Gabe had texted me in the morning to say he was sleeping in after spending most of the night working on songs. I had no clue about the how and why. We hadn't spent time talking about anything particularly deep and meaningful, and it still felt so surreal that I could have any impact on his writer's block—especially for a songwriter as prolific as Gabe Renard. Candy had told me how many albums Jacob's Ladder had out, so I knew if he was their main songwriter, he must've written over a hundred songs.

Then he'd met me for lunch at The Hitching Post, and this time I beat him to the punch by telling May I would be covering the bill. Although he initially protested me buying his lunch, he appeared very grateful in the end. When he'd texted me in the afternoon to ask if he could spend a few hours with me, I told him he could but said he'd have to come to the house. The one bright spot was that for the first time I could remember, I had the place all to myself. Aunt Sadie was at bingo over at the American Legion, Kennedy and Ellie had gone to Chattanooga to pick up supplies for their businesses, and Linc had gone over to my dad's.

Before Gabe had called, my plans for my evening at home had entailed baking. Once again, it was a prime example of how compared to him, my life was so simple. As I hurried out of the kitchen to get the door, I skidded to a stop in front of the gilded mirror in the hallway. I quickly checked my appearance before heading on into the foyer.

"Who is it?" I called.

"It's Gabe."

"Gabe who?" I teasingly asked.

"You know who," he retorted.

I laughed as I opened the door. "I thought you would be proud that I asked this time."

"Yeah, I'm thrilled."

"Come on in."

"Thanks."

After we walked into the kitchen, Gabe eyed the counters covered in groceries. "What's all this? Are you making me dinner?"

I laughed. "You wish."

He cocked his brows at me. "What's with all the bags?"

"Tomorrow is the PTA bake sale at Linc's school, and somehow he wrangled me into making his favorite turtle brownies."

"I thought your sister was the baker."

"She is."

"So why not delegate it off to her?"

"Because it's important for them to be made by my hands." When

Gabe continued staring blankly at me, I sighed. "You're not a parent, so you wouldn't understand."

"Let me guess: to show Linc that you truly care for him and his education, you are prepared to spend countless hours in the kitchen toiling away on baked goods after a long day at work."

I widened my eyes in surprise. "Exactly."

"See? I'm not a total parenting dumbass."

"I never said you were."

"Trust me, you implied it."

I held up my hands. "If I did, I'm sorry."

"Apology accepted." He then proceeded to start emptying one of the grocery bags.

"What are you doing?" I demanded.

"Uh, what does it look like I'm doing?"

"It looks like you're trying to help."

"Ding, ding, ding. That's exactly what I'm doing."

"*You're* going to help me make brownies?" It was one thing for him to hang out with me, but for a famous musician to actually participate in baking? It was way too crazy.

Gabe shrugged. "Yeah. Why not?"

"Excuse me for stereotyping, but you don't seem like the baking type."

"Once again, I would ask that you not make assumptions about me. Some people would stereotype my mother as being a typical passive pastor's wife, but trust me, she isn't. She made sure her boys participated in cooking just as her daughter did."

"I like your mother's style."

A genuine smile lit up Gabe's face. "She really is an amazing woman."

A storm of emotions rolled through me at his words and expression. "That's nice. You're really lucky to have a supportive and loving mom."

"Do you ever hear from yours?" Gabe asked.

"Nope. She's never even met Lincoln."

Gabe's brows popped up in surprise. "You're kidding."

"I wish. There have been a few phone calls here and there, but it's probably been at least five years now." I sighed. "She is the epitome of the old saying that you can't make a whore into a housewife."

"Damn," Gabe muttered under his breath as he opened a box of brownie mix.

I giggled at his reaction to my honesty. "Sorry, but I can't help calling it what it is. Sometimes I try to see things from her perspective. She wanted to get the hell out of her abusive home, and as a seventeen-year-old high school dropout, the only way to do that was through a man. She bounced from one to another trying to make one stay." I shook my head. "She struck gold the day she got her mitts onto my dad. He wanted to be the white knight who saved her, the one who changed her. After trapping him into marriage by getting pregnant with Kennedy, she then popped out me and Ellie in quick succession before realizing motherhood was not for her."

"That had to be hard on him," Gabe remarked.

"I'm sure it was. I mean, I can only imagine considering what I've been through myself, but when we were growing up, he never made it seem hard. It was just like everything flowed so effortlessly with him —well, almost everything." I grinned at Gabe. "He did sort of stumble with female hormones and our periods."

Gabe laughed. "I don't know many men who are comfortable with those things, least of all a father. It meant you guys were growing up, and I'm sure he hated that."

Once again, Gabe surprised me with the depth of his response. As I was getting to know him better, I could see he wasn't just a self-obsessed sex fiend. Although we'd only been hanging for a few days, I already felt a deep connection with him.

I cleared my throat. "Okay, let's get down to business. We need to start working on the brownie mix."

He jerked his chin at the cabinets. "Where do you keep your mixing bowls and baking pans?"

"Mixing bowls are in the top right cabinet. Baking pans are in the cabinet by the stove." As Gabe reached up for the mixing bowls, his t-shirt rode up, affording me an excellent side view of what I imagined was his very defined six-pack. Besides his perfect abs, I couldn't help noticing the tattoos. While he had one on his bicep and a few on his arms, I'd obviously never seen any under his clothes.

Before I could stop myself, I reached out and touched the ink. Gabe froze for a few seconds at my touch then slowly brought the mixing bowls down onto the counter.

After jerking my finger away, I said, "Sorry. I was just admiring the ink on your side."

"It's okay."

"It's in another language, isn't it?"

Gabe nodded. "Hebrew."

"What does it say?"

"It's the word for family. I got it done a few years back when I took a trip to Israel with Eli and my older brother, Micah. Since everything in my life personally and professionally is tied to my family, I thought it was a cool idea."

I smiled. "I really like it. My family means the world to me too. Maybe I should get a tattoo like yours."

Gabe eyed me curiously. "Do you have any tattoos?"

Groaning, I opened the carton of eggs. "Yes, I have two meaningful ones, and one I would like to forget."

"Don't tell me you got Linc's father's name tattooed on you somewhere."

With a laugh, I replied, "No, thank God, but I do regret being sixteen and sneaking off to get a tramp stamp."

"Hmm, let me see."

"Fine." Turning around, I untucked my shirt and held it up a few inches. "There it is."

"It's not bad."

I threw a glance at Gabe over my shoulder. "You're just saying that."

"I'm serious. I was expecting something like a tribal band or Chinese symbols."

I rolled my eyes. "I thought I was being so badass with those roses. I really want to get it lasered off when I get enough—"

My breath hitched when I felt Gabe's fingers on my skin. "I wouldn't get it removed."

"But, uh, it's…uh, a tramp stamp," I protested breathlessly.

"It's kinda sexy."

Oh God. Was Gabe Renard running his fingers lightly above the top of my ass while he called my tramp stamp sexy? I licked my lips as I couldn't help letting my mind wander to what it would feel like to have his whole hand on my ass…or maybe having that hand other places.

Dropping my shirt back down, I ended that train of thought. "Enough tattoo gawking. These brownies aren't going to make themselves."

After adding in the milk and eggs, Gabe began stirring the mix. When he got a little too overzealous in his ministrations, a cloud of mix flipped out onto his shirt. "Shit," he muttered.

"Do you need an apron?"

He shot me a look as he grabbed a rag off the counter and rubbed his shirt. "Let me guess, it would be something white and frilly to make me look ridiculous?"

I grinned at him. "Of course. Can you imagine how much money I could make on one of those gossip sites with a picture of you in an apron cooking brownies?"

Gabe returned my smile. "Does this mean I need to be watching my back to make sure you don't snap an incriminating picture of me?"

"While I might enjoy seeing you somewhat publicly humiliated, I would never do that."

"You would want me humiliated?" Gabe questioned.

Stilling my spoon, I said, "That's a harsher word than I'm looking for." I tilted my head in thought. "It's probably more like the saying in my family of bringing you down a notch." When Gabe stared at me blankly, I added, "You know, your ego."

"I get it." Once he'd gotten the chocolate powder off his shirt as best he could, Gabe tossed the rag back on the counter. "Man, I must've come off as just one more asshole to you."

"I'm sorry, but yeah, you were."

"Why are you apologizing? I'm the one who was the asshole."

"I know, but now that I know you better—"

Gabe shook his head. "Just because you know now, that doesn't excuse my behavior."

Ah, this was something I hadn't seen in him before: true repentance. I really appreciated that he was annoyed with how he first treated me. Was all of his cockiness just a façade?

"That's true. I guess you're right." I began stirring the caramels again. "I just wondered how much of your behavior was really bad and how much my view of you is skewed because you're a musician." *Were you real then, or am I seeing the real you now?*

Gabe leaned back against the counter. "I'd have to say after what you've experienced, you're very justified to feel the way you do."

"Well, because of those feelings, I might have been a little harsher on you than I had to be, at least that morning at the shop." I grinned at him. "I'm fairly certain you deserved everything I gave you that day in the woods."

Gabe smiled. "I probably did."

I moved around him to grease the baking pans. When I finished, Gabe held out his hand. At what must've been my questioning look, he said, "I'll pour."

"Oh. Okay."

Taking the large bowl of gooey chocolate in one of his hands, Gabe then poured mix into the two baking pans. After I smoothed it out with the spatula, I took them over to the oven.

"There. In just twenty to twenty-five minutes, I'll have baked my way into Linc's heart."

With a laugh, Gabe said, "You mothers are all the same, appealing to us through our love of food."

"Can you think of a better way?"

Tilting his head, Gabe replied, "Probably not."

"I rest my case." After eyeing the pile of dirty dishes, I groaned. "Now for the worst part of baking: cleanup."

"I'll help, and it'll go fast."

I shook my head. "Very impressive, Mr. Renard. Not only did you do most of the baking, now you're offering to clean, too."

Gabe grinned. "I just enjoy disproving your opinion of me."

"My opinion of you is certainly a work in progress."

"I'm glad to hear it."

We began working in perfect sync with Gabe washing the dishes and me doing the drying. When he picked up the mixing bowl, he paused. "Do you want to lick the spoon?" he asked.

"Yes, please."

As my tongue darted out, Gabe's eyes flared. Electricity crackled through my body, causing the hairs on my arms to rise. Time crawled by as we stood there staring at each other.

Gabe broke the silence by saying, "Fuck it." Tossing the spoon to the counter, he then reached out and jerked me to him.

"What are you—"

Gabe crushed his lips against mine, causing me to moan. His kiss was a combination of tenderness and insistence. His mouth moved against mine almost with desperation. *Sweet Jesus*, the man could kiss. He was even better at it in real life than he was in my dream. It didn't seem fair that he should be so good at so many things.

As Gabe plunged his tongue into my mouth, his hand slid around my ribcage to cup my breast and my nipple immediately hardened under his touch. He continued kneading my breast while his thumb brushed back and forth over my nipple, which drove me absolutely wild.

Then, as suddenly as it had all started, it stopped. Gabe jerked away from me, his wild gaze meeting mine as he jerked a hand through his hair. The kitchen was filled with the sounds of our heavy breathing. Before he could say anything, I leapt back at him, fusing my lips to his.

After knocking the leftover ingredients to the ground, Gabe grabbed me by the waist and hoisted me up onto the counter. "Too many clothes," he muttered as he eyed my chest.

Since I completely agreed with him, I grasped the hem of my t-shirt and quickly ripped it over my head then tossed it to the ground. Gabe's greedy hands jerked my bra straps down, freeing my breasts. He licked his lips before his mouth closed over one of my rock-hard nipples. "Mm, yes," I muttered as I pinched my eyes shut.

As Gabe's teeth grazed my nipple, his other hand came between my legs. Through my jeans, he rubbed the heel of his hand against my pussy. With a moan, I threw my head back. God, it felt so good to have his hands on me. I began arching my hips to get more friction. When it wasn't enough, I murmured, "Please."

Gabe replied by unbuttoning and unzipping my jeans. He pulled them down from under my butt...so easily. His hand dove into my panties and worked its way down to my pussy. When his fingers touched my clit, I once again cried out. As Gabe sucked my nipple into his mouth, he thrust one finger deep inside me. "Hmm, yes, more," I pleaded.

He obliged by sticking another finger into my pussy. Biting down on my lip, I rocked against his hand. His mouth and his fingers felt just as good as they had in my sex dream. When Gabe pulled his fingers out of me, I groaned in frustration. "I want to fuck you with my tongue," he said. *Um, okay.* He certainly wasn't going to get an argument out of me with that one.

But in the heat of the moment, as Gabe started to pull down my panties, I remembered how unprepared I was for this moment—like not lady-scaped at all kind of unprepared. It was one thing for his hand to feel it, but it was a completely different thing for him to see it. "Wait, no."

His dark brows furrowed. "What's wrong?"

"Um, it's, well..." Embarrassed heat rushed to my face.

"What?"

"I'm not ready."

A sexy smirk curved Gabe's lips. "Babe, you've soaked my fingers —you're more than ready."

I ducked my head. "Not like that. I mean, it's been a while, so I haven't taken care of things...down there."

He shocked the hell out of me by closing his eyes in bliss. "Are you telling me you have a full bush going on?"

I gasped. "Um, well, not a total bush, but it's certainly not how I'd prefer you to see it."

His eyes popped open. Before I could protest any more, Gabe jerked my panties down, and I shrieked when he widened my legs. Desire filled his gaze at the sight of what I felt was my overgrown jungle. "That is so fucking sexy."

"You're joking?"

He answered my question by burying his face in my pussy. I sucked in a breath before wheezing it out. "I guess you're serious," I said as I panted.

After his tongue traced in and out of my folds, he thrust it inside me. I moaned so loud it echoed through the kitchen. It had been so long since a man had gone down on me, and it had been even longer since it had been a man who knew what he was doing, one who swept his powerful tongue deep inside me. "Oh God, Gabe!"

"That's it, say my name, baby," he murmured, his voice vibrating against my sex.

I began lifting my hips to work against his tongue. Sweat broke out along my forehead. I was close—*oh, so close*—but it felt so damn good, I didn't want it to stop.

Just as I started to go over the edge, the acrid smell of smoke entered my nostrils. Wait, were Gabe's oral skills so good they'd set my vagina on fire? My eyes fluttered open to see smoke filling the kitchen.

"Oh shit! The brownies!!" I shrieked. I pushed Gabe's head away before I jumped down off the counter. On wobbly legs, I hobbled over to the stove. When I threw open the door, smoke billowed back at me.

"Got a fire extinguisher?" Gabe questioned.

"Pantry!" I shouted over my shoulder.

While Gabe rushed to retrieve it, I turned off the oven. After arming my hand with an oven mitt, I reached inside to take out the charred remains of the baked goods. When Gabe appeared at my side with the extinguisher, I shook my head. "Fire's out. Just open up the windows and doors to get the smoke out."

"Got it." After setting the extinguisher on the floor, he made quick work of opening the window over the sink and then the three over by the kitchen table. All I could do was stare at the mess on the stove. I didn't even care that I was standing almost buck-naked in my kitchen.

Fighting the frustrated tears that threatened to overtake me, I yanked my hand through my hair. "Shit!"

Gabe placed a comforting hand on my shoulder. "Take it easy. We can make another batch."

I glanced at the clock on the stove. "By the time I could get to Blair's, it would be closed.

"But it's only nine o'clock."

"You're in the boonies, city boy. Everything here closes early."

"What about a Walmart or another store open all night?"

I wiggled my bra back down over my breasts. "It's an hour away. I have to pick up Linc at Dad's before ten."

"Okay, while you go pick up Linc, I'll go to Walmart for the ingredients."

Gabe's offer sent warmth spreading through my chest; I couldn't believe he was so willing to do whatever it took to help me. But, the feeling of warmth was fleeting, and all too soon it was replaced by a sense of unease. Not only was what we had just done on the counter too fast, so was the whiplash of feelings I was experiencing about him.

"No, no, that's okay. You've done plenty," I replied as I hopped back into my panties and jeans.

"But I want to help," he protested.

Shaking my head, I replied, "Just go. I need to sort this out myself."

Gabe's expression darkened. "Why are you pushing me away?"

Because I'm mortified that I was so easy, not to mention I'm scared to death we've just screwed up what we had by almost screwing in my kitchen.

"I'm not. I just need to clean up this mess and go get Linc." When he started to protest again, I pinched my eyes shut. "Please. Just leave."

After huffing out a frustrated breath, he brushed past me. Closing my eyes, I listened to his heavy footsteps as they pounded against the hallway floor. At the sound of the front door slamming, I jumped. Now that I was alone, I allowed the tears to flow. This time they weren't about the burnt brownies. There was nothing I could do to rectify the mess I had made of those. Now I was thinking there was no way I could rectify the mess I'd just made with Gabe. So, my tears? They were all about Gabe.

I'M NOT sure how long I stood dumbfounded on Rae's back porch. This rejection stung in a different way than her others, and I wasn't just talking about my blue balls. Things had been changing emotionally between us, and I couldn't help being annoyed at her for cutting me off the same way she had before she even knew me. Okay, if I were honest with myself, I would say I really felt hurt more than I did annoyance. My dick felt the annoyance it hadn't gotten to come buried deep inside Rae's tight, wet pussy, but my heart was hurt by her dismissing me so quickly and once again alluding to the idea that I was just some self-centered prick. *You've done plenty.* What the hell did that even mean?

Even though she'd told me I'd done enough, there was no way in hell I was letting this one go. As I started down the porch steps, I dug my phone out of my pocket. After scrolling through my contacts, I hit dial, and I wasn't too surprised to hear Cumbia music blaring in the background when AJ answered. The drummer for Runaway Train, AJ Resendiz, always spent some of his down time in Mexico where his family was originally from. He and his wife, Mia, had a house in Puerto Vallarta.

"Hey Gabe, what's up?" AJ yelled over the music.

"Not much. Listen, I know you guys are out of the country, but I need a favor."

"Anything for you, my man."

"Do you think Mia could get me the hookup for about fifty to a hundred cannoli from Mama Sofia's?"

With a chuckle, AJ said, "You back on the weed and have the munchies?"

I snorted. "Not quite."

"Then what the hell do you need that many cannoli for?"

"It's a long story."

"If I'm going to have my wife call back to her dad's restaurant in Atlanta to request a shit-ton of cannoli, I think I'm owed an explanation." After he said something in Spanish, the loud music cut off in the background.

Inwardly, I groaned. The last thing I wanted to do was tell AJ what had happened with Rae—he and the other guys would rag my ass for days. "Fine, there's this woman named Rae, and I was—"

AJ sucked in a breath. "You've fallen for her."

"Whoa, whoa, I didn't say that," I protested.

"You didn't have to. I can hear it in your voice." Even though he was all the way in Mexico, I could picture the shit-eating grin on AJ's face. All the married Runaway Train guys were on Eli and me to settle down.

"You do realize we sound like two chicks on the phone right now, don't you?"

With a chuckle, AJ replied, "I couldn't give a shit less. I want to hear more about this Rae."

I could have found a million ways to describe her, but I merely replied, "She's my muse."

"Oh yeah, you're in deep."

"No, I'm not."

"Then why are you calling me?"

In a rambling mess, I said, "We just burned up the brownies when I was going down on her on the kitchen counter and now I need a replacement dessert for her son's school bake sale tomorrow so she doesn't hate me for distracting her with sex!"

Silence came from the other end of the phone. "Did you just say something about burned brownies?"

"Yeah, we were baking together…among other things."

"Yep, you've fallen big time."

"AJ, could you please cut the shit."

"I will after one more thing. You said she has a kid."

"Yeah. Lincoln's nine—well, he likes to be called Linc." I was rambling again.

"You don't do kids."

I scowled at the phone. "I'm aware of that."

"Then what the hell are you doing *baking* with a woman who has a kid?"

"I made a deal with Linc to give him a guitar if he would get his mom to hang out with me." Feeling like an old gossiping woman, I filled AJ in on everything that had transpired with the Jeep and the songwriting inspiration.

"I seriously do not have words right now, man."

"I doubt that."

"Okay, I have plenty but let me just ask you this: are you wanting to get the cannoli just to make it up to this Rae chick, or do you also want them so her kid will like you too?"

"What kind of question is that? This isn't about the kid—it's about Rae. If she stays pissed at me, my songwriting will get shot to hell again."

"I'm not buying it. You could have thrown some cash at Rae to help the situation, but instead, you're going to drive all the way to Atlanta tonight to pick up some desserts that are sure to be wildly popular at the bake sale, which in turn will make not only Rae but also Linc look good, not to mention that saving his mom's ass will make you look good in his eyes."

I remained silent for a few moments, processing what AJ had said. Surely he had to be out in left field with what he'd said about me wanting to impress Linc. This wasn't about him at all; it was about staying on Rae's good side. The only thing AJ was right about when it came to me and Linc was the fact that I didn't do kids. "You're full of shit, man," I finally muttered.

"You keep telling yourself that. The truth is, you like the kid."

"I never said I didn't. You're the one saying I'm trying to impress him, which I'm not."

"And just like the kid told you it would mean more to go out of your way for the breakfast, you're going out of your way for him."

I growled in frustration. "Fine. I want the kid to like me, okay?

And not just because I'm giving him a guitar as part of this hair-brained plan of ours."

"There. Now was that so hard to admit?" AJ teased.

"Be glad you're in Mexico right now, or I'd be kicking your ass."

"Ha! Bring it on."

"So, you've got my back?"

"As long as you're aware that these cannoli are going to cost you a fucking fortune."

With a laugh, I replied, "I don't care."

"Fine. I'll call Duke and tell him to start an emergency batch. They should be done by the time you make the trip from Bumblefuck to Atlanta."

Duke Martinelli was AJ's father-in-law. When he had retired from the NFL, he'd opened an Italian restaurant in the heart of Atlanta and named it Mama Sofia's, after his mother. "Tell Duke I'll owe him big time."

"Oh, I'm sure he'll let you make it up to him," AJ joked.

"Whatever, man."

"All right, I'm hanging up and calling him."

"Thanks. I appreciate it. I owe you, too."

"The only way I want to be repaid is for things to work out with you and this girl."

Rolling my eyes, I protested, "But you don't even know her. She could be a real bitch or a gold digger."

"I know what you've told me, and from that, I know she's someone worth pursuing—someone like my Mia."

I jerked a hand through my hair. "She could be. I just don't know."

"Then find out."

"Okay, I'll try."

"Talk to you later, man. Thanks."

"Yeah, later."

14

Rae

LONG AFTER GABE LEFT, my feet remained frozen to the kitchen floor. I would have been a complete statue of myself if I didn't continue running my fingers over my swollen lips. Each time I did, I closed my eyes and thought of Gabe's mouth on mine...his hands on my body...his tongue inside me. Just as I would flush with desire, mortification would once again crash over me.

As Aunt Sadie would say, I'd just behaved like a brazen hussy. I mean, how else would one classify my behavior? I'd allowed a man I'd known for less than a week to go down on me in my family's kitchen. Sure, he was a talented songwriter known around the world who called me his songwriting muse, but he was still a stranger to me.

While I'd been an avid watcher of *Sex and the City* back in the day, I'd only managed to live vicariously through their liberated sexual escapades. The five men I'd slept with in my life had all been within the confines of either a relationship or long dating period. Well, there was that one-night stand with a Falcons player, but I was only twenty at the time. I had certainly matured and become much wiser since then.

"What the hell?" Kennedy demanded.

Coming out of my stupor, I whirled around to face my sisters. Kennedy's wide gaze ricocheted around the room. "What happened?"

"Uh, I burned Linc's brownies."

Kennedy cocked her head at me. "Yes, I can smell that, but did a tornado blow through here as well?" She motioned to the floor where Gabe had swept the leftover ingredients and bowls to the floors before hoisting me up on the countertop.

"Gabe... He..." I pinched my eyes shut.

Ellie appeared at my side. "Did Gabe hurt you?"

My eyes flew open as I wildly shook my head. "No, no, no! It was nothing like that."

"Then what was it?" Kennedy asked.

"I thought my vagina caught on fire, but it was the brownies burning," I said absently.

Kennedy and Ellie exchanged a look. "Do we slap her or try to get some alcohol in her?" Kennedy asked.

With a scowl, I replied, "You don't need to slap me."

"Considering the state you're in and the way you're talking, that's still debatable," Kennedy said.

"While I don't need slapping, I could use a drink."

Ellie nodded. "Kennedy, grab the tequila from the pantry."

"I'm on it."

Steering me over to the table, Ellie said, "I think you need to sit down."

"That's probably a good idea," I replied as I flopped down in one of the chairs.

Kennedy returned with the tequila and three shot glasses. Always one for extreme bluntness, she asked, "Did you guys fuck on the kitchen counter?"

"If oral sex counts as fucking," I replied before throwing back the tequila. *Oh shit.* That was some extreme TMI I'd just unloaded on my sisters.

While Ellie's eyes bulged in horror, Kennedy paused with her shot glass in mid-air. "Whose ass am I going to be bleaching off the countertop?"

"Mine."

Kennedy bobbed her head. "He went down on you first. I like his style."

"Excuse me?"

"Most men only reciprocate oral sex. They want you to blow them before they'll eat you out."

I wrinkled my nose. "I seriously hate that term."

"What would you prefer I call it? Carpet munching? A c-swizzle? Eating the peach?"

Ellie slowly shook her head back and forth. "I seriously can't believe I just heard those terms come out of your mouth."

"It doesn't surprise me at all," I said as I reached for the tequila bottle.

Kennedy moved it away from me. "Easy there, Tex. Don't you have to pick up Linc at Dad's?"

I groaned. "Yes, dammit. I do." It was one of those moments when I really loved my son, but I also really wanted to get shit-faced with my sisters while sharing my jumbled feelings about Gabe.

"Then no more tequila." She jerked her chin at me. "Hurry up and spill it before you have to go."

With a sigh, I proceeded to tell the girls how Gabe's and my baking had turned into a smoking hot sexcapade that led to me letting the brownies burn, and in turn, how said sexcapade along with Gabe's care and concern led me to emotionally shut down and throw him out of the house.

When I finished, I'd managed to render both my sisters momentarily speechless, which was a feat in itself. Covering my face with my hands, I moaned. "Great, you guys think I'm just as psycho as Gabe probably does."

"No, we don't," Ellie protested.

"I think she's a little psycho," Kennedy replied. Then she grinned at me. "But I get where you were coming from. I mean, the fact that I had an affair with a married French man would be evidence of that."

"How am I ever going to face him again?" I pondered.

"By communicating to him what you've just told us," Ellie said sensibly.

I threw up my hands in frustration. "But I don't know how."

"Of course you do."

"I think the fact that I'm twenty-six and still single would say differently. I'm just no good when it comes to men."

"Just tell him you're sorry for freaking out on him. You just panicked because things were moving too fast," Ellie suggested.

"Then what? Ask him if we can go back to the way things were before he saw me naked and went down on me?"

Kennedy gave me an exasperated look. "Why on earth would you want things to go back to the way they were? You yourself said the man was a hell of a kisser, not to mention was he extremely talented at licking pussy."

"While I'm not sure I would have actually ever said the term 'licking pussy', yes, he was extremely good at it—like the best I've ever had."

"Then why go back to not being physical?"

"Because he has a job to do." At Kennedy's wicked expression, I said, "And it's not to be my official pussy licker."

"Ha, you said it."

"Whatever."

Ellie tilted her head thoughtfully at me. "Are you afraid if you guys keep going, Gabe might lose his songwriting ability again?"

"Something like that. I mean, things were rolling along perfectly well the way we were. He doesn't need anything to complicate it, and we all know how much sex complicates everything."

While Ellie nodded, Kennedy said, "But maybe what he needs now is some heat. Just because you guys start messing around, that doesn't mean he's suddenly going to be unable to write."

"I just don't want to rock the boat."

"I'm pretty sure from what transpired here this evening, Gabe would be more than happy to rock your boat," Kennedy mused.

"While somewhat misguided, I think Kennedy does have a point. You don't know how Gabe is feeling about all this, which is why you have to talk to him."

"Okay, fine. I'll call him in the morning. Hopefully he hasn't packed up and run back to Atlanta because his muse went crazy."

"I seriously doubt that," Ellie replied.

"What time is the bake sale?" Kennedy asked.

"Noon."

Kennedy nodded. "I can throw something together by then."

"You can?"

"While it'll be a complete, pain-in-the-ass inconvenience, of course

I can. You know I'd do anything for that kid." She smiled at me. "And for you, Rae. I always have your back. You know that."

I fought the tears that pricked my eyes. "Thanks, Ken. That means a lot."

"Now go on and get our boy."

"But the kitchen—"

"We'll clean it up while you're gone."

"I can't let you guys do that."

Ellie smiled. "We're family, silly. We always help each other out."

"Even if the other was practically fornicating on the kitchen counter?" I asked.

Kennedy snorted. "You sound just like Aunt Sadie, who, truth be told, probably has completely fornicated on that counter."

"Ew," Ellie and I shrieked. While I was aware of Aunt Sadie's sexual past, I certainly didn't want to think of her doing it, least of all in the same place where I had.

After grabbing my purse and keys, I said, "On that note, I'm out of here."

When my alarm went off the following morning, I fought the urge to pulverize my phone. While I might've had only one shot of tequila with the girls, I'd snuck the bottle into my room after I got home from picking up Linc. I'm not sure what it says about my state of mind that I wanted to drink on my own. It was actually pretty pathetic, now that I thought about it.

Three shots later, I'd stumbled over to my bed, and I must've passed out because I was still in my clothes.

"Fuck me," I grumbled as I pried myself off of the mattress.

Although I'd left Gabe with no reason to possibly text me, I still checked my phone to see if he had. Nope. Nada. Nothin'. Since I'd promised my sisters I would call him, I took a deep breath before texting, *Hey. I know we need to talk. Just name the place and time, and I'll be there.*

I sat there staring at the phone for a few minutes. I kept hoping I would see the little dots telling me he was texting me back, but they never appeared. With a grunt of frustration, I threw the phone over my shoulder before trudging across the bedroom floor and out into the hallway.

Thankfully, I found the downstairs bath empty. I knew I wasn't going to feel human again until I washed the alcohol stank off of me. Stepping under the scalding steam of water, I sighed. I had no idea what I was going to do about Gabe.

Even after the pep talk from Kennedy and Ellie, I still couldn't imagine facing him again after freaking out like I had. Surely, he had to have been completely turned off from me since I'd left him with both physical and emotional blue balls. He was Gabe Renard, for fuck's sake. He had women throwing themselves at him, and he certainly didn't need to waste his time with a head case like me.

Once I'd showered and gotten my makeup on, I headed back across the hallway to my bedroom. Instead of going to the closet to find something to wear, I made a beeline for the bed—specifically for my phone, which I'd tossed onto the bed. My heart plummeted when I still didn't have a response from Gabe.

Trying to talk myself out of the abyss, I said, "He's probably still asleep. He told you himself he's normally not a morning person."

Yeah, that was my story, and I was sticking to it. Pushing Gabe from my mind, I went about the rest of my morning ritual, including prying Linc from bed and downing a scorching cup of espresso.

Once Linc was finished with the scrambled eggs and bacon Kennedy had made for him, I asked, "Come on and get your things. Since we're running late, I'm going to let Papa know I'm dropping you off at school on the way to work."

"Okay Mom."

I stopped him in the doorway. "Do you have all your homework?"

"Yep."

"Your lunch money?"

"Yesss."

"Yeah, yeah, I get it—your mother is sooo lame for trying to make sure you have your shit together."

Linc laughed. "Yep, pretty much."

I rolled my eyes. "Fine. Then let's go." I'd started out the door when Linc grabbed my arm.

"Wait—what about my brownies?"

Ugh. Time to come clean. I'd gotten a small reprieve the previous night when Linc had fallen asleep on the way home, and I'd steered his drowsy ass to bed without any explanation of the brownies. Thanks to Kennedy and Ellie cleaning up for me, there wasn't any physical evidence either.

"You know, it's a funny thing about the brownies." Yes, ladies and gentleman, I was about to tell a complete lie to my child. "When I went to Blair's to get the mix, they were completely out."

"They were?" Linc questioned, his brow wrinkling. I could almost see the bullshit meter inside his head going off.

"Yep, and when I tried to make them from scratch, it turned into a big mess."

"Is that why the kitchen smelled so bad last night?"

My eyes bulged. "I thought you were too sleepy to notice."

"It reeked of something burnt."

"Sadly, that would have been the brownies."

"Oh," he replied. My heart plummeted at the same rate as his face.

"But don't worry, Aunt Kennedy is whipping up something extra super-duper special for me to bring for the bake sale."

"It won't be your brownies."

Forcing a smile to my face, I countered, "I'm sure it'll be ten times better than my brownies. Aunt K graduated from Le Cordon Bleu cooking school while your ol' mom here can barely make macaroni and cheese out of the box."

When Linc didn't reply, it felt like a knife twisting into my heart. I wasn't sure why mommy guilt had to be so damn painful. More than anything, I wanted him to yell at me, to throw his book bag while hurling an obscenity or two, but no, he remained quiet.

Feeling like an utter and complete asshole, I motioned for him to go on out the door. "Let's get you to school, sweetheart."

He nodded and then did a pitiful little trudge out the door. When I glanced back at Kennedy and Ellie, they both had downcast faces. "I promise I'll bring the best damn brownies I can make," Kennedy said.

"Thanks," I muttered before doing my own version of Linc's pitiful trudge. We made the drive to Hayesville Elementary in complete silence. I kept imagining this would be the day Linc told his therapist about, the one when he lost all faith in his mother, or maybe it would be the story he told his substance abuse counselor after my negligence sent him down a path of drug and alcohol abuse.

Instead of pulling into the carpool line, I eased into one of the parking spaces. While I could have called to inform the school about my utter fuck-up, I decided it would be better to tell them in person, not to mention the fact that I didn't want Linc walking into school empty-handed.

Of course, I should have remembered that at his age, my very existence was a complete embarrassment to him. He reminded me of that fact the moment I started following him into the building. "Seriously, Mom?" he hissed, his horrified gaze bouncing from side to side to check if anyone had seen.

I held up my hands. "My bad. You go on in." As he hurried away from me, I called, "Have a great day!"

I'm pretty sure he cursed me under his breath, but I decided to ignore it. Drawing in a deep breath, I walked inside the front lobby. I spoke to several of the parents I knew, many of which I'd gone to school with myself. It was pretty rare for anyone new to move into Hayesville.

When I got to the cafeteria, it was buzzing not only with the many kids who ate breakfast at school, but also with the moms setting up for the bake sale. Craning my neck, I searched the room for Pricilla Parton, the president of the PTA. I finally found her at one of the tables in the far corner of the room.

"Morning, Cilla," I said.

She whirled around, iPad in hand. At the sight of me, her eyes widened before a beaming smile lit up her face. "Well, hello, Rae."

"Listen, I have some bad news about the turtle brownies I was supposed to bring—"

Pricilla's auburn brow creased in confusion. "Turtle brownies? But you brought all that fabulous cannoli?"

I blinked a few times at her. "I'm sorry…what?"

"When we arrived this morning, we found five pans full of home-made cannoli. It had yours and Linc's names on it."

An awkward laugh bubbled from my lips. "Come on, Cilla, you've known me since our kids started school here together—would I even remotely know where to begin to make one cannoli, least of all five pans?"

Shrugging, Pricilla replied, "I just assumed Kennedy made them."

"No, she didn't. She's back at her shop right now trying to whip up some kind of replacement brownies."

"Then who sent all the cannoli in your name?" Pricilla questioned.

I sucked in a breath so fast I wheezed like a deflated balloon. "Oh my God," I hissed as it hit me just exactly who had saved my ass. I whirled around and searched the room for him. When I didn't see Gabe, I remembered what Pricilla had said about them finding the cannoli when they arrived. Gabe wouldn't have wanted to be seen at the school for all the craziness it might cause. *Oh God.* I had to see him —like, immediately.

Slowly, I started backing up from her. "Um, I've got to go."

"Wait, will you be back at noon to help with the sale?"

"Yes. I'll be here." I then turned and practically sprinted out of the cafeteria. At any moment, I expected some hall monitor to yell at me or threaten me with detention. Thankfully, I made it to my car without getting in any trouble.

When I slid inside, my hands were shaking so hard I could barely crank up. Gabe had outdone himself this time. Even though I'd pushed him away and practically thrown him out of my house, he'd still gone out of his way to do something so considerate for me and for Linc.

God, if I hadn't already been starting to seriously like this man, this was the gesture that would have sent me over the edge. But, as I drove down Main Street, all the voices of doubt chattered in my head. *It's too soon. It's too fast. He's just passing through.*

Shaking my head, I tried shaking myself free of the voices. I didn't want to deal with any of that right now. All I really wanted to concern myself with at the moment was getting to Gabe. I screeched into the driveway of the Grandview on two wheels. After throwing the car into park and killing the ignition, I once again broke into a run. When I burst through the front door, I screeched to a halt in the foyer. I was panting so hard I had to bend over at the waist to catch my breath.

"Reagan? Is that you?" Rejune questioned from the parlor.

"Yes. Mrs. Paulson," I huffed.

"Are you all right?"

"I've been better." With my breathing regulated, I straightened up to face her. "I'm here to see Gabe."

"I'm not sure Mr. Renard is receiving visitors at the moment." She lowered her voice. "I just heard the shower cut off a little while ago."

"I'll only be a minute."

A knowing expression came over her face. "Why I'm sure a strong, strapping young man like him takes far longer than a minute."

I rolled my eyes. "I'm just here to talk, Mrs. Paulson."

"If you say so." When I started for the stairs, she said, "Why don't you wait down here while I call up to his room to ask if he wants to see you?"

"I can find the way myself, thank you." While she continued to protest, I hurried up the two flights of stairs to the third floor. Although there were four doors to choose from, the strumming of a guitar helped steer me to the right room.

Rapping my knuckles on the door, I called, "Gabe?"

A screech came at the guitar strings. After a few moments, the door opened, and I gasped at the sight of Gabe before me. Rejune had been right about the shower—Gabe's hair was soaking wet, and he had a pale pink towel draped around his waist.

"Hey," he said.

"Hey," I muttered. We stood there for a few moments before I said, "Nice towel."

Gabe grinned as he glanced down at his waist. "It would appear that Rejune has a fondness for all things pink. I haven't been able to find a white towel or one without flowers the entire time I've been here."

"It's a good look on you."

"Har har."

Okay, Rae, get a grip and cut the flirty comedy routine. You came over to thank Gabe for saving your ass with the cannoli in spite of your insistence that you didn't need his help. I cleared my throat. "Listen, I just came from Linc's school."

The corners of Gabe's lips pricked. "I assumed as much." He held out his hand to me. "Do you want to come in?"

With a nod, I slipped my hand into his and let him pull me into the room. After he closed the door, he led me across the room to an overstuffed couch. "Have a seat while I go get dressed."

"You don't have to do that on my account."

His brows popped up. "Does that mean you prefer me half-naked?"

I laughed. "I meant, I'm not going to stay long, so you don't have to get dressed if you don't want to."

"I think it's best if I did."

I got Gabe's meaning immediately. Even after me pushing him away the night before, the sexual tension remained thick between us. I'd already fended off two imagined dirty scenarios of ripping off his towel and blowing him or ripping off his towel and then riding him like a crazed cowgirl.

I forced a smile to my now dry lips. "Yea, that's probably best." As Gabe started out of the living room and slipped into the bedroom, I got quite the view of his sculpted bare back. I fought the desire to run my fingers over the colorful ink splayed across the corded muscles. Once again, I found myself rolling my eyes and huffing in aggravation at my sex-crazed thoughts about Gabe. The last thing I needed at that moment was to give myself over to my desire for him.

When Gabe reappeared, he wore a red t-shirt that stretched across his heavily muscled chest. While his jeans weren't indecently tight, they certainly highlighted his wide thighs. Although it looked like he had toweled his hair dry a bit, it was still somewhat wet.

Sitting down next to me on the couch, Gabe asked, "Did you come here to tell me off?"

"Excuse me?"

"Because I went behind your back and took the cannoli to the school."

I widened my eyes at him. "Are you kidding me? I came here to *thank* you, like, eternally and from the bottom of my heart. I'm still in shock that you went to all that trouble. I mean, where did you possibly find cannoli here in the backwoods, least of all after nine o'clock?"

Gabe chuckled. "I called in a favor from a buddy of mine in Atlanta."

"You went all the way to Atlanta last night?" I screeched.

With a shrug, Gabe said, "Yeah. Why?"

"That's like five hours on the road."

"It gave me time to think. I also made a few phone calls, listened to part of the new Stephen King book."

I shook my head. "Now I feel even worse."

"Don't do that."

"But you went to so much trouble."

"Because I wanted to."

Cocking my head at him, I asked, "Why, after you did something so wonderful for me, did you think I was here to tell you off?"

"I knew I was taking that risk after you made it very plain to me last night that you didn't want my help." Gabe shook his head. "But I couldn't help it, Rae. I felt like I had to do something because it was partly my fault for distracting you and letting the brownies burn."

At his reference to distracting me, warmth flooded my face. "Yes, you were quite good at distracting me."

The smoldering look he gave me sent me squirming in my seat. "I would say I was sorry about that, but I would be lying," he said, his voice dropping an octave.

"Regardless of what happened, I wouldn't want you to be sorry for that—ever." I drew in a breath. "Me, on the other hand, I have a lot to be sorry for, starting with the way I freaked out on you."

"It's okay. I understand."

My mouth dropped open. "You do?"

"I may not have known you for long, Rae, but I do know what kind of woman you are."

"And what kind is that?"

"The type who normally doesn't almost have sex with a stranger."

I nodded. "Yeah, that's pretty much me. I mean, after the time we've spent together this past week, you're not a stranger. It's just... you're not someone I'm actually dating."

"And I get that. I really do."

"You do?" I repeated.

"While I'm sure you think the sex fiend in me is pissed we didn't get to finish what we started, that's not what upsets me."

Gabe's responses continued to surprise me. "It's not?"

"I got mad because you shut me out. You dismissed me like I couldn't possibly help you."

Wincing, I ducked my head. "I know, and it was wrong of me to do that. You were just being nice and trying to help me, and I freaked out and acted like a psycho." I peeked up at him. "Outside of my father, I'm not used to having a man help me." *Every other man has let me down. That's why I can't trust men.*

"I understand. I guess it's just going to take time for you to trust me."

"Yes, it is. I wish it didn't have to be that way, but I..." The truth was, my trust issues had begun even before I'd been so badly burned by Ryan. It went all the way back to when I was a three-year-old little girl, waking up one crisp September day to find my mother was gone. As the weeks turned to months, there was a reason I only trusted my dad, my sisters, and Aunt Sadie: they'd never left me. They'd never chosen something or someone over me.

But, Gabe hadn't had any part in what my mother had done so many years ago. I couldn't fault him for my past. I had to give him the benefit of the doubt. Staring intently at him, I added, "But I am willing to try."

"So am I."

I jerked my chin at his guitar. "Were you working on something new?"

Shaking his head, Gabe replied, "More like polishing one from earlier in the week." Reading what had to be my extremely curious expression, he asked, "Would you like to hear it?"

"I'd love to."

With a nod, Gabe picked up the guitar. "For the record, I'm not the best singer in my family."

"Oh, I'm sure you're a fabulous singer."

"We'll see about that."

Gabe began strumming the tune I'd heard when I got to his door. "Trapped inside these walls, I made a prison all my own. Lost and confused, I was always so alone," he began. While Gabe didn't have an amazing voice, I instantly fell in love with its coarseness. He was like a cross between Bruce Springsteen and John Cougar Mellencamp.

Closing my eyes, I focused on the lyrics floating through the air. For someone who had claimed to be unable to write, Gabe had penned a breathtakingly raw love song about a man who was saved by the love of a woman. Tears pricked my eyes at the haunting quality of the tune.

When Gabe sang the last note, I didn't know what to do. Considering how amazing the song was, it seemed cheesy to clap for him. Instead, I opened my eyes to let him see my tears. "Wow," I murmured.

Tilting his head at me, Gabe asked, "Wow as in 'Wow, that was a load of crap' or 'Wow, that was amazing'?"

"I can't believe you even have to ask for clarification. Don't the tears in my eyes tell you enough?"

"You could be crying because of how awful it was," he countered.

I swiped my eyes. "Well, I'm not."

A pleased look flashed in Gabe's eyes. "It was really that evocative?"

"Oh Gabe, it's beautiful. I love the symbolism of the man being a prisoner of his own insecurities, which causes him to be incapable of love—and then he finds the woman who sets him free." I swept my hand to my heart. "It's absolutely gorgeous."

"You know, you're the first person to hear it outside of my family. I played it for Abby and Eli the other day."

"What did they say?" I asked tentatively.

He grinned. "The same kind of things you did."

I playfully nudged his leg with mine. "Then why did you doubt yourself?"

His expression slowly darkened. "Because I remain in a constant state of crippling self-doubt," he said in an agonized tone.

I fought the urge to stare at Gabe in disbelief. I couldn't believe the words that had just come from his mouth. I doubted anyone outside of his parents or siblings had ever heard them. He was so reluctant to share personal things about himself, but this confession made him appear very vulnerable before me, and my heart instantly went out to him.

"That seems to happen a lot to creative people, doesn't it?" I questioned softly.

"It's our cross to bear."

"I wish I could take it from you—the self-doubt. Then you could have a clearly untainted view of how insanely talented you are."

"What you said just now—that's the other reason I wanted your opinion. You're a fresh ear, someone who isn't in the business."

"I don't know why you would want to listen to me. They're the ones who know and understand music."

"But you understand the emotion. Without an understanding and an appreciation for the emotion, a song is just a piece of music."

"And that's bad?" I questioned.

"To me it is. I want it to be an experience. When I write, I want my songs to be ones that take you back to a time or place or bring you comfort when you're going through a really difficult phase."

"That's so intense," I murmured.

Gabe chuckled. "What do you mean?"

"I've never met anyone who thinks as deeply as you do." I shook my head at him. "It's truly inspiring to hear you talk about songwriting."

"You're the inspiring one. Without you, this song wouldn't have happened."

"But how?" I murmured.

His lips curved into a smile. "Don't you get it, Rae? *You* are the song. You're within each and every line of the lyrics."

I wanted to argue with him that the beautiful meaning conveyed in the words of his song couldn't possibly be about me. I wasn't any of the things the heroine was—I didn't breathe life back into his dying body, didn't free him from the prison he found himself in.

As if he could read my mind, Gabe said, "Yes, you did."

Overcome by the emotion of the moment, I found myself stripped of the ability to speak. Although a myriad of emotions swirled in my mind, I couldn't find a way to string them together. Instead, I closed the gap between us on the couch and threw my arms around Gabe's neck before dipping my head to bring my lips to his.

I poured everything I couldn't seem to say into that kiss—all the appreciation and the longing, all the gratitude and the wonder.

When I finally willed myself to pull away, I stared into Gabe's hazy eyes. "Thank you for that," he said as he brought a hand up to cup my cheek.

"You don't have to thank me, silly. I'm the one thanking you—or at least I was trying to with my kiss."

"You did a damn good job."

I smiled. "I hope so." I could have stayed like that—wrapped up with Gabe staring adoringly at me—for the rest of the morning, if not forever, but my phone ringing in my pocket took us out of the moment. As I dug it out, I didn't have to look at the display to know who it was.

"Hey Dad," I said.

"Where are you?"

"And hello to you, too."

"It's after nine. You're never late."

As Gabe teasingly shook a finger at me, I rolled my eyes. "Today's the bake sale at Linc's school. I had to stop by there."

"Well, we've got an insurance adjuster here to look at that totaled Suburban."

"Okay, I'll be right there."

"See you in a few, sweetheart."

"Bye."

When I turned back to Gabe, he smiled at me. "You have to go."

"Unfortunately."

He swept a loose strand of hair back from my face. "It's okay. I didn't expect for you to be able to stay. You do have a job and a life."

Something in the way he looked at me made me sad. "I wish I could."

"I know."

After nibbling on my lip, I said, "You could come by later, if you wanted to. I have to go work the bake sale from noon to one, but after that, I'm free the rest of the day." I laughed. "Well, as free as one can be at their job."

Surprise filled Gabe's eyes. "I thought you didn't want me hanging out at the shop because I would stir up the men and confuse them about what's going on between us."

"They can say what they want to."

He grinned. "I see."

"Does that mean you'll stop by?"

With a bob of his head, he replied, "Just as soon as I catch a nap."

I grimaced. "Once again, I'm really sorry you lost sleep last night."

"Trust me. This"—he motioned between us—"made it all worth it."

"I hope so."

When I started to get off the couch, Gabe pulled me back down against him. Cupping my face in his hands, he leaned in and kissed me. Although I could tell he wanted it to be more just as much as I did, he somehow managed to maintain his restraint. When he pulled away, he smiled. "See you later."

"Sweet dreams."

"They will be if they're about you."

Sweeping a hand to my hip, I said, "I said sweet dreams, not sex dreams."

Gabe laughed. "Someone is pretty sure of themselves if they think I couldn't have a dream about them without it being about sex."

"I'm just speaking from experience."

When Gabe's eyes bulged, it was my turn to laugh. He popped off the couch like a jack-in-the-box. "You had a sex dream about me?"

"Maybe."

He growled. "Don't be coy now."

"Fine then. You were very good in it. Does that make you happy?"

"Like how good?"

I waggled my brows at him. "Like I came in my sleep kinda good."

A cocky smirk curved Gabe's lips as he puffed his chest out. "So I was *that* good?"

I am so not answering that. "Now don't go getting a big head. Just like with morning wood, women can have orgasms without any sexual stimulation."

Gabe's hand reached out to slide around my waist. As it started to dip down over my ass, he said, "I'm going to call bullshit on that."

Pushing out of his reach, I wagged a finger at him. "It's true. You can Google it."

"I'm not saying the orgasm thing isn't true—I'm calling bullshit that it wasn't *me* who made you come."

"Maybe. I guess we'll never know."

"We'll just have to rely on the orgasms I give you when you're awake."

Yes, I'd be really happy to rely on those too. "I guess so."

Tilting his head at me, Gabe asked, "You don't sound so certain about that."

"Oh, I'm certain about the orgasms you'll give me."

He grinned. "Okay, then what's the problem?"

You, Gabe. But really, it wasn't him—it was me. I hadn't slept with anyone for the sake of sex alone since I was in my early twenties. I'd grown not only older since then, but also wiser. I wasn't sure I could transition back to those early days, although Gabe had brought me awfully close to no-strings-attached sex—pun intended. I didn't know what was the right way to tell him that while I wanted to slow down, I didn't want to turn him off.

"I'm just not so sure I need them any time soon."

"Ah, I see. You're talking about putting the brakes on any more sexcapades." *Bingo.*

I giggled. "Sexcapades? Seriously?"

"I'm pretty sure what we did on your kitchen counter last night would be considered a sexcapade."

"Hmm, you're probably right."

"Of course I am."

"Okay, Mr. Cocky, you still haven't said whether you're okay with slowing things down."

"While I would prefer for us to stay in the fast lane, I'm totally fine with easing up a bit."

The breath I'd been holding whooshed out of me in relief. "Thank you."

With a wicked grin, Gabe waggled his brows. "You'd really be thanking me if I made you come."

I rolled my eyes. "And on that note, I'm out of here."

Gabe responded by playfully smacking one of my ass cheeks before pulling away. "I'll see you later."

After giving him a quick peck on the lips, I hurried out of the room. When I got to the top of the landing, Rejune scrambled off the bottom step where she had apparently been craning her head to eavesdrop.

When I passed her to go to the last landing of the stairs, I faked zipping up my jeans. "Have a good one, Mrs. Paulson." I winked. "I know I will."

Rejune's face flushed blood red, and I had to duck my head to keep from laughing. I wondered if I would even make it back to work before people in town heard the latest gossip of how Reagan Hart was fornicating with the out-of-town country star in broad daylight—and on a *Tuesday.*

Gabe

15

THREE DAYS *later*

I was in the middle of a hot-as-fuck sex dream about Rae when my phone woke me. At first, I thought it was my alarm since I was getting up early to have breakfast with Rae, but then I realized it was a call. "Hello?" I questioned drowsily.

"Good morning, Gabe. It's Pierce."

The mere sound of the label's exec had me shooting up straight in bed. "Hey Pierce, how's it going?"

"Good. I'm sorry to bother you so early, but I've just touched down at Hartsfield-Jackson. I was hoping to sit down with you and the band to hear your album's progress before I head back to LA this evening."

Fuuuuuck. This could not be happening. We weren't supposed to meet with Pierce and the other execs for at least two weeks. While I might've had the songs written, it wasn't like Abby, Eli, and I had gotten the chance to have any rehearsals. Sure, we'd done a few Face-Times over the phone, but it was not the level of preparedness a perfectionist like me would like to have.

"Well, I don't know. I'd have to speak with the others—"

"Xander and Paula have already been in touch with your brother and sister. They said they could be there, but I would need to check with you since you were out of town."

"Yeah, I'm up in the mountains. It'll take me a few hours to get back into town."

"Would noon be enough time?" *Like noon in two weeks' time? Sure. Noon today? Hell fucking no.*

"Sure. I could make it by then." Yeah, I was a spineless asshole.

"Good. I'll see you then."

Long after Pierce hung up, I held the phone in my hands, staring into space. While I should have been hauling ass to get packed up and out the door, I remained motionless. The only thing I could think about was Rae. What was going to happen to us if I left now? Things were just starting to flow, not to mention the cranked-up level of heat between us.

Since that day at the Grandview, we had been together each and every day. Although I wasn't completely on board with no more make-out sessions, the universe had clearly conspired against me because Rae and I hadn't found another long period of alone time. It seemed we were always accompanied by someone, be it Linc, her sisters, her dad, or the men at Hart and Daughter. My balls would've been turning the most brilliant color of blue if I hadn't been treating myself to a few fantasy sessions staring Rae.

Considering I was on a time constraint to get back to Atlanta, it made more sense to call Rae to tell her I couldn't make breakfast, not to mention that I was blowing town, but there was no way in hell I could be that big of an asshole. I had to say goodbye in person, had to tell her once again how much she had meant to my songwriting—and if I were honest with myself, how much she meant to me.

Then I would walk away.

Sure, I could prolong the inevitable by telling her I'd come back just as soon as the meeting with the execs was over. We could have several more weeks together before I had to leave again to record the album and I might finally get to bury myself deep inside her tight walls, but that was where it would end. I led a vagabond life on the road while Rae's roots were firmly bound to her small-town existence. I could never ask her to leave her responsibilities there, and I certainly couldn't leave the band.

With an agonized groan, I finally pulled myself up out of bed. After making quick work of packing up, I took a quick shower. Once I was dressed, I grabbed my bags and headed down the stairs. I made as quick of a getaway as I could with Rejune before hustling out to the Jeep. As I drove across town, dread washed over me. It was at a moment like this that I wished there was a liquor store in town. I could have used a hit of vodka to help get me through.

As I pulled into Rae's driveway, I was glad to see her car was still at home and I hadn't missed her. It would have been even worse if she had already left to take Linc to school and I had to hunt her down at the restaurant. There was no way in hell I wanted to do this in public. Glancing at the clock on the dashboard, I imagined she was just chugging down her second cup of espresso while she made sure Linc's lunch was packed into his backpack. *Holy shit.* I'd only been hanging out with Rae a little over a week and I was already in tune with the rhythm of her mornings. Man, that was intense.

After bounding up the front porch steps, I froze. Suddenly, AJ's words echoed through my mind: *I know she's someone worth pursuing —someone like my Mia.* Four years of being around AJ's wife had shown me that she was strong, fiercely protective, and extremely loyal to those she loved. She was also funny and had a heart of gold, especially when she would make extra food for me and Eli to eat while on the tour bus.

Strangely enough, everything I had just thought about Mia could be said about Rae. *I know she's someone worth pursuing.* Fuck, AJ had nailed it. Rae *was* someone worth pursuing, someone worth keeping. Was I really going to be an epic dumbass and walk away from the best thing that had happened to me in years? Sure, we had some obstacles in our path, but they weren't completely insurmountable. Wasn't it worth it to give it a try? Since I'd only experienced a handful of romantic relationships in my adult life, I really wasn't capable of answering that question. When it came down to it, I was just going to have to rely on the adage that there was a first time for everything.

With a renewed determination in my step, I reached out and rang the doorbell. After Rae peeked through the side curtain and saw it was me, her face lit up. She threw open the door and gave me a beaming smile. "Hey."

"Hey," I replied.

"What are you doing here? I thought we were going to meet for breakfast before I went to work."

"I'm going to have to get a rain check for breakfast."

Rae's smile slowly started to fade. "You are?"

I nodded. "My label called. They're asking to hear the songs I've been working on while one of the execs is in town, so I have to be back in Atlanta by noon."

"Oh," she murmured.

"I knew I had to come say goodbye in person, rather than just calling you."

"Goodbyes are pretty shitty no matter how you get them."

"True, but I also wanted to be able to thank you in person. I'd still be drowning in writer's block if it hadn't been for you. Hell, I wouldn't even be able to meet with the label today because I wouldn't have any songs to show them."

"I'm not sure you owe me any gratitude. I really didn't do anything but hang out with you."

I stared intently at her. "Yes, you did, more than you'll ever imagine."

With a smile that didn't reach her eyes, Rae said, "I'm glad I could help. For what it's worth, I enjoyed spending time with you this week."

"I enjoyed spending time with you, too." I took a step closer to her. "Listen, Rae, I—"

Linc popped out from behind his mother. "Hey Gabe, what's up?"

"Bad news."

"Whadya mean?"

"I gotta head back to the city sooner than I thought."

His expression instantly soured. "So you've come to say goodbye."

My gaze bounced from his to Rae's. "Just for now, not forever."

While a surprised look flashed in her eyes, I motioned to Linc with my hand. "Come out here with me for a minute."

Linc instantly obliged. When I glanced back at Rae, her face had filled with confusion. I knew she was wondering what in the hell it was I wanted to talk to Linc about. I walked him down the length of the porch to where we were out of earshot from Rae. In a low voice, I said, "Don't think for a minute that I've forgotten our deal."

His brows shot up. "You haven't?"

"Of course not. Did you think I was just going to run out on you?"

He shrugged. "Maybe."

An ache of sadness burned its way through my chest at both Linc's response and his expression. I reached out and touched his arm. "Hell no. Just as soon as I'm done with the label, I'll grab the guitar I owe you and come back."

"You will?"

"Damn straight."

He grinned. "Then I'll be waiting."

"You do that." Glancing back at Rae, I said, "Could you do me a favor and let me have some alone time with your mom?"

"You got it." He then hurried back down the porch and ducked inside the house.

"What was all that about?" Rae asked when I joined her again.

"Just a little man talk."

"I didn't know you and Linc had *man talk*," she said with a small smile.

"Yep, we do." Reaching out for her arm, I drew her out of the doorway. "I wasn't finished talking to you when Linc interrupted us."

"You already said goodbye—what else is there left to say?

"A lot." After steering her over to the swing, I eased her down onto the seat. "This morning when I got the call to go back to Atlanta, all I could think of was all the obstacles between us. I haven't really dated anyone in a long time, and it's been even longer since I tried to make things work with a woman. That said, I'd like to try with you."

Rae's eyes bulged at my declaration. "You would?"

I nodded. "I know your life is here with Linc, and my life is all over the place, but I still want to see where this could go."

"I don't know, Gabe. You're right about anything between us being complicated."

"When it comes down to it, when is life *not* complicated?"

As she nibbled on her bottom lip, I desperately wanted to kiss her. I wanted to take her upstairs and fuck her to make her truly mine, but I knew that wasn't likely to happen with the house full of her kid and her sisters. Finally, she exhaled a breath. "I-I don't know. The stakes seem kind of high."

"Come on, Rae. Don't be a chicken shit."

Her expression darkened as she jabbed a finger at me. "Don't you think I want to say yes? For once in my adult life throw caution to the wind and dive into the unknown? But I can't."

"Why the hell not?"

"Because I'm a mother. I always have to think about what is best for Lincoln before I think of myself."

"Look, I know I'm not a kid person, but I'm pretty sure Linc likes me."

"That's part of the problem. Linc's never reacted to any of the men I've dated like he has with you. If things don't work out between us, it won't just be me with a broken heart."

Rae's declaration left me somewhat speechless. For the first time in my life, I found myself wanting a woman with family obstacles. Before, the only issues I faced were getting them out of their clothes and finding a somewhat secluded place to screw backstage. Rae's and my challenges were monumentally more difficult to work through.

Linc's face flashed before my eyes as Rae's words about leaving him brokenhearted played in my mind. Since the day I'd met him at Hart and Daughter, the kid had certainly grown on me. Even AJ could tell that from over the phone.

"The last thing I would ever want to do is hurt Linc. I wish I could promise you it won't happen, but I can't. All I can promise is that I will do everything within my power not to hurt him."

Tears shimmered in Rae's eyes. "You really mean that, don't you?"

"Yes, I do. Just as I wouldn't do anything to hurt him, the same goes for you as well.

"I want to believe that...more than anything."

And I want you to believe in me, Rae. "All we can do is give it a chance. None of us knows what tomorrow will bring." Tilting my head at her, I asked, "In the future, would you want to look back and wonder what could have happened between us?"

"No, I wouldn't," she murmured.

"Then will you give us a chance?"

After a few agonizing seconds of silence, Rae finally smiled at me. "Yes, I will."

It took a few moments for me to breathe, let alone find my voice. "Hell yeah!" Drawing her into my arms, I brought my lips to hers. They felt just as amazing as they had the first night I kissed her in the kitchen—soft, sweet, and supple.

Just as we started to get a little carried away, a shrill whistle came from the sidewalk. "Get ya some, Rae!" a voice called.

Immediately, we jerked apart. Craning my neck, I said, "Who the hell was that jackass who just interrupted us?"

Rae giggled. "Martin Pauley from the hardware store."

"Remind me to go by there and knock him in the head with one of his shovels when I get back in town."

"I'll try to do that." After smoothing down her shirt, she said, "It's probably best. You need to get on the road, don't you?"

I grimaced. "Yeah, I do."

"Now that we're trying us, when will I see you again?" A hopeful gleam shone in her eyes. "Will you come back this weekend?"

A few hours without Rae's presence seemed too long, let alone a day, and that was how I knew I wanted this with her. I wanted a chance at something more. Suddenly, an idea struck me. "Come to Atlanta with me."

Rae appeared flustered at my request. "Wait, what?"

"You heard me."

"Yes, I'm aware of what you said. I'm just trying to process it."

"There's nothing to process. Throw a few things in a bag and come to Atlanta."

Rolling her eyes, Rae said, "Nothing to process? What kind of fantasy world are you living in? How about my kid and my job, for starters?"

"Let Linc stay with your dad, and you can take a mental health day from work." I gave her my best *How could you resist this face?* smile, hoping it might work on her.

"Pawn my kid off on my dad and play hooky from work?" *Guess not.* But, the more I thought about leaving her and not knowing when I'd be back, it just felt wrong.

"Yes, although I wouldn't exactly use those specific terms."

She swept one of her hands to her hips. "How about the fact that I've barely known you ten days and I'm going off with you for the weekend? You sure aren't one for moving slow, are you?"

"I think we sped past slow the night I went down on you on your kitchen counter."

Rae's cheeks flushed. "I suppose we did."

Placing my hands on her hips, I drew Rae closer to me. "I want more time with you." I slid my hands down over her ass. "I want more of you."

She sucked in a breath before pressing herself against me. "I want more time with you, too."

"Then please consider my request, Rae. Come to Atlanta with me. I know it's fast. I know it's not easy with the responsibilities you have on your shoulders, but I'd like to see us be an *us*. After I get done at the recording studio, we'll have the whole weekend together, just the two of us."

Tilting her head, she peered up at me with consternation. "Can you put on the brakes for just a minute to give me the chance to call my dad? As much as I want to run off for a carefree weekend with you, I have to make sure Linc is taken care of. I'm first and foremost a mom, remember?"

"Yes, I remember. You go ahead and call your dad, and I'll text Eli that I'm on my way."

I couldn't help feeling like an ass as Rae stepped back into the house. Of course she had to be considerate of her dad and Stella and make sure they could take Linc for the weekend. She wasn't the kind of mom to just dump her kid and run. She was thoughtful when it came to both her dad and Linc, which reminded me a lot of Abby.

Although I tried to give her some privacy, bits of the conversation floated back to me. "It's just until Sunday night. I'll be back to get him ready for school. It's just that Gabe's met all of my family, and I really want to meet his, not to mention hearing them perform the songs he's been working on." She paused for a moment. "I know it seems fast, Dad, but you've met him. Doesn't he seem like a nice guy to you?"

Jeez, I certainly hoped Abe liked me. I'd eaten dinner with him multiple times over the last ten days. More than anything, I hoped he wasn't trying to talk Rae out of coming with me. "I'm glad to hear you say that, and I'm glad you'll take Linc for the weekend."

Thank God. While inwardly fist-bumping myself, I heard Rae hang up. Within a flash, she had rejoined me. Smiling coyly up at me, she asked, "Can you give me ten minutes to pack?"

I grinned. "Considering I plan to keep you naked for most of the weekend, I would advise you pack light, and mainly lingerie."

She snorted. "Yeah, we'll just see about that."

After she wiggled out of my embrace, she jerked her chin at the door. "Come on. You can break the news to Linc that you're taking me to the city."

With a groan, I said, "Thanks for making me bad cop."

"It's good practice." She gave me a knowing look before slipping inside the house. I remained frozen in place, processing the enormity of her words. When I could finally put one foot in front of the other again, I rubbed my hand over my chest, where an unfamiliar ache had begun to spread.

AS GABE'S Jeep sped down the interstate toward Atlanta, I fought the urge to pinch myself for the thousandth time. It wasn't just the fact that I was playing hooky from work for the first time in my adult life and leaving Linc for the weekend; it was everything Gabe had said to me.

I haven't really dated anyone in a long time, and it's been even longer since I tried to make things work with a woman. That said, I'd like to try with you."

Gabe wanted to try a relationship with me. Mr. Rich and Famous Country Star wanted to try a relationship with *me*—a small-town single mother whose glamorous career was running a collision business. Who wouldn't feel like she was tripping in some alternate universe?

"You're awfully quiet," Gabe said.

"Just thinking."

"About leaving Linc?"

I turned in my seat to smile at him. I couldn't help loving that he imagined my thoughts were on my son and not him. "Actually, I was thinking about you."

Gabe's brows shot up. "Dirty thoughts?"

With a roll of my eyes, I replied, "Not quite."

"Bummer." He momentarily took his eyes off the road to grin at me. "What were you thinking about me?"

"At the moment, I'm thinking my original impression of you being a sex fiend still rings true."

Gabe laughed. "For real though, what were you thinking about?"

"How surreal this all is, how I never imagined when I woke up this morning that I'd be seeing the Atlanta skyline a few hours later."

"No regrets?"

"None yet."

"Good. I was afraid you might be regretting leaving Linc."

"Although I'm always sad to be away from him, it's not like he's an infant or it's the first time we've been separated. He went to Boy Scout camp for a week this summer."

"And you did okay?"

"I might've cried the first few days…and the day I went to pick him up."

Gabe smiled at me. "He's a lucky kid to have a mom who cares about him so much."

"I'm sure he would argue that he's not so lucky his mom cares because she's always on his ass."

"He might not appreciate it now, but I'm sure he will when he gets older. I know I did, and that's coming from a guy who had an ultra-strict missionary mom."

"Ouch. I'm sure that was pretty intense."

"Micah and Abby were always these angel kids, the ones who sat perfectly still in church and never had a hair out of place or dirtied their clothes." He glanced over me. "Eli and I were hell on wheels, practically from birth."

I laughed at his summation. "Surely you weren't that bad."

"I'm pretty sure we gave our parents all the grey hairs they have."

Tilting my head in thought, I said, "Out of me and my sisters, I would have to say that me and Kennedy probably tie for giving my dad the most grey hairs. Ellie was just like Micah and Abby—she's never been in trouble a day in her life. I got pregnant at seventeen, and Kennedy fell in love with a married man while she was in culinary school in Paris."

Gabe whistled. "I'd say you guys were neck and neck there for biggest troublemaker."

"Thankfully, we both got our acts together, and we haven't given Dad too much grief since—besides the being unmarried part."

"Is your dad on your case to get married like my parents are?"

"Yes and no. Although he knows my sisters and I are capable of taking care of ourselves, he wants us to have families of our own. I think he really wants us to have what he didn't—a happy marriage."

"My parents want that for Eli and me. More than that, they'd like us on a more straight and narrow path." He winked. "Give up a life of sin."

"I wondered what your parents thought of your career."

"They think we're incredibly blessed to get to make a good living doing something we love. At the same time, they'd appreciate a little less drinking and a little less..." He grimaced.

"Whoring around?"

"That's one way to put it."

"I'm not naïve, Gabe. I'm aware of the type of lifestyle you have."

"Had."

"What?"

He took his gaze off the road again. "It's the life I *had*. I don't have it anymore."

Immediately, the gravity of what he was saying hit me. The lovesick teenage girl in me wanted to clasp her hand to her heart. Of course, the adult Rae, who had been burned too many times before, rolled her eyes at the teenage girl part. I was way too wise to merely take his word. "Old habits can be hard to break," I murmured.

"I agree, but it helps if you have a reason for making the change, and you're my reason."

Turning in the seat to face him, I countered, "While that is immensely flattering, I would argue that it's easy to utter the words, but it's the actual action of changing that speaks louder." When Gabe opened his mouth to argue, I wagged a finger at him. "Don't even tell me your actions speak for you. It's not like you've had any temptation holed up here in Hayesville."

Gabe shook his head. "That's where you're wrong. I'll have you know, I've had other offers, and not just from Rejune."

"Ew."

He shrugged a shoulder. "Hey, I'm just being honest."

"And so am I."

"What exactly do you think is going to happen? I'm going to go back out on the road and start banging women left and right?"

Just the thought of Gabe looking at another woman, let alone having sex with one, turned my stomach. It wasn't just about the fact that I had yet to have sex with him, but it was more about my growing feelings for him. "Maybe."

With a grunt, Gabe replied, "Wow, I'm glad you think so highly of me."

"I do think highly of you."

"Could have fooled me."

"I know you're first and foremost a man, and men have urges. You're also an extremely good-looking man who is surrounded by beautiful women who want nothing more than to fuck you."

"Yeah, and that's it."

"Which part?"

"The part about the women who *just* want to fuck me." Gabe threw a glance at me. "They only want me because I'm Gabe Renard of Jacob's Ladder, or they want me for my money, but you"—he gave me an earnest smile—"you want me for *me*."

"Yes, I do," I replied softly.

"And that right there is worth turning away every stray piece of ass who throws herself at me." Taking one of his hands off the wheel, he reached out for mine. "I don't want to destroy what's between us before it even has a chance."

I dropped my gaze from Gabe's eyes to his outstretched hand. Nibbling on my lip, I weighed his words along with the sincerity with which he had spoken them. Deep down, I knew nothing he had just said really soothed my fears of his infidelity. The fear of being cheated on and abandoned was deeply rooted in my childhood, and nothing that had happened in my adulthood had managed to lessen it.

"Don't take your past out on me," Gabe murmured.

Sucking in a breath, I replied, "How did you know I was thinking about that?"

"Because I know you, and I know your past. I can understand why you don't want to trust me."

I shook my head at him. "I want to trust you. It's just hard."

"Then just promise me you'll try."

I slipped my hand into his. "Okay, I'll try."

Gabe turned his head to smile at me. "Good." After bringing my hand to his lips, he kissed my knuckles. As his breath fanned against my skin, I battled the annoying romantic in me that wanted to swoon at the gesture.

After dropping my hand, Gabe motioned to a sign above us. "There's our exit."

"I can't believe we're already here."

"Me either. The drive from Jake's farm usually feels like it takes forever, and it was even longer this time."

"It's totally cheesy, but I'm going to say it anyway: I guess it was the company this time."

Gabe grinned. "I totally agree with that one."

Once we exited off the interstate, Gabe made a turn onto a side street then we pulled into the parking deck of a high-rise office building. It was exactly the kind of place I expected to house a recording studio.

"Are you sure they won't mind that you brought me along?" I asked as he eased the Jeep into a parking space.

"I don't give a shit if they do."

"But this is important to you and your band."

Gabe turned to stare intently at me. "You're important to me."

Slowly, I shook my head back and forth. "Once again, is this real life?"

With a laugh, Gabe replied, "What do you mean?"

"I mean, am I really in the car with a handsome and famous musician who considers me his muse? Things like this just don't happen to girls from Hayesville. Surely I'm going to wake up to find this has just been a dream."

"You think I'm handsome?" Gabe asked, batting his eyelashes teasingly.

Holding my finger and thumb slightly apart, I answered, "Just a little." When he playfully swatted my hand down, I added, "Okay, okay, I think you're very, very handsome."

"Damn straight. And sexy?"

"Very sexy."

"And well-hung?"

I cocked my head at him. "Sadly, I can't answer that one."

"You could take my word for it."

"I think it's better if I get firsthand knowledge before commenting on that."

Gabe leaned across the console. "What does firsthand knowledge entail?"

"Hmm, I think both visual and physical contact would be necessary for me to do a thorough investigation."

"I see. I'd be happy to oblige."

Grinning, I said, "I'm sure you would."

Just as Gabe dipped his head to kiss me, his phone dinged. When he glanced at it, he took my hand. "Come on, we gotta hurry. Eli is asking where we are."

"Great. Not only am I going to be crashing your session with the label, I'm also the reason you're late," I protested as Gabe dragged me over to the elevators.

"Once again, I don't give a shit."

"You've really got to work on your professional attitude."

Gabe laughed as he punched the up button. "Trust me, the minute they hear the songs I've brought them, they'll forget all about me being a little late."

"And bringing some random chick."

"You're not a random chick to me. You're Reagan Hart, miracle muse."

I grinned at his summation. "Let's just see if the record execs think the same thing."

The elevator dinged on our floor, and we stepped out into the lobby.

A beautiful blonde practically leapt at us. "There you are. We thought you might be stuck in traffic since the Falcons are playing today."

"Sorry. It took a little longer to pack up and get here than I thought." Gabe glanced over at me. "I'd like to introduce you to some-one. Abby, this is Reagan Hart."

When Abby turned away from her brother to focus her curious gaze, I could see the questions rolling in her blue eyes. Since my name didn't seem completely foreign to her, I assumed Gabe had mentioned me, but from the extreme surprise on her face, I didn't think she'd expected to see me in person. After recovering from what I imagined was intense shock at my presence, Abby extended her hand. "It's so nice to meet you, Reagan."

"Actually, it's Rae, but thank you. It's very nice to meet you, too. Gabe has told me a lot about you."

"Oh he has?"

"Yes."

Abby grinned while eyeing her brother. "I hope it was all good."

I laughed. "Yes. It was all very complimentary."

"Phew, that's a load off my mind. I've heard very good things about you as well. Gabe told us how wonderful you've been for him creatively."

"Although I still don't quite understand his process, I'm really glad I could help."

Motioning with his hand, Gabe said, "We better go. From his text, Eli's inside keeping the execs company, and God knows what he's saying to them left to his own devices."

I followed Abby and Gabe through the lobby's heavy oak door, and a long hallway stretched out in front of us with different rooms on the left side. When I peered inside, I could see a small sound booth in each one. "This is where a lot of voiceover work is done," Gabe explained.

"This is amazing," I murmured. Even though I wanted to play it cool like I hung around recording studios every day, I was sure the mesmerized look on my face told the truth.

Gabe opened the door to a large office. When we walked inside, I saw three men and a woman sitting around a glass-top table. At our appearance, they rose from their chairs, and it took less than a second for me to spot Eli. As he strode over to us, it was like looking straight at Gabe.

"Glad to see you could finally bless us with your presence, bro," Eli said teasingly.

"Why don't you get off my dick?" Gabe shot back with a grin.

While the two of them hugged, I oh so eloquently remarked, "Wow, you two really are twins."

"Didn't Gabe tell you we're identical?" Eli asked.

"He mentioned it." I shook my head. "But it's not the same as seeing the two of you side by side."

"There are some small differences between us when you look really hard," Gabe said.

Eli winked at me. "Don't tell her that. If she looks too hard, she'll realize I'm the better-looking twin."

While I laughed, Gabe gave his brother a playful smack on the arm. "Keep dreaming, bro."

One of the men cleared his throat. "If you guys are ready, we'd love to hear what you have for us."

With a forceful nod of his head, Gabe replied, "We're ready, Pierce."

"Should I wait out in the lobby?" I whispered.

"If you went back to the lobby, you wouldn't be able to hear the songs." He stared intently into my eyes. "I want you to hear what you inspired."

His words sent my heartbeat accelerating, and I found myself unable to respond with anything other than, "Okay."

Taking my hand in his, Gabe led me over to a smaller room. Inside was what I assumed was the sound booth. The record execs had already taken a seat on the couches and chairs to the side. Instead of steering me over to them, Gabe took the extra chair and pulled it up beside the guy manning the soundboard. "Hey Johnny, how are you?"

"Doing pretty good. How about you?"

"Pretty good. This is Rae."

As I waved, Johnny said, "I'll take good care of her while I'm making you guys sound good."

Gabe laughed. "You do that."

After I sat down, Gabe kissed my cheek. "I'll see you in a bit."

I nodded. Since I didn't know exactly what to say to wish good luck to musicians, I said, "Break a leg."

With a grin, Gabe replied, "If I do that, I can't play the drums, and we're screwed."

"Whatever. You know what I mean."

"I do, and I appreciate it."

He then hurried out of the room and into the recording booth to join Eli and Abby. Since they weren't actually recording, he would be playing guitar instead of his usual drums. He handed the sheets of music to his bandmates, and they spent the next few minutes warming up and harmonizing a bit. Apparently, over the last week, he'd faxed them the songs he had been writing, and they'd even rehearsed once over FaceTime.

When their voices and instruments were once again silent, Gabe glanced through the soundproof glass to the execs. "I think this is the single we should lead with on the album."

He and Eli began strumming the opening of a slow song. During the time we'd spent together, Gabe had educated me enough about music that I knew to call it a ballad. Abby's beautiful voice filled the booth, and as her hand gripped the lyric sheet in front of her, her expression changed to reflect the emotions she was emitting through the song.

Trapped inside these walls,
I made a prison all my own

As I listened to the words, it amazed me how differently they sounded coming from Abby and not Gabe. Although his sister had a much better vocal range, I still preferred Gabe's singing. Maybe it was the rough, masculine quality of his voice that spoke to me both emotionally and physically.

Closing my eyes, I imagined myself back in that room with Gabe... the way the sunlight streamed in through the windows, basking him in an almost angelic light...the way his voice delivered the range of emotions the lyrics contained.

When the song ended, I popped my eyelids. My thought process immediately went from listening to the song to wondering what the execs thought. Glancing over my shoulder, I surveyed their expressions. When I saw that they appeared to be very satisfied, I exhaled the breath I'd been holding.

A tall, lanky man, who was the definition of California cool, stood up and came over to the soundboard. After holding down a button, he said, "I know we still have a lot to hear from you guys, but I'm really feeling that one as the first single, too. I should know by now to trust your judgement."

Gabe grinned. "Glad to hear it." Turning to his siblings, he said, "I'd really love to call the album *Ray of Light*."

"Works for me," Eli replied. He then gazed out of the sound booth at me and winked. I couldn't help smiling back at him.

"Abs?" Gabe asked.

Abby bobbed her head enthusiastically. "Not only do I love the song, I love the message the title would convey for the album."

A pleased expression came over Gabe's face before he glanced out at Pierce. "Then *Ray of Light* it is."

Pierce nodded. "I agree with Abby on liking the message." After the other execs murmured in agreement, Pierce said, "All right. What else do you have for us?"

"Two more ballads and then three upbeats."

"Okay. Take it away again."

As Gabe and his siblings played through the rest of the songs, I remained on the edge of my seat. I knew I was witnessing something special. I mean, how many people could say they'd seen the inception of a band's new album? I couldn't help feeling honored considering what an intimate moment it seemed to be for the band. Sure, they had an audience of execs, but there was something very pure about the process. It was three artists uniting to weave together the many pieces of a song.

After they played each song, I held my breath for Pierce's opinion. It felt like I was watching an episode of *American Idol* and waiting for the yes or no from each judge. Maybe it was because Pierce's British accent made me think of Simon Cowell.

Out of all the songs they played, there was only one Pierce and the others weren't too thrilled with. Even then, they only asked for the song to be reworked, not completely scrapped. From the light dancing in his eyes and his beaming expression, I could tell Gabe was on cloud nine. I couldn't imagine how proud he must be. It was like the old saying that after the darkness comes the dawn. He had trudged through the worst writer's block of his life to pen some truly amazing songs. I was so very proud for him and of him.

When Gabe and the others came out of the sound booth, I hopped off my stool and hurried over. Before he could ask my opinion, I blurted out, "That was amazing—*you* were amazing."

The most adorable blush fanned over his cheeks, one I'd never seen before. It was quite a difference from the usual smirk he wore whenever someone complimented him. "If anyone should be giving praise, it's me. Without you, none of that in there would have been possible."

Slowly, I shook my head back and forth. "It still floors me that I had any effect on your creative process whatsoever."

"Never doubt the effect you have on me." His voice had taken on a husky tone that caused goosebumps to pop out on my arms. Even though we were in small room filled with people, it felt like it was just the two of us. As the tension crackled, I inched closer to Gabe.

Just as my body was in reach of touching him, Eli popped up beside us.

"Hey guys, you wanna grab something to eat?" Eli asked.

Without taking his gaze from mine, Gabe replied, "Sorry, we have plans."

After glancing between us, Eli grinned. "Yeah, I can imagine what kind of *plans* you have and what you'll be eating."

While I didn't find the innuendo insulting, Gabe growled, "Watch your mouth."

Both Eli and I widened our eyes at his reaction. Holding up his hands, Eli said, "Easy now. I was just joking."

"Yeah, well, don't joke like that in front of Rae. She's not one of the guys." Gabe turned his gaze from Eli to me. With a smile, he said, "She's special."

Holy swooning hell. I fought the urge to melt into a puddle at

Gabe's feet. Sure, I knew he felt that way about me, but it was extremely sexy hearing him say it to his brother.

"I'm sorry for being offensive, Rae," Eli said sincerely. If I hadn't already liked him before, I especially liked him now. Even though Gabe hadn't demanded an apology, Eli was willing to give me one.

"Thank you, and it's okay. I'm surrounded by men on a daily basis, so I've certainly heard worse."

"Gabe told me you run a collision business back home."

"I do. I mean, I run the business side. I'm not actually welding on bumpers or anything like that."

Eli grinned. "It would be pretty cool if you did."

I laughed. "I'm sorry to disappoint you."

"Oh, don't get me wrong. I'm totally impressed that you run your own business, especially one that's so male-dominated."

I fought the urge to smile as I thought about how Gabe had been right when he'd called his brother a smooth talker. It was somewhat charming. "Thanks. I appreciate that."

"I'd love to hear more about it. Although you guys are busy today, maybe we can get together for drinks or dinner while you're in the city."

My gaze bounced from Eli's to Gabe's. When I cocked my brows at him, he nodded. "Sure. That sounds great."

Nodding, Eli said, "You guys just text me when you have a free moment."

"I'd love to come too," Abby piped up. I hadn't realized she had joined us. "I'm sure Jake would love to meet you."

"I'd love to meet him. I've loved Runaway Train for years," I replied.

While Abby beamed at my response, Eli cocked his head at me. "What about Jacob's Ladder?"

When I winced, both Abby and Eli laughed. Gabe saved me by saying, "Rae doesn't do country."

"Well, I didn't do country before I met Gabe," I added. I smiled at Abby and Eli. "After today, I'm a huge fan, and that has nothing to do with Gabe and everything to do with how beautiful the music is."

"Okay, I guess you're forgiven," Abby said.

Eli held up a hand. "Hold on—I would argue that since Gabe's the one writing the music, it's still all about him."

With a shake of my head, I replied, "It would only be his words on paper without you two. You guys came together to make music today, and it was amazing."

Eli's eyes bulged as he turned to Gabe. "Dude, she gets it."

Gabe grinned. "I know."

"What exactly is *it* that I get?" I asked.

"The process of making music."

I laughed before protesting, "But I don't play an instrument or sing."

"It doesn't matter. You either get it or you don't, and you totally do."

"Then I'm glad I do."

"So am I," Gabe replied.

Turning to his sister, Eli said, "Since Gabe and Rae have plans, why don't you let your big brother buy you lunch?"

"Actually, I was planning on using my child-free time to get a facial and a massage."

Eli bobbed his head in agreement. "I'm totally down for that—if we can grab a bite first."

I smiled at the two of them. "It sounds like you guys have an amazing day planned. I can't even remember the last time I had a facial or a massage."

Abby's eyes widened. "Oh my gosh, you should totally come with us. I mean, no offense to Eli, but it would be much more fun having a girls day."

"Thanks a lot," Eli muttered.

At the same time, Gabe stepped forward. "She can't go, Abby. She already has plans with me."

Something about his caveman attitude caused me to giggle, and then I knew I had to have some fun with him.

Moving away from Gabe, I linked my arm through Abby's. "Come on, Gabe. Would you really begrudge me a massage and a facial? I mean, don't I deserve a break?"

Gabe appeared so crestfallen that I struggled to hold back a laugh. Abby immediately picked up on what I was doing and held the hand linked through her arm so I was even closer to her.

"Rae's right, Gabe. From what you've told me of her running her own business and being a single mom, she deserves a little pampering, doesn't she? Forget just a massage—I think she should spend the whole day at the spa."

Gabe's expression was priceless, his gaze bouncing between me and Abby like he didn't know what to say or do. It was then that I lost it, and a very unladylike snort escaped my lips before I burst out laughing. My reaction caused Abby to lose it as well. Before I could say anything, Gabe untangled my hand from Abby's and practically dragged me away from her. I quickly waved over my shoulder to Abby and Eli, who were both laughing at their brother's antics. "Next time, Rae. I'll take you next time," Abby called.

"You. Are. In. So. Much. Trouble," Gabe growled. Naturally, it only made me laugh more.

When I could finally get words out, I said, "I'm sure you'll enjoy doling out the punishment, Mr. Renard."

That comment earned me a stinging smack on the ass, which had the opposite effect than Gabe had intended. It totally turned me on, and when Gabe looked at me, he saw exactly that. The smile on his face was not only a little victorious, it was also very sexy.

Jerking his chin at the door, Gabe said, "You know, they really liked you."

"Wait, how do you know? You guys didn't even get a chance to talk alone."

"I didn't have to talk to them about it. I could just tell."

A warm, fuzzy feeling filled me at his remark. "That makes my day. Even though I didn't get to spend much time with them, I really liked them, too. Abby just has this aura of sweetness about her, and Eli is amazing."

Gabe peered curiously at me. "You're not having second thoughts about me after meeting him?"

I rolled my eyes. "Have you lost your mind?"

"It's an honest question."

"No, it's not." I closed the gap between us to jab my finger in his chest. "There is no way I would *ever* be more attracted to Eli than I am to you. Sure, he looks just like you and he's funny, but the most important thing is, he's not you."

With a smirk, Gabe countered, "That is not necessarily a good thing."

"It is to me. There is no one else like you for me. I can't replicate what we have with Eli just because he looks like you, and even if I could, I wouldn't want to. *You* are the Renard brother for me. You're the reason I came to Atlanta. I only want to be with you."

"If you say so."

"Oh, I know so." I slid my arms around his waist. "I like you just the way you are, Gabe."

This time Gabe gave me a genuine smile. "Thank you."

If there was one thing I was beginning to see clearly, it was that Ryan had it all wrong. He had been so consumed by his own talent that he'd shut himself off from relationships with other people to chase dreams he'd never obtain. Gabe had immense talent. He had reached for the stars and surpassed his dreams. He was a man who had such a strong love for his family as well as possessing something else I was starting to truly admire: humility.

"You're welcome. You know what else I like?"

"What?"

"When you told your brother I was special."

Gabe bent over to kiss my forehead. "I meant it."

Gazing around the empty recording booth, I said, "Now that you're finished here, I guess we have the rest of the day to ourselves."

"Is there somewhere you'd like to go?" When I slowly nodded my head, he asked, "Where?"

"Your apartment."

A sexy smirk curved Gabe's lips. "I was hoping you would say that."

"Is it far from here?"

"Ten minutes across town, depending on traffic. Why?"

"Because I don't want to wait to be alone with you."

"Then let's get the hell out of here." He took my hand in his before gently tugging me forward, and I fell in step beside him as we made our way down the hallway of the studio.

Stopping in front of one of the dark and empty voiceover booths, Gabe turned to me with a lascivious leer. "We could slip inside and not have to wait."

I shot him a disgusted look. "You want our first time together to be some sleazy hookup in a voiceover booth?"

"Public sex is hot," he countered.

"That's true, but while I might sound like some doe-eyed virgin romanticizing the act, I want our first time to be special. Don't you?"

"I do, but my dick doesn't."

I laughed. "For once, think with the head above your shoulders, not the one below your waist."

Gabe exhaled a ragged sigh. "Got it." He then pulled me on down the hallway toward the elevators at a frantic pace.

"Would you slow down?" I called.

"I'm just trying to get you back to my place."

"Well, I'd like to get there with my arm still in my socket, and at the rate you're pulling on me, it's questionable whether it's going to stay in."

Gabe laughed. "Okay, okay. I'll take it easy."

"Thank you."

True to his word, Gabe managed a leisurely pace to the car. After he started the car, he even said, "If you're hungry, we can grab something to eat."

While my stomach did feel a little empty, I didn't think my nerves would allow me to eat anything. Normally, I didn't get too anxious when it came to having sex. Sure, there was a little apprehension the first time with someone, but I'd never quite experienced what I was feeling at the moment. "I'm good."

"Are you sure?"

"I am."

Gabe grinned. "I was so hoping you'd say that."

I laughed. "And I'm so not surprised that you were."

As we drove across town from the recording studio, Gabe and I rehashed everything that had happened in the studio. After thankfully not getting into much traffic, we also made a quick stop at a sandwich place, despite having said we would skip lunch. Since neither one of us had eaten breakfast, we were starving. After eating outside at one of the umbrella tables, we then made our way back to the car, and it was only a few more minutes before Gabe pulled into a gated high-rise building. He punched in his code on the keypad, drove through the gate, and then pulled into a numbered parking space not too far from the building's entrance.

"I see you're a VIP even in the parking lot," I mused.

Gabe laughed. "As much as I pay for that penthouse, I deserve some VIP status."

I widened my eyes at him. "Penthouse?"

He nodded. "I bought it off the drummer of Runaway Train. After he got married and had a family, he needed more space."

Sucking in a breath, I asked, "AJ Resendiz?"

"You know AJ?"

"Well, I don't *know him*, know him, but I do listen to Runaway Train."

"Just not my band."

"You're country, remember? Not my favorite."

"Yeah, yeah. I get it. You hate country music and have a lady boner for AJ."

With a laugh, I replied, "I do not have a lady boner for AJ. Do I find him good-looking? Yes, I do. There's just something about the whole Latin lover thing."

"The dude's married with two daughters."

I shrugged. "Just because I can't touch doesn't mean I can't look."

Gabe grunted as he shook his head. "If AJ finds out you think he's hot, he'll never let me hear the end of it."

"Thought," I corrected.

"Huh?" Gabe questioned.

"I *thought* he was hot, not think he is hot. I only have eyes for you now."

"You better."

I smiled at him. "I promise."

"Come on. Let's go."

After Gabe grabbed my bag out of the back of the car, we headed inside. When we stepped onto the marble-tiled foyer, I couldn't help craning my neck to take in all the opulence. "Wow. This is…wow," I murmured. Not my most eloquent moment.

"Does that mean you like it?" Gabe asked with a smile.

"How could I not?"

"Sometimes I think it's a little over the top. I think I'd like something a lot simpler." He dug his wallet out of his pocket then pulled out a keycard. "I mean, this whole process is a little excessive."

"True, but it's also probably a necessary evil for someone like you. It helps to ensure your security."

"I seriously doubt there's anyone out there obsessing over me."

After he swiped the card, we stepped into the elevator. To make it to the penthouse, he had to insert the keycard into a slot above the buttons. "Oh, I'm sure there's a horde of women out there obsessing about you, dreaming about the day they can get their hands on you."

Scratching his chin thoughtfully, Gabe replied, "I do have quite a lot of female admirers."

I cocked my brows at him. "How about focusing on the one female admirer in front of you?"

Gabe grinned. "It would be my pleasure. In fact, I plan to focus on every aspect of the sexy-as-hell female in front of me."

"Which aspect do you plan to focus on first?"

After closing me into the corner of the elevator, Gabe loomed over me. His nearness coupled with the lust glittering in his blue eyes made me shudder. "Your lips."

"Interesting choice. I imagined you starting farther south."

He slowly shook his head back and forth. "Ah, but any good lover knows you need to capture the north before you divide and conquer the south."

I laughed. "Is that right, General Renard?"

"Yes, it is."

The elevator dinged, and the doors opened to reveal Gabe's penthouse. Neither one of us moved.

Reaching out, I ran my thumb over his bottom lip. "So I should start here"—with my other hand, I reached out to cup his jean-clad cock—"instead of here?"

As I rubbed his growing erection, Gabe threw his head back and groaned. "Screw it. What do I know about military tactics? Just keeping touching my dick." When I pulled my hand away, he hissed.

"But I want your mouth on mine," I said quietly.

"And I want your mouth on my cock," Gabe growled.

Tsking at him, I replied, "Patience."

"Fuck that!" he exclaimed before pouncing on me. The next thing I knew my feet were flying off the floor as Gabe drew me up into his arms to carry me into the penthouse.

"I'm very capable of walking you know," I protested.

"It would take too much time," he replied as he power-walked me through the foyer.

Tilting my head, I gazed up at the glittering chandelier. "That's so beautiful."

Gabe's response to my compliment was to sprint through the living and burst into the bedroom.

"You know, you're acting like a released convict desperate for sex. Did you even stop to think I might have enjoyed a tour of your place?"

"I'll give you a tour after we have sex." After easing me back onto my feet, Gabe grinned down at me. "And as for the convict part, I can promise I'll last longer than a released convict."

"I certainly hope so."

"Trust me, Rae. You never have to doubt my stamina, especially not where you're concerned."

"Hmm, I think I'm going to need you to prove that to me before I can believe it."

"My pleasure." Once again, Gabe leapt at me like a wolf with its prey. We became a tangle of arms as our tongues battled each other, and there was a frantic desperation in Gabe's kisses. While wetness pooled in my underwear from the excitement of his need, I didn't want it to be so fast. I wanted to savor the feel of his hands on me. I wanted a small ember to grow into a crackling flame.

As Gabe's hands fumbled with the button on my jeans, I tore my lips away from his. "Slow down," I panted.

He gazed at me, eyes hooded with desire. "But I just want to be inside you. After having my fingers and tongue in you, I've been fantasizing for days about what your tight walls will feel like around my dick."

I shoved Gabe away. "No," I said firmly.

His hazy eyes stared questioningly at me. "No?"

"Sit." I then pointed to his bed across from us.

Gabe's brows shot up at my command. Instead of arguing with me, he obediently began backing away. I followed close behind him, keeping my eyes on his. When the backs of his knees hit the edge of the mattress, he flopped down on the bed.

Jabbing a finger into his bare chest, I said, "Now you listen to me: we're not going to rush into this like two horny teenagers pawing at each other in the back seat of a car."

"We're not?"

"No. We're going to fuck like adults who know about the merits foreplay and delayed gratification."

"Can't we at least have a horny teenager quickie and then move on to fucking like adults?" Gabe suggested.

I shook my head at him. "I'm not one of the groupies you stick your dick in for a quick release. I'm special, remember? I'm your muse, and I demand more." *Holy shit.* Had I actually just said that to him? Even though it was exactly what I was feeling, I couldn't believe I'd had the balls to say it. I sucked in a breath as I waited for Gabe's reaction.

"You're right. You don't just demand more—you deserve more."

My heartbeat accelerated at his words. "Thank you for acknowledging that."

Gabe slid his hands around my waist. "You drive a hard bargain, Rae Hart."

I reached out to cup the bulge in his jeans, causing Gabe to suck in a deep breath. "Mm, yes, very hard."

"You. Are. Killing. Me," he bit out.

With a wink, I replied, "Oh, but I've only just begun."

NOW THAT I had Gabe on the bed, I started initiating my slow-down plan. Even though he couldn't have cared less, I wanted to make our first time memorable. Although it was too soon to be mentioning anything about love, I wanted our first time to be about more than sex. I wanted it to be more like making love.

With my gaze locked on Gabe's, I brought my hands to my breasts, cupping them over my shirt. When I squeezed them, Gabe sucked in a breath. Turning my fingertips downward, I ran them down over my hardening nipples toward my waist. When my fingers reached the hem of my shirt, I gripped the fabric. Slowly, I inched the shirt up over my abdomen. The closer I got to the underside of my breasts, the farther Gabe leaned over on the mattress toward me.

Taking him by surprise, I did a quick whip of the shirt up over my head then tossed it at him. After it smacked him in the face, it dropped into his lap. He picked it up and brought it to his face. Closing his eyes, he inhaled deeply. "God, you smell good."

"Thank you." Now that my shirt was off, I brought my attention to my jeans. After unbuttoning and unzipping them, I turned my back to Gabe. "Hey, what—"

His words cut off when I bent over, sticking my ass in the air. I then worked the material down slowly over my hips to the floor. Glancing over my shoulder, I wiggled my thong-clad ass in Gabe's face.

I yelped with surprise when he brought his palm down across one of my cheeks, but I also enjoyed the sensation. "Did you like that?" he asked, his voice gravelly with lust.

"Yes. Do it again."

Gabe sent a stinging slap against my other ass cheek, causing me to moan. Just when he leaned forward to grab ahold of me, I sidestepped away and out of his grasp. Now it was his turn to moan, but this time it was from disappointment.

I turned around to face Gabe again. Bringing one of my hands up, I eased the left strap of my bra down my arm. When it almost revealed my breast, I stopped and went to the right one. Once again, I turned my back on Gabe. My hands came around to the clasp of the bra. After I undid it, I kept the material flat against my breasts. Slowly, I slid around to where I was facing Gabe again.

Leaning into him, I said, "You can take my bra if you want to."

"Hell yes," he replied.

When he started to reach for it, I shook my head. "You can't use your hands."

Confusion momentarily filled his face at my request. Then it appeared he had a light-bulb moment because he dipped his head, his warm breath fanning against my chest. When he opened his mouth, his lips brushed against the top of my breast before he took the material between his teeth. With a growl, he tugged it away from me, leaving my breasts exposed. He jerked the bra out of his mouth before tossing it to the floor.

Pure hunger burned in his eyes as I took a step back. I slid my thumbs into the lace at the tops of my hips. Teasingly slow, I started easing the fabric down. Gabe licked his lips as he stared expectantly below my waist. I knew he was wondering if I had taken care of business down there since we had last been together.

When I danced the thong down past the top of my pussy, his eyes flared. While I had done a little trimming, I had left enough to please him. His gaze bounced from my nether regions to my eyes. He grinned. "Thank you."

Although it felt slightly odd to have a man be grateful for pubic hair, I replied, "You're welcome." I then brought my panties back up my hips.

Gabe furrowed his brows. "What are you doing?"

"I think it's time we focused on you."

"Can't you focus on me with your pussy bare?"

I grinned. "All in good time."

Stepping into the gap between his thighs, I leaned over to undo the top buttons on his shirt. After I whisked it over his head, I stopped for a moment to admire his chest. "Hmm, so sexy," I remarked.

"It's all yours, Rae," he rasped.

I slid my fingers down his chest, adding pressure with my nails as I got closer to the waistband of his jeans. Gabe sucked in a breath, flexing his washboard abs. After undoing his belt buckle, I unbuttoned his jeans and then slid the zipper down.

Bending over, I closed my mouth over one of his nipples. "Fuck," Gabe muttered, as I suctioned the hardening point. When I started kissing down his chest toward his dick, Gabe's hands came to grip my shoulders. Gently, he pushed me back.

Tilting my head, I asked, "You don't want me to put you in my mouth?"

Groaning, Gabe replied, "After your striptease, I'll come in your mouth."

"Is that such a bad thing?"

"Normally, I would say no, but in this case, I want to come balls deep inside you."

Shivering at the imagery in my mind, I replied, "That works for me, too."

Before I could stop him, Gabe reached out to bring his hands between my legs. "Hmm, looks like you're ready for me."

I sucked in a breath as he stroked and rubbed my clit over my panties. The material brushing against me coupled with his finger was some delicious friction. Gripping his shoulders, my hips rocked hard against his. Pushing the material aside, Gabe thrust a finger deep inside me. "Oh yes," I murmured.

"Do you want to come on my fingers?"

"Mmhmm."

Gabe slide another finger inside my wet core. As he fucked me with his fingers, his thumb rubbed my clit. As I started to go over the edge, my nails dug into Gabe's flesh. "Yes, Gabe!" I cried. I threw my head back and rode out the waves of pleasure.

When my walls stopped convulsing, I brought my gaze to Gabe. He was licking me off of his fingers, and the sight caused another shudder of pleasure to ripple through me as I remembered well what his mouth and tongue felt like on my pussy.

"Ready?"

"More than ready," I murmured.

Gabe rose off the mattress, dug his wallet out of the pocket of his jeans, and pulled out a few condoms. After tossing them back onto the bed, he jerked his jeans and underwear down and off his hips. When his cock sprang forward, I couldn't help inhaling a sharp breath.

Gabe glanced up from stepping out of his pants to smirk at me. "Impressed?"

"Very."

"Wait until you feel it inside you."

Licking my lips in anticipation, I replied, "I can't wait." God, was that an understatement. I was *so* ready. It wasn't just about being ready to have sex again after an almost yearlong drought; it was about the fact that I was going to have sex with *Gabe*. He was all male and so very sexy. Just looking at him standing before me was turning me on.

While sliding the condom on with one hand, Gabe took my hand in his other and tugged me to him. After I fell against his chest, he turned us around then eased me down onto the mattress. Once I was lying on my back, Gabe climbed on top of me. I was secretly thankful he had gone for the missionary position. Sure, it was basic and lacked any kinkiness, but there was something to be said for having the weight of him on me while staring into his handsome face.

With his gaze locked firmly on mine, Gabe slowly eased into me. I gasped as the fullness of him spread through my lower half. Dipping his head, Gabe kissed me. His tongue swirled inside my mouth, and I felt completely and deliciously filled with him. More than that, I loved the look of adoration that swam in his eyes. I didn't think any man had ever looked at me like that when we were having sex. Maybe this was different because it was making love. Since we'd only known each other ten days, I knew it was too soon to be thinking about love, but it was certainly different than what I'd experienced before.

While Gabe's thrusts had been slow and steady in the beginning, he began to speed up his pace. Our breaths began to come in rushed pants. He rose up to sit on his knees before sliding his arms under my knees. "Oh fuck," he grunted as the change in position allowed him to go even deeper."

"My sentiments exactly," I panted.

He began driving into me at a maddening pace. I gripped the fitted sheet to hold me in place. Our moans and gasps of pleasure swirled in the air along with the heady smell of our sex. When I felt my walls begin to tighten, I bit down on my lip. Gabe pounded into me once again, and I came, screaming his name, my nails digging into the mattress. As I rode out the waves of pleasure, Gabe continued thrusting into me. After a few moments, he threw back his head and grunted with pleasure as he spilled himself inside me.

Slowly, he unhooked his arms from my knees before sliding out of me. While I stretched my aching muscles, Gabe slid the condom off and tossed it in a trashcan beside the bed. Then he snuggled beside me. Whoa. That was a surprising development. I was staying the weekend with him, so it wasn't like he wasn't going to offer to take me home or have me leave. But I never imagined Gabe was a man to cuddle.

We lay in silence for a few moments before he turned his head to look at me. "Rae?"

"Yes?"

"Was it good for you?"

Slowly, I craned my head to look at him in disbelief. I seriously couldn't believe what I just heard. As I stared into his handsome face, it shocked me to find his usual inflated ego gone. Instead, it was replaced with an earnest look—like he was really concerned that I had enjoyed the sex. "Um, yeah, I'd say it was more than good. It was pretty damn amazing."

A grin inched across his face before he was finally beaming ear to ear. "Really?"

"Of course. I can't believe you even have to ask. I mean, I came twice. That's truly outstanding."

"I know you did, but I just wanted to hear it from your lips." He reached over to cup my cheek. "It's important for me to please you."

Well damn. I was a few moments away from melting into a puddle at his feet. "It's important for me to please you, too. Maybe more so."

"Why would you say that?"

Suddenly, I felt very vulnerable lying there naked in his bed. I tugged the sheet around me. "Because you've been with so many women. I need—"

Gabe brushed his hand over my mouth. "You don't need to do anything or be anyone else, Rae. Just be you."

Although I should've been touched by what he said, I brushed his hand away. "If I decided I was through giving blow jobs, or I wouldn't let you take my ass, you'd be perfectly fine with that?"

Gabe's eyes widened before a laugh burst from his lips. "Does that mean you're down for ass play?"

I scowled at him. "Would you be serious?"

"I'm always serious when it comes to anal sex."

"Gabe," I hissed.

"Okay, okay. I'll be serious."

"Good."

"Of course, I would be disappointed if you *stopped* giving blow jobs, especially since I haven't had the pleasure of having your mouth around my cock yet. Not to mention burying myself in between your creamy ass cheeks…"

"You're losing focus."

"My dick isn't, because it's getting hard again."

"Seriously?"

After taking my hand in his, he brought it to his half-mast erection. "Nice refractory time, eh?"

I couldn't help laughing at the absurdity of his statement in the middle of what I wanted to be a serious conversation. "Yes, you have a nice refractory time for an older guy."

Gabe sucked in a harsh breath. "Did you just call me…*old*?"

"You are thirty."

"Which sure as hell isn't old the last time I checked."

"It's middle-aged for a dick when you consider the number of men in their forties and fifties on Viagra."

"I'm not sure I like the direction this conversation has taken." He glanced down at his slackening erection. "Not to mention what it's done to my dick."

"Maybe you should have focused on what I was saying."

"Fine." He pulled himself into a sitting position. Turning back around, he stared down at me. "Rae, while I would be initially heart-broken over the loss of your oral and anal skills, it would not be a deal breaker for me."

"Yeah right," I huffed.

"You know, you have more worth than what is between your legs."

"You sound like Aunt Sadie."

"Well, she's a wise woman."

"I'll be sure to tell her that."

"Make sure you do. In the meantime, get it through that thick skull of yours that the other women are in the past, and you, *just you*, are here now in the present." He gave me a genuine smile. "And hopefully the future."

His words put my unease to rest, at least for the moment. Changing topics, I rose to sit on my knees beside him. After I brought my lips to his, I reached between us to cup his slackened cock. It jumped in my hand as Gabe jerked his mouth from mine.

"What are you doing?"

"I thought it might be time to acquaint you with my oral skills."

"Is that right?"

"Mm-hmm."

As I began to slide my hand up and down his cock, it began to grown once again. "Yes, very nice refraction."

"I'm glad it pleases you," Gabe mused.

"Lie down."

He licked his lips. "Fuck, I love it when you tell me what to do."

I grinned at him as he proceeded to lie back down on the mattress. Now it was my turn to lick my lips before I bent my head. With hooded eyes, Gabe stared in anticipation at me. Instead of taking his dick in my mouth, I instead flicked my tongue against the head. Slowly, I swirled it around and around the tip.

Gabe groaned and bucked his hips up. Once again, I was going to tease him until it drove him wild. I turned my attention away from the tip and began licking him from root to the head. I flattened my tongue against his cock before sweeping it upward. Gabe threw his arms over his eyes, and as his teeth dug into his bottom lip, I felt a rush of wetness between my legs. There was something about watching him enjoy being pleasured that did me in. *I wanted more of that. For him. For me.*

After licking him sufficiently, I finally sucked the tip of him into my mouth. "Oh fuck," Gabe muttered as I suctioned the head of his dick. I went back and forth from sucking him hard to then easing up the pressure. When he groaned once again, I took him in even deeper. I then began bobbing up and down while also using my hand.

When I increased my pace, Gabe grunted. "Fuck, Rae, I'm going to come."

At the feel of his balls tightening in my hand, I let him fall free of my mouth. After grabbing a condom out of his nightstand, I tossed it at him. "I want you to come in me."

Gabe flashed a sexy smile at me before unwrapping the condom. "Your wish is my command."

After he slid the condom on, I threw my right leg over to straddle him. Taking his dick in my hand, I brought it to my already slick entrance. Slowly, I started easing down on him. Once he was buried deep inside me, I placed my hands on his chest before starting to slide on and off of him, rising up then sinking back down. Gabe began raising his hips to echo my movements.

Leaning forward, Gabe's mouth closed over one of my nipple. He sucked it into a hardened peak. While his mouth kept a delicious assault on my breast, he brought his hands to my waist. He began to lift me even faster and harder off of his dick. When his teeth nipped and grazed my nipple, I felt myself going over the edge. Gripping his shoulders, I rode out the intense orgasm. Gabe thrust into me a few more times before he came with a string of expletives.

We collapsed back onto the mattress in a tangle of arms and legs. It took us a few moments to get our bearings as well as catch our breaths.

"Once again, that mind-blowing," I murmured.

"Hell yeah it was."

With a grin, I asked, "Should I be anticipating another refractory period from your dick, or can I maybe grab a shower?"

Gabe laughed. "I think he's good for the night, so you can shower. But on one condition."

"What's that?"

"You let me in there with you."

"It's a deal." As Gabe and I climbed out of bed, I added, "After our shower, can we order in and watch movies?"

"Sure thing." He winked at me. "As long as you don't talk during the movie."

FOR THE FIRST time in almost two weeks, I woke up in my own bed. Although it was nice to be back home, it was even nicer to have Rae's lush body pressed against mine. As my mind went back to the night before and our amazing sex, I couldn't stop the smile of satisfaction from curving my lips.

Closing my eyes, I inhaled the sweet coconut smell of Rae's hair. She had been more than worth the wait. Sure, it had barely been two weeks, but that was an extremely long time for me to wait to have sex. Usually, I was naked with a woman less than two hours after we first met, but Rae was different. She had always been different, and she always would be.

I had to give Rae credit for knowing how to play the delayed gratification card. Making me wait until we got back to my apartment was one thing, but holy shit when she started that striptease, I seriously thought I was going to come in my pants.

Pulling her hair back, I began planting kisses down her neck. When I got to her shoulder, I began to lick and nip my way across her soft, creamy skin. At her long sigh, I paused. "Good morning, beautiful," I murmured into her ear.

She smiled at me over her shoulder. "Good morning."

"Did you sleep okay?"

"Yes. I don't think I moved once during the night."

Her laugh vibrated through her body. "You certainly did." Pressing her ass back against my morning wood, she said, "I see he's not worn out."

I sucked in a breath at how fucking good her ass felt as it cushioned my cock. "He's insatiable."

"Much like the man he's attached to."

"That's true." My hand snaked around her waist and up around her ribcage to cup her breast. Brushing my thumb back and forth over her nipple, I then pinched it, causing Rae to gasp. "God, I love how responsive you are."

"And I love the feel of your hands on me."

When I slid my palm down over her abdomen and between her legs, I found Rae deliciously wet. "Ah, I see this isn't worn out."

"A little sore, but no," she murmured breathlessly.

The mere mention of her being sore appealed to the caveman in me. I wanted Rae's body to remember the feel of my dick inside it, to crave the feeling of being stretched and filled.

I pulled my hand away. "Don't move."

Once I fished a condom off the nightstand, I tore into the wrapper and rolled one down the length of my throbbing cock. The mattress dipped under my weight as I slid back under the sheets to Rae.

After lifting her thigh with one of my hands, I guided my erection in. When I thrust balls deep into her tight, slick walls, we both moaned with pleasure. My free hand came to cup her breast again and I tweaked her hardening nipple, pinching the swollen flesh.

As I continued to twist and roll Rae's nipples between my fingers, my mouth came to her earlobe. I kissed my way down the shell before licking my way back up again. Rae gasped and bucked her ass back against me, causing me to go even deeper inside her.

Taking one of her hands, I guided it between her legs. "Touch yourself," I commanded as I once again focused on licking the sensitive flesh of her earlobe."

Rae obliged by slowly stroking her clit. When she whimpered, I asked, "Does that feel good?"

"Yes," she panted.

"Faster," I ordered. As she began to rub herself more furiously, I sped up the tempo of my thrusts. When I slid in and out of her, her fingers grazed my dick, slickened with her arousal. Since I was getting close, I closed my hand over hers and began to work her clit even harder.

"Oh...ahhh, yes!" she moaned as she worked closer and closer to coming. As her walls began to convulse around me, she screamed, "Gabe!"

Hearing her call my name with such pleasure as she came caused a shudder to ripple through me. As a desire to mark Rae as mine entered my mind, I began to my slow down my pace. "I want to come on you," I grunted into her ear.

Glancing over her shoulder at me, Rae said, "Then do it."

With a groan, I pulled out of her. After tearing off the condom and tossing it to the side, I brought my hand to cup my cock. As I prepared to jerk off on Rae's back, she shocked the hell out of me by rolling over to face me. It was her hand, not mine, that finished me. As I came, I spurted across her beautiful round globes.

"Fuck, Rae," I muttered before collapsing on the bed beside her. We both lay there, staring at the ceiling and trying to catch our breath. Turning over on my side, I grinned at Rae. "Damn, I hope it's always going to be that good between us."

"Mm, I hope so, too." Glancing down at her chest, Rae said, "I think I could use a shower now. How about you?"

"The caveman part of me wants you to stay marked by me all day."

Rae wrinkled her nose and laughed. "You're so possessive."

"I am of what's mine." I brought the sheet up to slowly wipe me off her breasts. When she was sufficiently cleaned off, I met her gaze. "You're mine, Rae."

She blinked at me. "Am I?"

"Yes. You are. You were emotionally mine in the way you became my muse, and now you're mine physically in the way I've claimed your body."

The corners of her lips quirked. "Do I get a say in this, caveman? Or are you just going to drag me by the hair back to your cave?"

I reached up to intertwine my fingers in her hair. When I tugged, she gasped as her eyes widened with desire. "I guess so," she replied.

With a grin, I released my grip. "Oh. I know it."

'We'll just have to see about that."

I wrapped my arms around her. "If it involves pulling your hair or spanking your ass, I'm all for it."

"Right now I'm more interested in showering and getting something to eat."

"You go grab a shower, and I'll go raid the fridge."

Rae grinned. "Okay."

After Rae showered, she rejoined me for a lazy breakfast in bed. Since I'd forgotten to tell my housekeeper not to restock the fridge while I was gone to Hayesville, I found fresh strawberries and blueberries along with some croissants and muffins. After we embarked on a mid-morning sexathon, we remained in bed, cuddling and watching movies for the remainder of the day.

It was just after four when Rae glanced up at me. "I have a question for you."

"Shoot."

"Are you going to keep me held hostage as your sex slave all weekend?" Rae asked.

I chuckled. "Would that really be so bad?"

She smiled. "Not really but I would like to do something romantic tonight."

"You mean watching Netflix and ordering in isn't romantic?" I teased.

Rae playfully smacked my bicep. "No. It isn't."

"You seemed to like it last night."

"Because I wanted to stay naked and not leave the house, but that's not what I want to do today."

"It sounds like a winning plan to me."

"Seriously, Gabe."

"Okay. What did you have in mind?"

She shrugged. "I don't know. We have a city full of culturally stimulating places right outside our door."

"And with it being a Saturday night, all those culturally stimulating places, as you call them, are going to have an hour to an hour and a half wait," I mused.

As her expression darkened, Rae untangled herself from my arms and sat up in the bed. With her bare back to me, I felt somewhat shunned. "What's wrong?"

"Admit it—you don't want to take me out."

"What? I never said that."

"You didn't have to."

"All of this attitude just because I made the remark that we're going to have to wait forever to get a table?"

Rae threw a glance at me over her shoulder. "I'm wondering if you said that because you don't want to take me out."

"Why in the hell wouldn't I want to take you out?"

"Because you're ashamed of the paparazzi seeing you with someone like me."

"You don't seriously think that...do you?" When Rae didn't respond, I snapped up to sit beside her. Taking her face in my hand, I forced her to look at me. "That is absolutely not the truth. I would be honored to be seen with you."

"Really?"

"Of course. There's no reason in the world I would ever be ashamed of you."

Rolling her eyes, Rae said, "I'm just a hick from the sticks. I'm not the model type people expect to see you with."

"That's bullshit. You're fucking gorgeous, not to mention sassy and sexy and smart."

A small grin played at Rae's lips. "Nice alliteration there with the descriptions."

"I try." I leaned in to kiss her. Pressing my lips against hers, I hoped to quell the fears swirling in her mind. When I pulled away, I stared intently at her. "I'm not only honored to have such a beautiful woman in my bed, but I'd be happy for every photographer in town to snap a picture of us."

"Really?"

"Hell yeah."

Putting her head in her hands, she groaned. "You must think I'm a real nutjob for feeling this way."

"No, I don't."

She peeked at me through her fingers. "You're just saying that because you think my pussy has magical powers."

I laughed as I pulled her to me. "Yes, it's true that your pussy is magical, but I get that it's hard to date someone famous."

Rae peeked at me through her hands. "You do?"

"Micah's wife, Valerie, had a really hard time at first when she started dating him. And the band wasn't even remotely as famous then. I can't imagine how she would take it now. So, yeah, I do get it."

"Thank you. I'll try not to be such a crazy person next time."

"Just keep being yourself."

"Psycho and all?"

"Yep."

Rae rolled her eyes but smiled in spite of herself. "The fact that you can be okay with me being crazy makes me think you're still in the pussy haze."

I snorted. "How long do you think it will take for me to get detoxed, exactly?"

"I'm not sure." A sly look entered her eyes. "But I think it would be most beneficial to reduce temptation by getting you outside of this apartment."

"I already said we'd go out." Cocking my head at her, I added, "And how do you plan on reducing my temptation? Are you going to leave your pussy behind?"

Rae giggled. "It will be covered, thus out of sight and out of mind."

"While it might be out of sight, your pussy will never be out of my mind." She snorted at that.

"Why does that not surprise me?"

"Okay. Let's go get a shower, and then we'll hit the town."

Rae's face lit up. "Really?"

"Yep. Dinner, dancing—the works."

"You would seriously take me dancing?" Confusion filled me at the sudden change in Rae. How could she even doubt I wouldn't want to be seen with her? Back home, she was a fearless badass, yet here....Oh right. *She's out of her element.* It was time for me to work double time to reassure her.

"Rae, while dancing is not my favorite thing, I do know how to dance, and would love to be out on the town dancing with you tonight."

She smiled, and it was the sweet smile, which told me I'd said the right words. She seemed less . . . vulnerable. Rae then quirked a brow at me. "Is there a single part of me that screams dancer?"

And Miss Sassypants was back. "Not exactly. I just find it hard to believe that someone who manages to do such amazing things with her hips in bed doesn't know how to dance."

With a laugh, Rae replied, "Thanks for the hips compliment."

"You're welcome."

"For the record, I can dance like in a club. It's waltzing and all that kind of stuff that I don't know how to do."

"Then I'll have to teach you."

"Tonight?"

"If you want to." Since Rae's expression was skeptical, I replied, "Or we could just take in some of the sights the city has to offer."

Rae nodded. "The last few times I've been here, it was either for a Falcons game, or to take Linc to the zoo and aquarium." She grinned. "I'd like to see more adult sights."

"I can certainly arrange that." After I kissed her, I said, "Go get that fine ass of yours in the shower. We have a date to get ready for."

19

AFTER I SLID a gold tube of lipstick across my lips, I surveyed my appearance in the bathroom mirror. Although I was never one to be an ego tripper, I had to admit I looked pretty damn good. Sexy and sultry even. Before I'd left the house, Ellie had insisted on sending me with one of her swanky dresses. Since the only dresses I owned were the ones I wore to church or parents' night at school, I happily accepted it.

The deep purple material fit like a second skin against my body while the spaghetti straps left little to the imagination when it came to my cleavage. Kennedy had taken care of that department when she had sent me with a bustier to maximize my assets. While I was wearing my sisters' dress and underwear, I was happy to say that the strappy black heels were actually mine, as well as the calf-length black dress coat I would be adding when we started to leave.

Since Gabe was a fan of my hair being down, I'd merely pulled it back on the sides after adding in some waves. I fluffed it one last time before adding in a little setting spray. I wanted to keep the waves, but I also wanted Gabe to be able to run his fingers through it easily.

I smiled as I thought of him. He had insisted I get ready in his bathroom while he collected his things and went to the guest bedroom. Although I could have preened a few more minutes in front of the mirror, a gentle knock came at the door. "Rae? We need to leave in five minutes to make it to our reservation."

I exhaled a breath before replying, "Coming." I allowed myself one last glance in the mirror before I threw open the bathroom door.

When I stepped out, Gabe had his back to me while digging in his dresser drawer. My heart did a flip-flop at the sight of him in dress pants and a dress shirt. I'd never seen him so dressed up, and I had to admit the partial suit porn was very swoony.

As Gabe pulled out a watch and started to put it on, I softly said, "I'm ready."

Gabe whirled around. After taking in my appearance, his eyes bulged, and his jaw dropped open. "Holy shit, Rae. You look out-of-this-world stunning."

Inwardly, I did a victory dance at his reaction. Outwardly, after doing a little twirl to give him a view of my backside, I asked, "Does that mean you like the dress?"

"Like it? I fucking love it." Gabe shook his head. "I don't think I've ever seen you in anything but pants or jeans."

"Although I much prefer pants, I will occasionally put on a dress for special occasions."

Bending over, Gabe ran his hand up my thigh. "Mm, I do like the extra skin showing." He paused at my thigh-highs. "What do we have here?"

"Before you get your hopes up that they're some sexy garters, they're only Walmart thigh-highs."

Gabe grinned. "I don't give a shit where they came from. I love the way the lace feels." He flicked the hem of my dress so he could get a look at them. "And I really love the way they look."

"I'm glad you like it."

"I'm sorry to say it, babe, but you're really going to have to wear dresses more often."

"Is that right?"

"Yes, but I have ulterior motives for liking them."

"Oh, you do?"

His hand came between my legs, causing me to gasp and a wicked grin to curve on his lips. "I love the easy access."

I smacked his hand away. "You're detoxing, remember?"

Chuckling, Gabe shook his head. "I have a feeling I can't be rehabilitated. I'm an addict."

"You're going to have to try harder. Now come on, let's go get something to eat. I'm starving."

As we started onto the elevator, I asked, "Do you really think we'll have to wait over an hour to eat?"

"Normally we would, but while you were in the shower, I pulled a few strings to get us a reservation."

"You mean you used your VIP status to worm your way in?"

"Pretty much."

With a smile, I replied, "Normally, I would find that type of elitist stuff disgusting, but considering how hungry I am, I'll make an exception this time."

Grinning, Gabe said, "I'm glad to hear it."

As we started into the elevator, I asked, "Where are you taking me?"

"Nikolai's Roof."

"That sounds interesting. Is it Russian?"

"Both Russian and French."

"Really? Hmm, I've never had Russian food before." As we started our descent down to the ground floor, I gave Gabe a sheepish grin. "If I'm honest, the only French food I've had is what Kennedy has cooked for us."

"You don't need to feel embarrassed that you don't have a distinguished food palate. Even when I was in Moscow for a few days, I didn't eat Russian food."

"You didn't?"

Gabe shook his head. "Nope. While Eli was trying all the local cuisine, I was living off McDonald's and chicken."

I laughed. "Then why did you pick a restaurant that serves Russian food?"

"You forget that it also serves French food."

"Yes, that's true."

"The main reason I chose it is because of the gorgeous views of the skyline, and they have a hell of a wine list."

The elevator doors dinged open, and Gabe and I stepped out into the lobby of his building. "An impressive wine list? Does that mean you have plans to ply me with alcohol to get me back home early and into your bed?"

Gabe waggled his brows at me. "Maybe."

"I'll make sure to sip slowly then."

He laughed. "Wait until you taste some—you'll be draining it in no time."

"We'll see about that."

When we walked outside into the setting sun, I expected to go over to Gabe's car. Instead, he motioned to a black Mercedes under the building's awning.

"You ordered a car for us?"

Gabe nodded. "I want to be able to drink without having to worry about getting behind the wheel." He then winked at me. "Not to mention it makes tonight a little more romantic, right?"

Okay, he had me there. I'd never been driven around in a chauffeured car before—and no, the limo Ryan and his friends had rented for junior prom didn't count. I'd lost my virginity that night in a cheap motel outside of Chattanooga. At the time, I thought it was terribly romantic. Later, I realized how cheesy it had actually been.

"Hey, what's wrong?" Gabe asked as the chauffer held open the door.

"Nothing. Why?"

"You got this sad look on your face."

With a wry smile, I replied, "I'm sorry. An unpleasant memory from the past hit me."

Cupping my cheek, Gabe said, "No more bad memories. Tonight is all about us and the present."

I nodded. "Yes, it is." I then ducked down inside the Mercedes. After sliding across the leather seats, Gabe dropped down beside me. I snuggled up beside him as we then made our way through the crowded streets of Atlanta.

When we pulled up outside the Hilton, I shot Gabe a look. "You just happened to pick a romantic restaurant within a hotel?"

Gabe chuckled. "Are you insinuating I planned dinner around having easy sex access?"

"That's exactly what I'm insinuating."

He held up his hand. "I swear, it had nothing to with sex and everything to do with the French food and the views."

"Just remember, there's no sex until we get back to your penthouse. Tonight is about romance."

After saluting me, Gabe said, "Yes, ma'am."

As I stared at the jaw-dropping handsomeness before me outfitted in the most scrumptious suit porn, I *hoped* I would exercise the same self-control I'd asked of him. *Don't drool, Rae. Don't.*

WHILE I WOULD HAVE PREFERRED KEEPING Rae all to myself in my penthouse, I had to admit that I was enjoying the hell out of our date. There was something to be said for getting dressed up and going to a nice dinner. After a three-course meal with dessert and copious amounts of wine, we then headed down the elevator.

Closing her eyes in bliss, Rae leaned against the back of the elevator car. "Oh my God, I'm so stuffed."

"I second that."

Her eyes opened to smile at me. "This has been such a wonderfully romantic night."

"I would argue that the night is still young."

With a giggle, Rae replied, "It's almost nine o'clock. That's like midnight back home."

"I had something else in mind for us to do."

As we stepped off the elevator and into the hotel lobby, Rae eyed me suspiciously. "It doesn't involve getting a room here, does it?"

I laughed. "Would you give me a little credit on the sex-fiend front?"

Her face softened. "Okay. My apologies."

When we walked outside into the chilly night air, I motioned to the horse-drawn carriage among the taxis and Uber drivers. "Would a carriage ride be considered romantic or cheesy?"

"It would be romantically cheesy." Rae winked. "And I would *love* it."

"Then your carriage awaits, Cinderella." Holding out my hand, I helped her into the carriage. After Rae was seated, I climbed in beside her.

"Is this something else you arranged while I was getting ready?" Rae asked as the carriage lurched forward.

"Yes. I sure did."

With a teasing smile, Rae asked, "What would have happened if I'd turned my nose up at the idea?"

"I would have pretended not to have anything to do with it while secretly paying the driver through my Apple wallet."

"I see," Rae replied with a laugh.

I winked at her. "But I had it on good authority that you would probably like it."

Rae's brows creased. "Good authority?"

"I texted Kennedy and Ellie to get their opinion."

"Then I'll have to make sure I thank them as well." After leaning her head against my shoulder, a happy sigh escaped Rae's lips. "Thank you for a truly beautiful date night."

"I did do pretty well on short notice, didn't I?"

She grinned up at me. "Yes, Mr. Egomaniac, you did."

"In all seriousness, I'm glad you've enjoyed yourself. I can't remember the last time I had such an easy and relaxed night in the city. I've loved every minute, Rae." *It had been so long since I'd wanted to put so much effort into one night.* When did I become so shallow and . . . easy? Once again, she had brought something out in me that had been somewhat suppressed. *Defeated.*

Rae's happy expression faded slightly. "While tonight is so very magical, I'm already dreading tomorrow when my carriage turns back into a pumpkin."

"What are you talking about?"

"When you have to take me back home tomorrow."

I shook my head. "Just because you're going back home, doesn't mean we'll never see each other again. I plan to stay in Hayesville with you."

Her eyes widened. "You do?"

"At least for the next week or so until I'm needed in the studio." After her stunned silence, I added, "Well, that's only if you want me to stay."

She grinned. "Of course, I want you to stay. You just took me off guard."

"Not only are you surprised, I'm sure Rejune will be thrilled to have me back at the Grandview."

Rae groaned. "I swear, if we had any spare room at the house, I'd have you stay with me."

"For some reason, I don't think that would go over very well with Aunt Sadie or your dad."

"Probably not, but I'd be willing to risk their wrath to have you out of Rejune's clutches."

I chuckled. "Babe, you have nothing to worry about in that department."

"I know, but I'd also prefer to have you as close to me as possible."

"I like that idea as well." Nuzzling her neck, I added, "Especially when it came to bedtime."

A snort escaped her lips. "Of course you would mention bedtime."

"I can't help it. You drive me absolutely fucking wild with desire."

As Rae gazed up at me, I saw the question in her eyes. I shook my head at her. "You really don't know how incredibly sexy you are, do you?"

"Maybe." She smiled. "But I wouldn't mind you telling me more."

"If I tell you more, I'm going to want to ravish you."

As lust glittered in her dark eyes, it seemed Rae had abandoned her *all-romance-and-no-sex* resolve. "I can live with that." Oh yeah, she'd definitely abandoned it.

When I pulled the blanket over our laps, Rae gave me a questioning look. "What are you doing?"

"Keeping us warm."

"But it's not that cold outside."

"I'm aware of the temperature." I slid my hand up her thigh and then between her legs.

"What are you doing?" she hissed as her wild gaze spun from me to the driver and then back.

"Shh, just go with it."

"But the driver—" I cut her protests off by rubbing her pussy.

Pinching her eyes shut, Rae bit down on her lip. As I worked her clit over her panties, she began to slowly raise her hips.

Dipping my head, I whispered into her ear. "Would you like more?"

"Yes," she panted.

"What do you want?"

"Your fingers inside me."

I obliged her request by slipping two fingers into her panties and then plunging them deep inside her. "Oh God!" she shrieked.

Her reaction caused the driver to glance at us over his shoulder. "You better be quiet or the driver is going to keep watching me finger-fuck you under this blanket."

She bobbed her head while once again biting down on her lip. As I increased the pace of my fingers, Rae began working her hips faster against my hand. When I felt her walls begin to tighten, I said, "Go on, babe, let yourself go. Come out here under the skyline."

Rae didn't have to be told twice. As her walls tensed around my fingers, one of her hands gripped my shoulder while the other gripped the seat. Even as her eyes rolled back in her head with pleasure, she somehow managed not to cry out.

Once her walls had stopped convulsing, I drew my hand out of her panties before bringing my fingers to my lips. Rae gazed at me through hooded eyes as I licked her off my fingers. When I finished, she adjusted her skirt before she sat up straighter in the seat. She threw a glance at the driver before turning to face me. "I think it's time to repay the favor."

"You do?"

She cupped my erection under the blanket. "It's either that or have you walking funny when the ride ends."

I grinned. "I suppose we don't have a choice."

After she unzipped my fly, her hand dove inside my pants. I sucked in a breath when she took my cock in her hands.

"I wish I could have my mouth around your dick right now instead of my hand."

"You do?"

"Mmhmm. I love the way it feels to have my mouth filled with you."

"What else would you do if my dick was in your mouth?"

"I'd lick the head before I sucked it deep inside. Then I'd slide you in and out, twirling my tongue around your underside. I'd pump you with my hand just like I'm doing now."

Oh fuck. Rae and the dirty talk were driving me wild. Throw in the fact that I was getting a public hand job, and I was flying high.

"When I tasted your pre-cum, I'd slide you deeper into my mouth while my hand worked you even harder. With my free hand, I'd cup your balls, kneading them between my fingers. Then when you got close, I'd keep you buried in my mouth."

"You'd let me come in your mouth?" I said, panting and raising my hips against her hand.

"Oh yes. After you came in my mouth, I'd swallow all of you down. Then I'd make sure to lick every drop off your cock."

Her words and the mental imagery had me throwing back my head as I blew my load on her hand and the blanket. Giving Rae a satisfied smile, I said, "That was fucking mind-blowing."

"I'd have to agree."

After I cleaned myself off Rae's hand, I balled the blanket back up into the floor. I looked up to find the driver had pulled the carriage over to the sidewalk at the Hilton. "Okay. That's the tour."

"Thanks, man," I said as I hopped down. After I helped Rae from the carriage, I pulled my wallet out of my suit pocket and took out two crisp one-hundred-dollar bills.

When I handed them to the driver, his eyes widened. "Thank you, sir."

"You might not be saying that when you have to throw that blanket away."

"Excuse me?"

"Let's just say that tip also covers a new blanket."

As the realization of what I meant washed over him, he quickly nodded his head. "Got it." At the same time, Rae squeaked and hurried away. I knew I had embarrassed her by mentioning our escapade in front of the driver.

When I finally caught up with her, she was waiting in front of the Mercedes—her face still flushed from mortification. Although she protested slightly, I pulled her into my arms and kissed her. It had been too long since I'd had her lips on my lips, her taste in my mouth. God, I would never get enough of her. "I'm sorry for embarrassing you," I murmured against her lips.

"You better be."

"Is there some way I can make it up to you?"

Tilting her head, she looked thoughtfully up at me. "A chick flick on Netflix followed by some orally induced orgasms."

I laughed. "Hmm, I think that can be arranged."

"Good. I'm also going to want French toast from Rafferty's on the way home."

"You don't want much, do you?" I countered as we slipped into the car.

With a smile, she snuggled against me. "Would it be too much to ask for you, too?" Hell, no. I was hers. Undeniably, irrevocably hers.

"You have me—mind, body, and soul."

"And heart?"

"Always." Without a doubt in my mind.

ONE MONTH later

It was just a usual Friday morning that found me out working in the warehouse, rather than behind my desk. Armed with my clipboard of paperwork, I was inspecting the progress on some of our latest jobs. Since I'd starting dating Gabe, Fridays were spent counting down the hours until I could see him. Either he would drive up to Hayesville or I'd drive into Atlanta, and sometimes we would meet halfway to stay in the guesthouse at Abby and Jake's farm.

True to his word, he spent two weeks with me before he had to return to Atlanta to begin work in the studio. We'd have breakfast together at my house. Then I'd go to work, and he'd go do what I joked were his *musicly* things. When lunch rolled round, he would bring food to the shop. Most days, he would bring lunch for my dad as well, and the three of us would eat together. He'd quickly picked up the names of most of the men who worked for us, and like Dad, he would hang around shooting the shit, until it was time for Linc to get in from school.

Sometimes we would sneak in a quickie. We'd gotten pretty creative with picking locations, and some of my favorites were banging in the back seats of some of the abandoned cars in the junkyard.

Once Linc arrived home from school, Gabe's attention became focused on him. He helped him with his homework and made sure he had a somewhat healthy afterschool snack. They would sometimes disappear for hours on end somewhere away from the shop. Whenever I would question what they were doing, Gabe would tell me they were just throwing a football around. I knew he was secretly hoping to get me to lighten up on Linc's desire to play guitar.

Although I'd been heartbroken when he'd had to go back to

Atlanta, Gabe worked double time to make it seem like we weren't apart. There were Facetime chats through the day, as well as some late at night for phone sex. While I'd been skeptical at first about if we could make a long-distance relationship work, things had rolled along well these last two weeks. Still, I did worry about what it would be like when Gabe went back on the road. Even though he assured me it wouldn't be as bad as I feared, I still couldn't help being worried.

I'd just finished inspecting the replacement of a rear deferential when I heard my name called. When I looked up, I saw one of the mothers from Linc's class in the doorway. I hurried across the floor to meet her.

"Hey Britt. What seems to be the problem?"

An embarrassed flush filled her cheeks. "I sort of ran off in a ditch on the way home last night. I think I've done something to the front wheels."

Smiling, I said, "Well, you've certainly come to the right place." I scribbled on my notepad. "I'll get someone to head outside and check on your front-end alignment."

"Thanks, Rae." As I started to call for one of the guys, Britt said, "You know, I didn't think I'd find you here this morning."

"Oh? Why not?" I questioned absently as I craned my neck to see who might be free.

"I figured you'd be at the school."

Shiiiiit. With being hot and heavy with Gabe, had I somehow forgotten something important at Linc's school? "Uh, remind me again what's happening at school today?"

"It's the talent show." Britt rolled her eyes in a huff. "I would be there myself if Mackensie hadn't chickened out at the last minute and refused to do the number she's been practicing for weeks on the piano."

I furrowed my brows at her. "What does the talent show have to do with Linc?"

"He's playing *Love Me Tender* on the guitar."

"Excuse me?"

Britt looked taken aback. "That's just what the program said."

I shook my head. "There must be some mistake. Linc doesn't even own a guitar. How could he be performing today?"

After digging in her purse, Britt produced a folded red sheet. "Here. See for yourself," she said as she handed it to me.

When I gazed down at the program, I couldn't believe my eyes. There it was in black lettering: *Lincoln Hart—Love Me Tender, guitar solo.* Blinking, I tried fighting the feeling that I had slipped into some alternate universe. The one thing I did know was that I needed to get to the school and find out what the hell was going on.

"Thanks, Britt. I, um, I gotta go."

"Rae?" Britt questioned as I sprinted past her and out the door. Of course, I realized halfway to my car that I didn't have my keys. After turning around, I hurried back inside, and Britt once again asked, "Rae?"

"I'm sorry. I just came back in to get my keys." Once I had retrieved my purse from the office, I grabbed the first man I saw, which happened to be Donnie Granger. "Go take care of Britt's car."

Wide-eyed at my breathless request, Donnie nodded. After getting in my vehicle, I tore out of the parking lot on two wheels. I didn't bother telling Dad or the others where I was going. Although it took less than five minutes to walk to Hayesville Elementary, I didn't want to waste any time.

After slinging my Passport into the first empty parking space I came across, I flung the door open and jogged inside the building then hurried down the empty hallways to the auditorium. When I threw open the door, I heard an upbeat tempo blaring from the speakers. A group of girls was doing a choreographed hip-hop dance.

When the routine ended, the principal came to the microphone. "Thank you Jenna, Keri, and Melissa for that wonderful dance. Next up we have Lincoln Hart."

My heart leapt into my throat at the sound of his name. Although I should have been glad I hadn't missed his performance, it just drove home the fact that it was really happening. Linc was playing the guitar —and not only was he playing the guitar, he was doing it in front of an audience. I suddenly had a flashback of middle school when Ryan had sung and played the guitar part for The Thunder Rolls by Garth Brooks. "This seriously can't be happening," I murmured.

As Linc walked out from behind the curtain, my chest ached. My somewhat shy son was beaming as he gazed out into the crowd. Somehow between home and school, he'd added a tie to the white button-down shirt he had put on that morning. He must've packed it in his backpack where I wouldn't see it.

Linc sat down in a chair in the center of the stage. After adjusting the guitar on his lap, he began to strum the opening chords. It made sense that he had chosen Love Me Tender—Dad was a huge Elvis Presley fan, and I was sure he'd heard the song countless times.

He played the entire song flawlessly. When he finished and applause rang out in the auditorium, his smile stretched from ear to ear. After standing up, he even took a bow. In that moment, it seemed as if he was born to perform.

Agony burned its way through my chest while tears pricked my eyes. So much of me wanted to be applauding just like the others in the auditorium, but I just couldn't bring myself to do it. I felt like the worst mother in the world for not embracing not only my son's talent, but also his pure unadulterated happiness, but each time I started to bring my hands together, I flashed back to that scene with Ryan.

No. No. No! I couldn't let that happen. I couldn't lose Linc to music. Even though it seemed extreme, I just couldn't let him become his father.

After he disappeared behind the curtain, I made my way backstage. Part of me felt like an asshole for confronting him now, like I should have let him bask in his moment of glory for the day before coming down on him when I picked him up from school. But, the other part of me wanted answers to the questions burning through my mind. How and when had he learned the guitar? After I had refused to get him one, where on earth had he gotten a guitar?

Weaving my way through kids and parents, I finally saw him. He had his back to me and was chattering incessantly to someone just outside my field of vision. He gesticulated wildly while bouncing on the balls of his feet. Just as I got to him, the person leaned in to hug Linc.

My heart shuddered to a stop, and I fought to breathe.

Gabe?

I shook my head furiously from side to side as if I could somehow clear my head and not see him before me. He couldn't possibly be standing with my son and congratulating him on doing something he knew I had forbidden. Surely Gabe would never go behind my back like that. He'd said he'd support my decisions as a parent.

When Gabe's image remained in front of me, bile rose in my throat. I swept my hand over my mouth, as I feared I'd vomit then and there.

After he pulled away from Linc, Gabe caught sight of me, and the smile on his face vanished. Sensing something was wrong, Linc turned around. His eyes widened. "M-Mom? W-What are you doing here?"

Yeah, that a good question. He'd already changed into someone I didn't know. He didn't even want me to hear him play. I'm going to be sick.

"I could ask you the same thing." My gaze flickered from Linc's to Gabe's. "*Both* of you."

Gabe jerked a hand through his hair before he stepped forward. "Listen, Rae, I can explain."

I crossed my arms over my chest. "Explain what, exactly? How you're secretly here in town and didn't think to pick up the phone to call or text me? Or how when I talked to you on the phone last night, you didn't bother to tell me my son was in a talent show? Or maybe how you seem to be supporting my son playing the guitar when you know how I feel about that?"

"You have every right to be angry with me and Linc."

Narrowing my eyes at him, I countered, "Angry? I think fucking livid is a better description for it."

After glancing around, Gabe said, "Lower your voice, okay?"

"Don't tell me what to do!" I hissed.

Linc stepped between us. "Mom, don't yell at Gabe. It's not his fault. It's all mine. I was learning to play long before Gabe came to town."

"Wait, what?" It was like I could see Linc's mouth moving, but I couldn't make out the words.

"Joey's brother has been teaching me guitar for about six months."

I stared at my child like he had suddenly grown horns. How was it possible my perfect angel had been going behind my back to do something I had *forbidden him* to do? Deceiving me. It was like he had become a perfect stranger.

Linc sighed. "I know you're mad, and I didn't mean to go behind your back. It's just I really wanted to learn the guitar."

Shaking my head, I countered, "But you know how I feel about it. You know why I don't want you to do it, yet you still did it."

The corner of Linc's lips turned down in a frown. "I know, but I thought once I learned and you saw how good I was, it wouldn't matter."

"It *does* matter. It always has, and it always will. There's no way I can just let this go."

Wincing, Linc asked, "Am I grounded?"

"Yes, for the next month."

"A month?" he questioned.

"You also won't be allowed over at Joey's house for the foreseeable future, and you give the guitar back to whoever gave it to you."

Linc's eyes bulged in horror while his lip trembled. "You mean I can't play the guitar anymore?"

"You were never supposed to play it in the first place."

"But Gabe gave me a guitar."

The world shuddered to a stop around me. Once again, I couldn't believe what I was hearing. I hoped against hope I hadn't heard correctly. "He what?"

Gabe winced before taking a step toward me. "I'm sorry, Rae. I should have come clean about this a long time ago."

"What do you mean?"

"That day at Hart and Daughter when you turned me down the

second time, I ran into Linc outside your office. Since he'd heard our conversation, he and I made a deal together."

"Let me guess—a deal for a guitar?"

Gabe nodded. "I would give him a guitar if he could get you to hang out with me."

Oh. My. God. Not only had Gabe given my son a guitar, he had manipulated me into hanging out with him. My mind spun back to seeing him after that morning. "That night when we ran into you at The Hitching Post?"

Linc swallowed hard. "I told him that was where we would be eating."

I shook my head. "I can't believe this. The two of you have been conspiring against me this entire time."

With a roll of his eyes, Gabe countered, "Don't be so dramatic. It was just that one dinner. Once you really got to know me, you were hanging out with me of your own volition. There was no collusion whatsoever."

"It doesn't matter what happened after that first night at The Hitching Post. It's the principle of the matter." Turning away from Gabe, I jerked my chin at the guitar case at Linc's feet. "Give the guitar back to Gabe." At Linc's hesitation, I growled, "Now."

The look Linc directed at me held the same punch as if he'd kicked me in the gut. While I'd already feared I was being too harsh in his punishment, the pure anguish mixed with hatred told me I'd made a serious mistake. I knew I should have taken a moment, or even a few hours to try to gather my emotions before I started doling out punishments. I wasn't just dealing with my anger and hurt with Linc; I was also dealing with my heartbreak over Gabe's involvement. *He knew why this was so vital to me. I had opened up my heart to him.*

Whirling around, I stalked over to him. "I want to talk to you—*alone.*"

"Fine," Gabe muttered.

After dragging him over to a secluded corner, I hissed, "Let's get one thing straight: Linc is my son, not yours. You don't get to voice an opinion on how I raise him, especially after going behind my back like you did with the guitar."

"I'm fully aware he's your son, but would you stop and listen to yourself? You're getting absolutely hysterical over nothing." *Hysterical. Over. Nothing.* He didn't wake up to an empty house and wonder where Mommy had gone. He didn't watch the father of my son *run* from the hospital room. *It was not nothing to me.*

"Don't you get it? It isn't nothing to me. I've worked Linc's entire life to keep him away from the guitar, and you blow in and take it upon yourself to screw all that up."

"Hey, don't pawn this all off on me. Linc was learning the guitar before I even got to town, and so fucking what if he was doing it behind your back? He loves it, not to mention, he's good at it—like really good."

"That's all you have to say to me? Did you think you should be apologizing for undermining me *and* my parenting?"

"I can't be sorry for something I really don't feel remorse for. As far as undermining your parenting, maybe someone needs to do it since you're screwing up your kid's happiness because of your own warped issues." *What the hell? Who was this man?*

I jerked my head back at Gabe's response. The Gabe I knew would never be so cruel. "My warped issues? How can you say something like that?"

"I guess I'm just a bastard like your ex. I mean, I am a musician, so I fit the mold, right?"

Shaking my head, I replied, "How could I have possibly wasted the last couple of months on someone so insensitive and clueless?"

Gabe's eyes narrowed at me. "Maybe it was just for the great sex. After all, a bastard musician like me was only ever going to be good enough to be in your bed and never fully in your life or your kid's life, right?" *That's what he thinks? Wow.*

"You seriously disgust me."

"Hmm, that's quite a change from when you're begging and pleading for me to make you come. But I'm only good for one thing, right? I guess you are like your mom—both of you needed a little musician dick to get you through the rough times."

At Gabe's comparison of me to my mother, a blood-red haze ran before my eyes. Before I could stop myself, I swung my arm out and brought my flattened palm across his face. The smack echoed through the now silent area behind the curtain.

Gabe rubbed his cheek before smirking at me. "I guess that's my cue to leave."

While I expected him to sidestep me and go out the back door, he surprised me by walking over to Linc. My heart shuddered to a stop when Gabe opened his arms, and Linc fell into them. Instead of me comforting my child, it was Gabe.

"And the winner of the Hayesville Elementary talent show is Lincoln Hart!"

Hearing Linc's name called out, coupled with everything that had just happened with Gabe, sent shockwaves reverberating through me. I knew I couldn't stay there one second more. I then did something so uncharacteristic of me.

I ran.

Sprinting out the backdoor of the auditorium, I bypassed my car and kept going on foot. Although the winter air stung my lungs and my muscles began to burn, I kept running. I didn't stop until I skidded through the front door of Harts and Flowers.

Kennedy glanced at me from behind the counter where she was adjusting some freshly baked cupcakes. After taking one look at me, she cried, "Ellie, get out here!"

"Can't it wait? I'm trying to get the last of the arrangements together for Mr. Johannsen's wake."

"*Now*," Kennedy demanded.

My frantic gaze bobbed from Kennedy over to the back of the store where Ellie had poked her head out of the curtain. "Oh shit," she murmured before she came striding toward me.

"Please tell me you guys have a tequila reserve hidden somewhere in here?" I said, barely managing to get it out as I panted.

"No tequila, but there is some rum."

I nodded. "Get it, and don't bother with a glass. I'll drink straight from the bottle."

"Oh shit," Ellie repeated.

After I collapsed on one of the overstuffed couches in the bakery area of Harts and Flowers, I watched my sisters scramble around to fulfill my request. Although I'd originally envisioned drinking from the bottle, Kennedy ended up pouring glasses for the three of us. While Ellie sat down beside me on the couch, Kennedy pulled a chair over to sit across from us.

Once I'd downed my glass and half of another one, I unloaded on Kennedy and Ellie about what had happened with Gabe and Linc.

"Fuck," Kennedy muttered.

"Yep. That pretty much sums it up."

After we sat in silence a few moments, Kennedy leaned forward in her chair. "Okay, don't kill me for this since you can be a mean drunk, but would it really be that bad for Linc to keep playing the guitar?" Kennedy asked.

I widened my eyes at her. "Whose fucking side are you on?"

"It's not about sides, Rae. It's about what's best for your son."

Pouring myself another glass of rum, I sighed. "I honestly don't know." And that was the honest to God truth. My mind kept flashing back to how happy Linc had looked playing, but it wasn't just about him being happy—he was good at it. Had I been wrong all these years about him playing an instrument? I mean, he'd been the same sweet and kind Linc these past weeks while he was playing the guitar. So far so good, right?

Ellie traced the rim of her cup, a contemplative look on her face. "You know, I've read about how being involved in music raises a child's intelligence. It can also give them a focus they can use to stay out of trouble."

I swallowed down another burning gulp of rum. "I know. I've read all that shit myself."

Kennedy snorted. "Then what's the problem? Are you afraid of being wrong?"

"Maybe…or maybe I'm afraid Linc will be a small percent the jerk his sorry excuse for a father was."

Shaking her head, Kennedy said, "Maybe it's time to realize that Ryan is Ryan and Linc is Linc. I mean, if we were really ruled by our DNA, all three of us would be fucked based on what Mom did. Last time I checked, none of us were quitters like her. Sure, we've made our fair share of mistakes when it comes to men, but we've never abandoned our family."

Ellie nodded. "Ken's right. Thankfully, we've all carried on the wonderful traits Dad gave us. The same can be said for you and Linc."

"I want to believe that—I really do. I just worry what will happen to him when he becomes a teenager."

"He's going to be a little shit as a teenager regardless if he's playing the guitar or not. I mean, remember us as teenagers?" Kennedy said. After glancing at Ellie, she grinned. "Okay, so maybe it was just me and you, Rae. Maybe he'll take after Ellie and be an angelic teenager."

Ellie and I laughed. "I could live with that," I said.

"At the end of the day, Linc is a hell of a kid with a good heart. I can't imagine him being a truly terrible teenager," Kennedy said.

Tears stung my eyes. "God, I treated him so horribly this morning. When I think of how he looked at me when I told him he had to give up the guitar…" I shuddered. "He despises me now."

"There's nothing you did or said that Linc won't forgive you for. He loves you more than anyone or anything in the world." Kennedy winked at me. "Even the guitar."

I hiccupped a laugh as I ground the tears from my eyes. "I hope so.

"I know so," Kennedy said.

Ellie nodded. "Me too."

With a groan, I eyed the coffee mug-shaped clock on the wall. "Ugh. I need to get to work."

Shaking her head, Kennedy said, "I think you need to take a mental health day today. Take an hour or so to sober up and then go back to the school and talk to Linc."

"You're right. I'm not going to be any good today until I've made things right with him."

"And what about Gabe?" Ellie cautiously asked.

An agonized sigh escaped my lips. "I can't think about him today."

"Okay, whatever, Scarlett O'Hara. When will you think about him?" Kennedy inquired.

I rolled my eyes. "Of course I'll be thinking of him. I've already thought about him the whole way over here, especially as I sucked down that rum. I just can't deal with my feelings about him today."

Ellie placed her hand on my thigh. "If he calls you, will you at least agree to talk to him?"

Yeah, I don't think I'll hold my breath for him to call. That wasn't going to happen. Not after the way we'd shredded each other. I knew how he felt about me now. I'd seen it in his eyes. Heard it in his voice.

After all, a bastard musician like me was only ever going to be good enough to be in your bed and never fully in yours and your kid's lives, right?

"I doubt he'll call, Ellie. He wasn't sorry at all for his actions. He knew I asked him to be careful about getting invested in Linc and me, because I was terrified of how he'd hurt Linc when . . . if he left. He's made his pretty position clear on what he thinks of me, my parenting, and well . . . everything."

"But if he calls—"

"I can't, not now. I need some time to think."

"Just don't take too much time," she cautioned.

"I'll try." I rose off the couch. "Now if you'll excuse me, there's a pot of coffee with my name on it just waiting to sober me up."

———

Standing outside the school's cafeteria, I waited on Linc's class to come to lunch. My skin singed under the stares of the other parents who had come to eat with their kids while my ears burned with the whispers around me. There was no doubt that what had transpired between me and Gabe had made its way through the gossip mill.

Although I would have died a thousand deaths to save myself the humiliation of facing people at the school, I knew I had to make things right with Linc. While my heart ached with what had happened with Gabe, my soul was in agony at what I had said and done to Linc.

As Linc came down the hallway toward the lunchroom, his downcast face broke my heart. While his friends chattered around him, Linc didn't appear to hear them. He was locked in his own world of grief.

"Linc!" I called.

When his gaze connected with mine, pure panic flashed across his face. Since he looked like he might bolt at any moment, I rushed forward. His friends scattered, leaving him all alone.

Tears pooled in my eyes as I hurried toward him. By the time I reached him, I was crying so hard that his image was blurred before me. Although I knew I ran the risk of driving him away by embarrassing him, I still knelt in front of him. "Oh baby, I'm so, so sorry."

"Mom?"

Swiping the tears from my cheeks, I nodded. "I would give anything in the world if I could take back the things I said to you this morning." I placed my hands on his shoulders. "Worst of all, I'm sorry I embarrassed you in front of all those people. It was your big moment, and I selfishly ruined it for you. You've worked so hard and did so well, and I'm so, so sorry."

"It's okay."

I shook my head. "No, honey, it's not. It's never okay to yell at you in front of other people, not to mention what happened with me and Gabe."

"But Mom, I'm sorry, too. I'm sorry I went behind your back to have Jeremy teach me how to play, but most of all, I'm sorry I asked Gabe to give me a guitar."

Cupping his cheek, I said, "It's okay. I understand why you did what you did."

Linc's dark eyes widened. "You do?"

"Yes, I do. Not only that, maybe you playing the guitar is not so bad."

If I hadn't been so emotionally downtrodden, I might have found

Linc's extreme expression of disbelief comical. I didn't know his mouth could open that wide. "Are you serious?" he demanded.

"Yes, I am."

"Why?"

"I had a little talk with Aunt Kennedy and Aunt Ellie."

Linc slowly shook his head back and forth. "You're really going to let me play guitar?"

Although I still wasn't completely sold on the idea, I knew I had to let go. Linc wasn't Ryan any more than I was my mother. "While I would prefer you didn't play, I will support you if that's what you want to do."

Linc took me off guard when he launched himself at me, bowling us over onto the floor. "I guess this means you forgive me?" I asked.

"Yeah, I do." Linc pulled back to give me a serious look. "But don't worry, Mom. I would have forgiven you even if you hadn't let me play guitar again."

"I know. I believe you."

When I started to lean over to kiss his cheek, Linc's eyes bulged in horror. "Mom, no! Someone will see."

I laughed. "I'm sorry. I just wanted to show you how much I love you." My chin trembled a little. "And I do love you, Linc, more than anyone else in the whole wide world. The decisions I make are ones I think are the best for you, but sometimes, I make mistakes."

"I make them too, Mom. And I love you, too."

God, it was so good hearing those words come from his mouth. I knew that this wasn't happily ever after. There were going to be tough times ahead of us; it was just part of being a mom and raising a child. I just hoped and prayed we would always have moments like these where we could say we loved each other. Where we could admit when we're wrong and forgive each other too.

"Okay, that's enough loving for now. I'm going to need you to get out of here. *Now*," Linc said, his gaze bouncing around the hallway.

And just like that, the moment was broken, but I didn't mind one bit. My boy had forgiven me, so all was right in our world.

Gabe

28

THE DOOR to Eli's guest bedroom swung open, and then a pair of heavy feet stomped across the floor and over to the window. When the curtains were jerked open, sunlight streamed into the darkened tomb of a room. Swinging an arm over my eyes, I growled, "Go away."

"It's three in the afternoon."

"I don't fucking care what time it is."

The next thing I knew, Eli had jerked my hand away from my eyes and was staring daggers down at me. "Oh, I'm well aware you don't care about the time. You also clearly don't care about any type of personal hygiene since you haven't showered for days, and you obviously don't give two shits about your liver since all you've done for the last week is drink vodka like a fucking fish."

A week ago when my relationship with Rae had gone down in flames, I'd taken refuge at Eli's townhouse. Like a pussy, I couldn't bring myself to go back home because I didn't want to be reminded of my time there with Rae. When I was completely smashed, I'd seriously contemplated burning the place down. Now I was a little more sober, I'd decided to put it on the market and start fresh somewhere new. Of course, that would require me getting out of bed and putting on clothes, which I had no desire to do.

With a grave expression, Eli shook his head at me. "I can't continue watching you do this to yourself, bro."

Sitting up, I glowered back at him. "Fine. If you're going to give me shit, I'll just go home."

"I'm not giving you shit. I'm genuinely worried about you."

Deep down, I knew he was. It was written all over his face. Especially in the dark circles under his eyes. While I tended to sleep when I was worried or depressed, Eli experienced crippling insomnia. "I do appreciate your concern. But I'd really prefer to go back to sleep."

When I started to lie back down, Eli punched me in the arm. Hard. "What the hell?" I demanded as I rubbed my aching muscle.

"You're not going to drown yourself in more booze while swimming in a pity-party. You're going to get your sorry ass up and figure out how to get Rae back."

"And what if I don't want Rae back?" I shot back. Yeah, I didn't believe me either. I was just spouting lies to cover for the fact I would never get Rae back.

"I can't be sorry for something I really don't feel remorse for. As far as undermining your parenting, maybe someone needs to do it since you're screwing up your kid's happiness because of your own warped issues."

God, how could I have said something so hurtful to her? Rae didn't have warped issues. Next to my mother and sister, she was the most devoted mother I'd ever seen. Nothing she had ever done warranted my extreme criticism.

"Give me a break, G. You call out her name in the night."

Oh shit. Had I really been doing that? "Yes, you have," Eli said, answering the questions in my mind.

"I don't know if I can get her back."

"But you haven't even tried? Have you once tried to call or text her?"

"No."

"Then how to do you know?"

My mind flashed back *again*—like it had ten thousand times in the last week—to our horrible showdown behind the curtain of the elementary school auditorium. The insults we'd hurled at each other might as well have bullets or grenades. They'd had the same wounding power. "The way we ended was brutal."

"But what if it's not the end? You may have lost the battle, but there's still a war to be won, but only if you're willing to fight."

"You've been watching *Saving Private Ryan* again, haven't you?"

Scowling at me, Eli replied, "Would you please focus on you

and Rae?"

"I am. The opening beach scene at Normandy? Yeah, that was what happened between us." With my hands, I imitated bombs bursting and machine-gun fire while simultaneously making the noises with my mouth.

I must've sounded and looked fucking crazy because Eli frowned at me. "I think we need to get some food into you. There's an IHOP right around the corner. Nobody will be expecting to see us there."

Raking my hand over my face, I groaned. "I can't look at a plate of French toast."

"Oh Jesus," Eli muttered. It seemed he remembered me telling him about going to Rafferty's to get Rae's favorite breakfast. Although he looked ready to run out of the room and never look back, he surprised me by easing down on the bed beside me. "There's something I feel I need to tell you."

Since his tone was slightly freaking me out, I replied, "Uh, okay."

"I envy what you have with Rae."

My jaw dropped down to my chest. I didn't know if I was still intoxicated, or if I'd actually heard Eli say he was envious of me. *Me.* The man who had the world at his feet was jealous of *me*? That was unfathomable. "Seriously?" I croaked.

He nodded. "You found your true other half. Rae is everything you're not, and you're everything she's not. You complete each other."

"Wow," I murmured.

"Don't you realize how special that is? I've been searching for the last two years, and I can't find it. I gotta say I'm pretty pissed that you weren't even looking, and something truly incredible fell right into your lap."

That was the truth. Rae had been incredible from the very first moments I spent with her. All sass and spark. Oh, God. Even though I was still angry at her, I knew she was the most amazing thing that *would ever* happen to me. She hadn't that I was *just a musician* and *not better for anything else.* That was on me. So on me. She'd rightly criticized me for undermining her place as decision maker for her son. *For their lives.* Her anger had been justified. And her son? That kid?

Fucking phenomenal. There was no way if I walked away from her, I would ever find something so indefinable with someone else. But if there was one thing that was also completely clear, it was this. It wasn't just about her—I would never find another Linc.

Tears stung my eyes. Feeling like an epic pansy, I ground them away with my fists. "But the things I said to her." I cringed. "I don't think I can come back from that."

"I can't imagine there's anything you said that could have been that terrible."

"I told her she was screwing up her kid's happiness. I compared Rae to her mother, who ran away with a musician. Told her that she'd just been desperate for some musician dick."

Eli recoiled back from me. "What the fuck, man?"

"She'd wounded me, and I wanted to wound her back."

"You did a fanfuckingtastic job." *Yep. That about sums it up.*

"I'm well aware of that."

Eli raked his hand over his face. "You of all people should know the power of words."

"Once again, tell me something I don't know."

"I am. You're going to have use your power for words to get Rae back."

"What do you mean?"

"Come on, asshole. Think of what brought the two of you together."

My fucking writer's block brought us together, but I had to con my way into her world to be anywhere near her after that first inspiration hit. She'd hated me. Despised me without giving me a chance. But I had been a dick to her, so I had deserved it. How did Eli think that would help win her—

Fuck.

I'm such idiot.

The power of words.

Rae understood me within the words of my songs. She had right from the beginning when I showed her the lead song on the album.

I love the symbolism of the man being a prisoner of his own insecu-

rities, which causes him to be incapable of love. And then he finds the woman who sets him free.

Was I truly incapable of love? Or had I not found the right person to love?

One thing I was absolutely certain about was that Rae *had* set me free. *In more ways than one.*

It had been right in front of my face all along. All the things I wanted to say to Rae but I didn't think I express verbally I could put into a song. "I could write her a song and then sing it to her."

"Exactly."

I nodded. "Okay, I'm going to need some things from you."

"Shoot."

"First, I need some Thai or Indian takeout. Something about spicy food gets the juices flowing."

Eli grinned. "As well as your sinuses."

I laughed, both the sound and sensation of it feeling so foreign. It had been well over a week since I'd found anything remotely funny to laugh at. "Exactly."

"What else?"

"While you order the food, I'm going to grab a shower."

"Thank God. You seriously stink to high heaven, bro."

"Whatever."

Cocking his head at me, Eli asked, "Once you have a shower and takeout, what next?"

"I'm going to need some privacy. Do you think you could manage not to burst in here for the rest of the night?"

"Now that I don't have to fear you're in here impaling yourself on your drumsticks, I will be happy to leave you alone. In fact, I'll go one step further and call Ashton to see if I can go over to her place."

Ashton was one of the backup singers for Jacob's Ladder, and Eli had been on and off again with her for over a year.

"Still trying to make it work with her?"

"Yep. Even though she's not the one, she's a lot of fun to be with." He waggled his brows. "Not to mention she gives the best head I've had in years."

I groaned. "Like I needed to know that."

"She sucks like a Hoover."

Holding up a hand, I replied, "Enough. If you don't stop, I am going to impale *you* on one of my drumsticks."

Eli laughed. "Okay, okay. I'll shut up and go order both Thai and Indian takeout." He winked at me. "I don't want there to be anything stopping you from penning just the right words to get Rae back.

"Why, Eli?"

"Because you're a great fit, G. She's your one."

When he started to rise off the bed, I reached out for his arm. "Thanks, Eli. I owe you hell of a lot."

A sincere smile spread across his face. "Glad you came to me."

"Always be there for you, man."

"I know that. You're my brother—my twin." Eli started for the door and then stopped. Turning around he said, "You know, Gabe, it's not just you having Rae that I envy."

My heartbeat skidded to a stop before restarting. "It's not?"

"I know you think—that you've always thought—you got the short end of the talent stick between the two of us and with Micah and Abby, but you are so much more than you realize. What you do with the words and the music you weave together is something I will always be envious of."

I swallowed hard, willing myself not to cry. "Fuck," I croaked.

With a chuckle, Eli said, "Now there's something. I've made the master of words speechless."

"You have, and it pisses me off because I would really like to tell you what it means to me."

"It's not necessary. I can see everything you want to say in your eyes."

I furrowed my brows. "You can?"

He nodded. "And you're welcome." Jerking his chin at the bathroom door, he added, "Now go clean yourself up. No woman would want your stinky ass."

With a laugh, I rolled my eyes. "Yeah, yeah, I'm going."

SEVEN DAYS. No, I wasn't referencing the horror movie *The Ring*, although my appearance had started to resemble Samara's over the last week. I was talking more about how long it had been since I'd seen or heard from Gabe. The last image remained burned into my mind—the one of him hugging Linc before I blew out of the auditorium and started my Forest Gump run to see Kennedy and Ellie.

For the first few days, I continuously checked my phone every other minute to see if he'd reached out to me. After I didn't receive a text or call for him, I stopped checking every few seconds. Yesterday I'd made it half the morning before I checked.

I wasn't sure why I expected him to call—I certainly hadn't left him with any indication that I wanted him to. That day at Linc's school, we'd both slung enough hurtful words at each other that I wasn't sure who had said or done worse. For the life of me, I still couldn't bring myself to be the bigger person and call him. I wanted to tell him I had been wrong about Linc playing the guitar and knew I had completely overreacted about him giving Linc a guitar.

But I didn't. I moped around the shop and the house. While I barely ate, I did manage to drink a little too much. It was quite unseemly, as Aunt Sadie would say, since I did a lot of it alone in my bedroom.

This day found me sitting outside in the front porch swing. I didn't know how long I'd been staring into space, when I heard a voice from the doorway. "Would you like some company?"

"I'm not sure I'm one for company these days," I answered honestly.

Aunt Sadie bobbed her head before ambling down the porch to the swing. Jabbing her cane at me, she said, "Scoot over."

"Fine," I muttered.

Once I'd given her adequate room to sit, she plopped down beside me and peered at me with a wry smile. "In a small town, it's much more proper if you do your grieving inside the walls of your house, rather than on the front porch."

"Is that what people are saying? That I'm grieving for Gabe?"

"No. I think the people in town are still hung up on the fact that you had a public breakup at the elementary school talent show."

I groaned. "I figured as much."

"The part about grieving inside the house came from my meddling Great-Aunt Alva after I lost George in the war." Aunt Saddie patted the bottom of the swing we sat in. "I don't know how many months I sat here, hoping against hope, that somehow the military had been wrong and he would come bounding up the sidewalk for me."

"I'm sorry for your loss, Aunt Sadie, and I really mean that. I've always felt so sorry for you that you lost the only man you ever loved."

Aunt Sadie swung her knees over to where they bumped into mine so she could face me. "Do you know why I never married?"

"Because you lost George."

Slowly, she shook her head back and forth. "George was the first love of my life, but there was a second love, one that almost broke me."

"Holy shit," I muttered. Normally, I would've tempered my language some in front of Aunt Sadie, but this earth shattering tidbit warranted a little cussing. Leaning closer to her, I asked, "Who was he?"

"His name was Elliot, and he worked at Hart Collision with your father."

Suddenly, it hit me. I remembered a man name Elliot. He had always had candy for me and my sisters when we were really little and visited my dad at the shop. I also remembered him being at the house once or twice. "Wait, did this happen like over twenty ago? Like before Kennedy, Ellie, and I were in school?"

"No, it was more like forty years ago."

I furrowed my brows at her. "But I remember an Elliot."

"As you should. He worked at the shop until he died twenty years ago." A ghost of a smile appeared on her lips "Just because we broke up, that didn't mean I had him wiped off the face of the earth or fired from his job. I can be pretty petty, but not that petty."

"What happened between you two?"

"While there were other men after George, none of them were Elliot." Drawing her shoulders back, she added, "I'll cut to the chase and leave out what led to me finding true love again at fifty, because the most important part of the story is how I lost him."

"Okay," I said tentatively.

"There was another woman in town, Viola, who Elliot had dated before me. When she saw we were getting serious, she started a campaign to make me believe Elliot still loved her. One day he didn't come over to walk me to church, and when I went by later to check on him, I found Viola leaving out his back door."

"Oh, hell no!"

"Yes, I thought as much too."

"What did you do?"

"Why I marched right up the front steps and banged on the door. When I confronted Elliot, he promised me nothing had happened, said he'd been sick and stayed home from church then when he woke up, he found her there in his house." Narrowing her eyes, she said, "He tried to say she still had a key from when they had dated, but I wasn't buying it. I told him he must have thought I was an idiot to believe such a story, and I left. For days after that, Elliott pleaded with me to believe him. He swore on his life that nothing had happened with Viola and said he could never love anyone like he loved me. Finally, he got so frustrated, he stopped calling or coming by. Although I would see him in town from time to time, he never talked to me again."

Since I knew how the story ended, I asked, "Why couldn't you believe him?"

"Plain and simple stubbornness." She gave me a knowing look. "The same kind of a stubbornness that is keeping you from calling Gabe and trying to make things work."

"Wait a minute. What happened between you and Elliott is not the same as what happened between Gabe and me," I protested.

"Is it not?"

"No. You believed a lie of betrayal perpetuated by a jealous woman where Gabe truly betrayed me."

"Betrayal is a pretty strong word for what Gabe actually did."

"Aunt Sadie, I told Gabe my history. He knew about Ryan and Mom, and how because of music, they had left me. He knew how I felt about Lincoln having a guitar, and how I feared I would lose Linc too. Is that irrational? Now, I can probably say yes. But at the time, I was terrified. Linc is my world. How do I trust someone who didn't show any remorse for helping my son to not only disobey his mom, but to do so publically?"

"Yes, I'm well aware of that."

"Are you sure you are because it doesn't seem that way from what you're saying."

Aunt Sadie pursed her lips at me. "Yes, Gabe broke your trust. And yes, in the moment, he claimed he didn't feel any remorse. But you and I both know in the heat of the moment, we say things we really don't mean. Perhaps time has tempered *his* anger. Maybe he's had time to contemplate more about the complexities of parenting a child, and how the adults must stand by each other's decisions, and never sabotage them."

I contemplated what Aunt Sadie was saying. "I guess."

"You have to remember that Gabe's insensitivity comes from the fact he's never been a parent. It was his ignorance that led him to say and do the things he did. The Gabe I know would never knowingly hurt you or Linc."

"I really don't think he meant to hurt us either," I said softly.

She nodded. "Relationships are hard and people make mistakes. Sometimes they make colossal mistakes, and sometimes they are minute ones. In the end, it isn't the mistakes themselves, but it's how you handle them. It's the ability to look past the mistake and see the heart and motive behind it."

Reaching over, she cupped my chin. "Reagan, I love you very much. I've always been immensely proud of you for finishing high school and going to college when the chips were stacked against you.

Not only are you a wonderful mother, but you're also a very good businesswoman."

I swallowed hard. Although the words seemed inadequate for how I was feeling, I replied, "Thank you, Aunt Sadie."

"So hear me out. You're being a stubborn idiot over this mess with Gabe." When I opened my mouth to protest, she shook her head. "And he is too, because he hasn't tried to reach out to you. But you know as well as I do that men are emotional babies. Trust me, you don't want to end up like me—alone and having to live each day with regret. I'll never know what could have been with Elliot where you have the chance with Gabe. You need to decide if you can look past the mistake. He needs to decide if he can learn from it and avoid making it again. And then you both need to begin to forgive and heal."

After surveying her words, I slowly nodded. "Okay. I'll try to talk to Gabe."

Relief filled her eyes. "I'm so glad you saw things my way."

I laughed. "You certainly didn't give me much choice. I was waiting for you to beat some sense into me with your cane."

She gave me a sly smile. "Well, that was my plan B."

"I'm glad it didn't come to that."

"Me too." She reached over and patted my leg. "I'm so glad you said you would talk to Gabe."

"Really?"

With a nod, she replied, "Well, firstly, he's terribly handsome."

"Aunt Sadie!" I laughed.

"But mostly because he's on his way here."

My stomach plummeted to my feet. "Excuse me?"

"I said Gabe is on his way to see you."

"But…what? I mean, how do you know that?"

"He called about an hour ago to make sure you were here." Winking, she added, "I was going to have to fake a stroke or something if you tried to leave."

I bolted out of the swing. "I can't believe you didn't tell me until now. I can't let Gabe see me like this!" I gesticulated wildly to my grease-pit hair, lack of makeup, and the Star Wars pajama pants I was wearing.

"He was in Ball Ground when he called."

"Oh shit! That means he could be here any minute. Shit!"

"Go ahead and get in the shower, honey. I'll stall him for you."

As Aunt Sadie sat there leaning on her cane, I couldn't help but think how much she reminded of me of Olenna Tyrell from *Game of Thrones*. All she needed was the medieval headdress thing and she could be her twin.

"Okay. You do that." I sprinted away from Aunt Sadie and into the house.

"Mom, can you—" Linc started to ask.

"Nope, can't. Ask one of your aunts." While I did momentarily pause to make sure he wasn't maimed or bleeding, I blew on past down the hall to the bathroom. Once again, I wouldn't be winning any Mother of the Year awards any time soon.

I was pretty sure there hadn't ever been a time I'd managed to shower and wash my hair in under ten minutes. Maybe back when I was playing for the league because I'd always feared some creep had put cameras in the showers in the locker room—it had happened to one of the other teams—but I was almost certain this time was a personal record.

After my shower, I left my hair wet while I slathered on foundation and eyeliner as fast as I could. Once I finished with my makeup, I dried my hair. Since I had yet to decide what to wear, I wrapped a towel around me. I burst out of the bathroom door and into a wall of hard flesh.

Oh shit. It took me less than a second to realize who I had bumped into. When I jerked away, I glanced up into Gabe's eyes, and I saw so many emotions burning in his baby blues: fear, amusement, hurt, anger. I was sure the same emotions were reflected in my own.

"Um, hello."

God, I'd missed hearing his voice. The deep, rumbling timbre that could make me feel comforted in one minute and incredibly horny the next.

Drawing my towel tighter around me, I said, "Hello."

"I'm assuming since you don't seem too shocked to see me, Sadie must've mentioned I was coming."

Double damn. He knew I knew, which meant he knew I had just fixed up for him. "Yes, she mentioned it." Smooth, Rae. Very smooth.

"You look good."

"Excuse me?"

Gabe winced. "I mean, you look like you're doing good."

"Thank you."

After jerking a hand through his hair, Gabe exhaled a ragged breath. "Why don't you get dressed, and I'll wait for you in the living room?"

"Maybe we should sit outside so we can be alone."

The corners of Gabe's lips quirked. "We are alone. The others just piled into Kennedy's car and left."

Well, wasn't that an interesting development? I was standing in front of Gabe half-naked while we were completely alone in the house. "I see."

"I suppose they felt we needed some privacy."

"I guess so." Before things could get any more awkward between us, I said, "Okay, I'll go get dressed, and you make yourself comfortable in the living room."

"Okay, I will."

Gabe and I then proceeded to do that awkward two-step where one person moves forward and the other one does at the same time. Each time we tried to outwit each other, we ended up bumping together again. Finally, Gabe pressed himself up against the wall and motioned for me to go. I hauled ass into my room and then slammed the door.

Since Gabe had seen me in a towel, I figured there was no point worrying about what I was going to wear. I threw on my nicest pair of jeans along with a Hart and Daughter sweatshirt. After taking a deep breath, I opened my door and started down the hall to the living room.

When I got there, Gabe was sitting on the couch, his head in his hands. At the sound of me entering the room, he jerked up. After opening and closing his mouth several times like a fish, he blurted out, "I'm a fucking asshole."

I blinked at him. "Nothing like cutting to the chase."

Shaking his head, Gabe said, "I'm sorry. My head is spinning with all the things I want to say to you. While it wasn't the most eloquent thing I could have come up with, it certainly expresses how I feel."

Easing down beside Gabe on the couch, I said, "I suppose we can start with that. You're an asshole, and I'm a bitch."

Gabe's brows shot up. "You are?"

"Don't tell me you thought I was blameless in what happened between us?"

"No, I just wouldn't put you in the bitch league."

"Oh yeah, I belong there. I was a bitch to both you and Linc." I drew in a deep breath. "Not only was I a bitch, I was wrong."

"About what?"

"Linc playing the guitar. He isn't his dad just like I'm not my mom."

At the mention of my mom, Gabe winced. "Rae, I'm so fucking sorry I compared you to your mom. I was so hurt by you that I wanted to hurt you too."

"Deep down, I know you didn't mean it. It was just hard for me to hear."

"Please know that I've regretted it every single day. It was the reason why I haven't called you."

"What do you mean?"

"I was afraid that because of the things I said, you'd never forgive me."

I widened my eyes at him. "I thought you hadn't called because you didn't *want* to forgive *me*."

Gabe smiled. "It sounds like we could really improve on our communication skills."

"I'd say so."

"You know, I wrote a song for you about what happened between us."

"You did?"

"Yes, but it's terrible."

I smiled. "That's what you always say, but your songs are always works of art."

Gabe chuckled. "No. Trust me. This one was so bad that Eli made me swear I wouldn't sing it to you."

"You're kidding?"

"I wish I was. He thinks I could probably sell it to one of those screamer bands or some goth group."

"Sounds like it was pretty dark."

With a nod, Gabe said, "It was reflecting where I've been the past week without you. More than anything in the world, I wanted to make a grand gesture to show you how sorry I was, but no matter how hard I tried, I couldn't make the right words come, the words beautiful enough to show you just how much I care for you."

I swallowed hard. "You got writer's block again?"

"I just can't seem to write a song without you, Rae."

With a sigh, I countered, "I can't be with you just so you can write songs."

"I'm well aware of that, and it's not the reason I came to see you." Leaning forward, he took my hand in his. "I can't seem to do *life* without you."

"You can't?" I questioned softly as I fought to regulate my out-of-control heartbeat.

"If there's one thing that has become abundantly clear this week, it's that I love you."

Oh God. He had said those three little words—the ones that any woman desires to hear from the man she cares about. Not only was my heart beating erratically, but now I found it hard to breathe as well.

Cupping my chin, Gabe tilted my head to look at him. "I love you, and I don't want to be without you. I don't know if you can ever forgive me for what I did, but I want you to know how sorry I am. If you do give me a second chance, I swear I will never undermine your parenting ever again. I will always be upfront and honest with you about even the tiniest detail of my private life. I promise that I'll—"

"I love you, too, Gabe!"

A beaming smile lit up his handsome face. "You do?"

"Yes, I really do."

"And you can forgive me?"

"Yes, but it's going to take some time."

Gabe's elated expression slowly faded. "It is?"

"Just because we said we're sorry to each other doesn't mean our trust in each other is magically repaired. It's going to take a little time to build it back. To look beyond our mistakes."

"You're right, it will." With a grin, he added, "I'll do everything I can to speed the process along."

"I hope so."

Taking my face in his hands, Gabe said, "I love you so much, Rae Hart."

"And I love you, Gabe Renard."

He tilted his head in thought. "How long do you think it'll be before we'll be able to get things back working in the bedroom department?"

I laughed. "Why am I not surprised you brought that up?"

"Some things never change."

"We do have the house to ourselves…"

While Gabe appeared to be momentarily lost in lascivious thoughts, he shook his head. "No. I believe we need a little romance first."

"We do?"

"Have you eaten?"

"No."

"Then I think the two of us should have a night out on the town in Hayesville."

"Which would be dinner at The Hitching Post and in bed by nine o'clock," I replied with a smile.

"It sounds wonderful." Gabe rose off the couch and then offered me his hand. "Are you in?"

"Yes, I'm in."

As we started to the door, Gabe flashed me a wicked grin. "They don't have any horse-drawn carriages around here, do they?"

NINE MONTHS later

At the screech of the guitar strings, I winced while Linc muttered, "Dammit."

I cocked my brows at him. "Hey man, watch it with the language."

"You say worse," Linc countered.

"That's no excuse. You're supposed to do as I say, not as I do."

Linc rolled his eyes. "Now you sound like Papa."

"Yeah, yeah, I'm some old fart. Now back to the music. That was supposed to be a B flat to an E flat, not a G flat." When Linc followed my instruction this time, he hit the chord perfectly. "There ya go. Now try it a few more times."

Almost a year had passed since I'd first made the deal with Linc to get a very reluctant Rae to hang out with me in return for getting him a guitar. In some ways, it seemed like just yesterday, while other times, it was hard to imagine a time in my life when Rae and Linc hadn't been a part of it.

With Rae now on board with Linc learning the guitar, he was progressing way past what he'd done in the talent show. I also liked to think he was excelling because of my expert tutelage, although with me back on tour with Jacob's Ladder, our time was somewhat more limited. Of course, whatever musical talent Linc's father had seemed to be magnified in Linc. I could totally see him pursuing music as a career, although I tried not to say that in front of Rae. While she might've made peace with Linc playing the guitar, I knew there was no way in hell she wanted him to become a musician.

As for the two of us, things were progressing as well. She'd flown out almost every weekend we'd been out on tour. Sometimes she brought Linc, but most of the time, she came by herself. While trying to have private time with my girl, I could see why each of the members of Runaway Train had eventually bought their own tour bus when they settled down. Even though she got along great with my siblings and the road crew, I didn't like sharing what time I had with Rae with the others. I also didn't like our lovemaking being tempered because Rae was afraid Eli and the others would hear her.

Others might have thought we hadn't been together long enough to be thinking of the long-term, but I really didn't give a shit what they thought. I knew without a shadow of a doubt that there was only one woman in the world for me, and I'd found her in the backwoods of Georgia. I wanted to build a life with Rae, and because of that fact, I'd been doing some serious thinking about popping the question. I just needed to talk to Linc first, and when I glanced up to look at him, I knew there was no time like the present.

"Can you put the guitar down, buddy?" I asked.

When he scowled at me, I felt like I was looking at Rae. "But we still have fifteen minutes of practice time."

"I know that. It's just, I need to talk to you about something... something really important."

"If this is the facts-of-life stuff, I already know it."

"You do?"

"Yeah. Papa talked to me about it last year."

"While I'm glad you're informed about sex, that's not what I want to talk to you about."

"Fine," Linc muttered. He swiveled in his chair to put the guitar back in its case. Once he was finished, he peered expectantly at me. "So, what's so important that it cuts off my music lesson?"

Now that I had his full attention, I found myself feeling extremely nervous, like I was sitting in an interrogation room with a light beaming down on me. I wiped my suddenly sweaty palms on my jeans before I cleared my throat. "Your mom and I have been dating for a while now."

Tilting his head, Linc appeared lost in thought. "How long has it been?"

"Eleven months."

"Is that a long time?"

It is when you've previously been a commitment-phobic asshole.
"For some people, it is, and for others, it isn't. I feel like it's a long
time for your mom and me—long enough for me to know how I feel
about her."

"You're not breaking up with her, are you?"

I chuckled. "Hell no. She's the only woman for me, ever."

Linc exhaled a relieved breath. "You scared me there for a minute."

"I'm sorry." I leaned forward in my chair. "Not only do I love your
mother, I want to spend the rest of my life with her. I'm planning on
asking her to marry me."

"You are?"

"Yes, I am."

Linc shot out of his chair to throw his arms around my neck.
"That's awesome. And you'll be my stepdad?"

"Yep, I sure will."

He pulled back to stare wide-eyed at me. "I can't believe it."

I chuckled. "I'm glad you're happy about it."

Confusion suddenly replaced the elation on his face. "Wait, you
said you were *planning* to ask Mom to marry you. Does that mean you
haven't asked her yet?"

"That's right."

"Shouldn't you be telling her first before you tell me?"

I smiled. "In a way, yes, but here's the thing: there's an old custom
where a man asks the father of the woman he loves if he can marry her.
It's a way to show respect to your future father-in-law." I reached out
to place my hands on his shoulders. "Instead of going to your Papa, I
wanted to ask you if I had your permission to marry your mother."

Linc's mouth gaped open. "You want *my* permission?"

"Yes, I do. Although your mom loves her dad very much, you are
the center of her world. You will be the one most affected by us getting
married, so it only seemed fair to ask you."

When Linc's brown eyes pooled with tears, my throat constricted,
and I felt like someone had punched through my chest to squeeze
my heart.

"You're the only guy in the whole wide world I'd want to marry my mom."

Linc's statement sent me over the edge. Overcome by emotion, I jerked him against my chest. "You don't know how proud I am to hear you say that, buddy." After squeezing him tight, I eased him back to smile at him. "I promise I'll be a good husband to her, and I'll do my best not to hurt her or you."

"You better."

"I will."

A quizzical expression came over Linc's face. "Have you gotten Mom a ring?"

Once again, I had to laugh at just how much of an old soul he was. "No, not yet. I wanted to make sure things were square between the two of us before I dropped a chunk of change on a ring."

"Can I help you pick it out?"

"Sure you can. You probably know more about what she likes when it comes to jewelry than I do."

He frowned a little. "I don't know. Maybe I could also ask Aunt Kennedy and Aunt Ellie."

"Actually, buddy, I'd like to keep this just between the two of us."

As Linc nodded, he held up his right hand. "I won't say anything. I promise."

I grinned at him. "I trust you. You did a great job of keeping our guitar secret."

"I did, didn't I?"

"Yep." I jerked my chin at his guitar case. "Speaking of, we better pack up the sheet music and head out. Your mom will kill us if we're late for dinner."

"Okay." He started shuffling the music back into his folder. When he reached to pick up his case, he froze.

"What is it?" I asked.

He turned to stare intently at me. "Are you guys going to have kids?"

Holy shit. He wasn't holding back with that loaded question. I swallowed hard. "Uh, well, we really haven't talked about it."

"I think Mom would like to have more kids, maybe a little girl," Linc replied thoughtfully.

"She probably would." I smiled to myself at the thought of having a sassy little girl with Rae.

"What about you? Do *you* want kids?"

Since I knew Linc deserved absolute honesty, I decided it was best to tell him the truth and not sugarcoat it. "You know, I wasn't sure I really wanted kids before I met your mother." I smiled at him. "But then I met you, and everything about you has changed my mind." When Linc remained quiet, I asked, "What about you? Are you on board if we decide to have more kids?"

He nodded. "That would be cool."

"Then what's with the mood change?"

After nibbling on his lip—a trait that was so much like his mother —he peeked up at me. "I was just thinking that even if you guys did have kids, maybe you might adopt me."

Talk about feeling like I'd been sucker-punched and roundhouse-kicked in the balls. Linc had really pulled out all the stops with that question. Although I had thought about it before, it hadn't seem real until the words had come from his mouth. I guess I'd never stopped to imagine that he would want me to adopt him. Sure, I thought he would be fine with me being his stepdad, but there was a whole new level of meaning with taking on my name and legally being my child.

I drew in a deep breath. "Even though I don't need to have a piece of paper that tells me you're my son, of course I would want to adopt you. It's just…complicated."

With his eyes lit up like one of the stage lights during a show, Linc danced around my chair. "I can't believe I'm going to be your son!"

"Wait a minute, Linc, didn't you hear me when I said it would be complicated?"

"Why does it have to be complicated?"

"Because of a lot of legal bullshit. First, we'd have to get your mom on board—"

Sweeping his hands to his hips matter-of-factly, Linc asked, "Do you seriously think she would say no?"

I laughed. "No, I don't think she would, but she's only a small step. The big step is your real father has to give up all his rights to you. That means your mom would have to track him down and then he would have to sign the legal papers."

Linc's face fell. "Oh. That does sound complicated."

Reaching out, I ruffled his hair. "Complicated, but not impossible."

"Does that mean you'll try?"

"Of course I will. After I talk to your mom about it, we'll start looking into it before we get married." With a laugh, I shook my head. "I'm probably putting the cart before the horse on that one considering I need to ask her to marry me first."

"When do you think you'll do that?"

I shrugged. "I dunno. After I get the ring, I'll wait until the moment feels right."

"That sounds like a good plan."

When my phone dinged in my pocket, I grabbed Linc's guitar case. "Come on. I bet you a hundred bucks that's your mom giving me grief for being late."

Linc rolled his eyes. "Just tell her you're a man and you'll come to dinner when you're good and ready."

Tsking at him, I said, "And here I thought you had women all figured out."

"Jeez, give me a break. I'm only ten."

TWO MONTHS *later*

"Pinch me," I murmured.

Gabe laughed. "Only if I can pinch your ass or your nipple."

I smacked his arm with my free hand. "Way to ruin a moment."

"My apologies." Gabe released my other hand and brought his hand to my arm then gave it a gentle pinch. "There, how was that?"

"I'm still standing in front of the Eiffel Tower, so it's not just a wonderful dream. It really is real life."

Many, many months ago, I'd told Gabe how I wanted to eat French toast or crepes in Paris. Somehow, he hadn't forgotten that random comment, and when my birthday month rolled around, he presented me with two first class tickets to Paris. We'd arrived the previous day just in time for my birthday the next day, and even though our hotel suite boasted the most amazing view of the Eiffel Tower, I hadn't actually gotten to stand in front of it until this moment.

After breakfast in bed led to a lengthy sexathon and subsequent nap, it was after five o'clock before we dragged ourselves out of the hotel room. After three orgasms, I certainly wasn't complaining about being slightly delayed in seeing the tower in person.

As I stood staring up at the intricate metal structure, I found it surreal that the girl who had barely been outside of Georgia was about to celebrate her twenty-eighth birthday in Paris. "I feel just like Carrie in *Sex and the City*."

With a chuckle, Gabe replied, "Does that mean I'm your Big?"

I grinned. "Yes, except without all the douchey behavior."

"I'll take it." He wagged his brows. "Especially the big part."

Elbowing him, I said, "Don't make sexual innuendos in front of the Eiffel Tower. It's far too classy."

"Babe, I'm pretty sure it's heard much worse, not to mention what it's seen." As he shielded his eyes from the setting sun, he added, "Man, it must be a rush to fuck up there."

"Only you would stand in front of the Eiffel Tower and think about sex. Besides, I seriously doubt that happens."

"Oh, I'm sure numerous people have been caught, not to mention the ones who threw enough money at the guards to have some after-hours fun." Gabe waggled his brows at me. "Want me to see what the going rate is for a post-sunset quickie?"

Although I normally wasn't one to shy away from sex in public places, I didn't think I could possibly have sex on the Eiffel Tower. I mean, what if we got arrested? How would I ever explain to Linc why I was being detained in a Parisian jail? I quickly shook my head back and forth. "No. I'm good."

Gabe bent over to place his palm on my bare thigh. As his hand started underneath my skirt, he asked, "Maybe a finger bang in a corner?"

With a shriek, I jerked away from him. "Once again, I'm going to have to say no."

"I'm really digging you in this dress. It's very *accessible*."

I jabbed my index finger into his chest. "That's it—no more horny sex-talk. I don't want to hear anything else come out of your lips that isn't romantic."

"Exactly how would you define 'romantic'?"

Rolling my eyes at him, I replied, "Um, hello, you're the song-writer. Figure it out."

Gabe chuckled. "Fine. You win."

I cupped my hand over my ear. "And what sweet nothings would you like to say to me?"

"That even though you're a pain in my ass, I love you very much."

"You're impossible," I huffed.

Tilting his head at me, Gabe smiled. "There isn't another woman on earth I'd rather talk dirty to than you. You are my ultimate fantasy, live and in the flesh. I dream of your mouth against mine, your lips on my skin, the feel of your soft curves beneath my body. There is no greater heaven on earth than being buried deep inside you, our bodies joined together as one."

His words sent a shudder through me. I didn't know why I was surprised that he had found a way to mix in sex with the romance. He was a songwriter for goodness' sake. Pressing myself against him, I murmured, "Thank you."

"You're welcome." He dipped his head to bring his mouth to mine, his lips soft and tender against my own. Each and every time he kissed me, I fell just a little more in love with him. There was something about the way he exuded such emotion through his kisses. Even though he could pen such words of love in his songs, sometimes he still had a difficult time vocalizing them.

When he finally pulled away, I was breathless, and damn him if I didn't have a slow ache burning between my legs. I became utterly and completely wanton when it came to Gabe, an insatiable sex fiend who craved more and more.

At what must've been the lust burning in my eyes, he grinned at me. "Ready to go to dinner?"

"Yes, asshole," I grumbled.

With a hearty laugh, Gabe replied, "We can always go back to the hotel room."

I shook my head furiously from side to side. "Oh no, mister. There's no way I'm missing out on my VIP dinner at Jules Verne."

Gabe held up his hands. "It was just a suggestion."

Pointing at the elevators, I commanded, "Let's go—now."

"Yes ma'am."

After emitting a moan of pure ecstasy, I lay my napkin down on my now empty plate. "Oh my God, I don't think I've ever been so stuffed."

"What about dessert?" Gabe asked.

I widened my eyes. "Are you kidding me? I'm not sure I'll eat the rest of the trip, least of all try to eat anything else tonight."

He chuckled. "Then how about we go up for drink at the champagne bar and take in the views?"

"As long as it's okay that I'm waddling slightly, then I would love to."

After Gabe paid the check, he held out his hand to me. "Come on, my little Oompa Loompa," he teased.

I playfully smacked his arm. "While I might feel like an Oompa Loompa, I most certainly don't look like one."

"You are wearing a purple dress," he remarked as he we headed to the coat check.

"Keep it up, Mr. Renard, and you'll be able to tell Trip Advisor how well that couch in the suite's living room sleeps."

Gabe smirked. "Like you would really toss me out of bed."

"You should know me well enough not to tempt me," I countered.

Dipping his head, Gabe whispered in my ear, "But who would be there to give you orgasms if I wasn't in bed with you?"

I flashed him a wicked grin. "Considering this is Paris, I'm pretty sure I could find many devices to satisfy me."

"None of those devices are as good as my tongue or my dick."

"While I might disagree, there's nothing like you spooning me or waking up beside you."

With a smile, Gabe said, "That's more like it."

After Gabe helped me into my coat, he slid his on as well, and we then took the elevator up to the champagne bar. After weaving our way through the crowd, we got in line for a glass of bubbly.

When we reached the front, a man in a crisp black suit asked, "Good evening. The rose or the white?"

After glancing over at me, I said, "The rose."

Gabe nodded. "We'll take two."

Once we had our glasses, Gabe and I moved to one of the less crowded corners of the observation deck. My hair and clothes rippled in the gentle breeze, and when I shivered in the cold, Gabe wrapped an arm around me. "Are you okay?" he asked, concern vibrating in his voice.

"I'm fine." Gazing out into the glittering night sky, I murmured, "Have you ever seen anything more beautiful?"

"Yes."

I smiled up at him. "After traveling so much, I'm sure you have."

"Actually, I have the pleasure seeing my most beautiful every day."

When I got his meaning, my heartbeat thrummed wildly. "Aw, thank you, babe. I'd have to say you're pretty impressive to look at every day, too."

Gabe grinned. "But do I compare to this view?"

"You far outrival it." Bolstered by both the champagne I'd been sipping along with the slight headiness the altitude brought, I leaned in to whisper in his ear. "I'd say your cock alone is far more magnificent."

A shudder rippled through Gabe, and I wasn't sure if it was because of my flirty words or because of the cold.

"I like your way of thinking," he said with a smirk.

I giggled. "I thought you would."

Pulling back from him a bit, I leaned in to get a closer look through the crisscrossing wire. "It's amazing how many buildings are squashed into such a small area. It's so much different than home," I mused while taking another sip of champagne.

Suddenly Gabe wasn't beside me anymore. When I glanced over my shoulder to see where he had gone, a screech erupted from my lips and my hands flew to cover my mouth. "Oh my God," I murmured as I spun around to face Gabe. The man I loved with all my heart and soul was down on one knee with a turquoise box in his hands. Although I might not have been out of Georgia much, I knew that box could only be from one place—Tiffany's. Once again, the only words I could muster were, "Oh my God!"

Gabe smiled up at me. "Reagan Margaret Hart, my muse and my love, I want to spend the rest of my life making music with you. Two months ago, I asked Linc if I could have your hand in marriage. Today, I'm asking you." When tears pooled in Gabe's eyes, it was my undoing. "Rae, will you marry me?"

His image blurred before me as I let myself go and sobbed openly.

245

I couldn't believe what he was saying. He had asked Linc's permission to marry me. He loved my son enough to ask him if he would be okay with us getting married. Gabe loved me enough to want to include my son in one of the biggest decisions of his life. Just when I thought I couldn't love him any more than I already did, my heart grew just a little more.

"Rae?" he questioned.

"Yes! Yes, of course I will marry you!" I cried as I lunged forward. I threw my arms around his neck and the momentum sent us toppling to the ground. As I lay there entwined in Gabe's arms, I began kissing every square inch of him that I could reach—his cheeks, his nose, his mouth, his neck, his temples. I tried to emulate what he did with his kisses, to show him just what I wanted to say but somehow couldn't. I wanted him to know he had made me the happiest woman on earth by loving me and loving my child.

At the sound of applause behind us, I couldn't help laughing at the absurdity of the moment. There we were rolling around on the top floor of the Eiffel Tower while tourists clapped for us. I knew this was a moment I would remember for the rest of my life.

"I guess we better get up," I said.

"They could just step over us," Gabe suggested with a grin.

"Whatever. Come on."

Once I pulled myself off him, Gabe rose to his feet. When we were both upright again, He reached into the turquoise box in his hand. I was shocked that he had managed to hold on to it after me tackling him.

Taking my hand in his, he slid the ring on my finger. "Now it's official. You are the future Mrs. Gabriel Renard."

Although it was dark outside, I held my hand up to gaze at the ring. "It's beautiful."

"You really like it?"

"I love it. It's everything I could have hoped for." I winked at him. "Okay, maybe it's a hell of a lot bigger than what I ever hoped for, but I'll take it."

Gabe laughed. "While I normally like to think when it comes to rings, go big or go home, it was Linc who brought me down a carat."

I widened my eyes at Gabe. "You picked a bigger ring?"

He nodded. "But Linc made the very good point that it wouldn't be very practical in your line of work."

I realized then that he had not only asked Linc's permission to marry me, they had gone ring shopping together. "I've got to say I would have loved to have been a fly on the wall when you two were looking at rings—and when in the world did you take him to Tiffany's?"

"When you guys flew up to New York for the opening of the tour."

I laughed. "Now I remember. You guys were acting so weird that day, and although you said you were just going shopping, you wouldn't let me come with you."

Gabe nodded. "I had to lie and tell you we were going to hit several music stores to shop for guitars, which I knew was the easiest way to get you to stay at the hotel."

"You're right, but it never dawned on me when you two got back that you didn't buy anything."

"Oh, trust me, we bought something."

"I can't wait to call him and tell him the news. Let's see, if it's nine o'clock here, then it's three o'clock there. What would he be doing right now?"

"Your dad will have just picked him up from school, and they'd be heading back to the shop or to his and Stella's house. They'll probably make a pit stop at Harts and Flowers for Linc to get a snack and for your dad to get a coffee."

It warmed my heart that Gabe knew the little ins and outs of Linc's schedule. "You're right. We'll call him the minute we get back to the hotel room."

"Speaking of the hotel room, what do you say we head on back?"

"But it's only nine o'clock—the night's still so young. I mean, they don't call it the City of Light for nothing," I protested.

Gabe pulled me into his arms. Nuzzling my neck, he asked, "Don't you want to go back and make love for the first time as an engaged couple?"

As his warm breath fanned over my skin, I shivered. "Yes, I do," I murmured.

"Then let's get the hell out of here."

Although I wanted to stroll the streets until the wee hours of the morning, I decided to give in to both my fiancé's voracious sexual appetite and my own—but I wasn't going down without a fight. "Let's make one thing clear, Mr. Renard: tomorrow there will be no sex of any kind until I've toured the Louvre and seen Notre-Dame."

"What happens if I wake up with morning wood?" Gabe asked as we started for the elevator.

Batting my eyelashes, I replied, "You can jerk it out during the shower you'll be taking so we can leave the hotel to see the Louvre and Notre-Dame."

Throwing his head back, Gabe chuckled heartily. "Wow, I thought the sex wasn't supposed to wane until after the wedding, not after the engagement."

"I only said I was momentarily withholding in order to see the sights. Once I've seen those two things, you can take me back to the hotel and ravish me continuously until it's time to go to dinner, which will be at a romantic restaurant of my choosing."

"Damn, you drive a hard bargain," he replied playfully as we got on the elevator.

"But you love me anyway, don't you?"

He smiled down at me. "I sure as hell do." He dipped down to plant a tender kiss on my lips. "I love you more than I can ever say, even with the words I can string together in the lyrics of a song."

"I think you did a pretty amazing job with the ones on *Ray of Light*."

"True, but I wrote those before we were engaged, before we were really truly and completely in love. I can't imagine how I will write now."

When he furrowed his brows, I gasped. "Don't tell me you think you're going to get another case of writer's block?"

"Are you kidding? Between getting engaged and getting married, I'll have plenty of material to work with."

I exhaled a relieved breath. "You had me worried there."

"Sorry. I was only trying to think how I could possibly put everything that has happened this last year into just twelve to fourteen songs."

"If anyone can find a way to do it, it's you. You're an amazing songwriter, not to mention an amazing fiancé."

"And lover?"

"Oh yes, very much an amazing lover. You're going to be an amazing stepfather to Linc, too."

As we started out into the crowd leaving the Eiffel Tower, Gabe said, "I'm not so sure about being Linc's stepfather."

His words and tone caused my heart to shudder and restart. "You aren't?" I asked tentatively.

Gabe shook his head. "He and I were talking, and I think it would be better if I adopted him."

Oh. My. God. Had he just said what I thought he had? My knees gave out and I lunged forward. I would have face-planted in front of the Eiffel Tower if Gabe hadn't caught me.

"Jesus, Rae, are you all right?" Gabe demanded as he slid a strong arm around my waist.

"I'm fine. It was just a little bit of a rush."

Since I was still a little shaky, Gabe steered me over to a bench. After I sat down, he knelt in front of me. "Feeling better?"

"Yes."

Frowning slightly, he said, "If you don't want me to adopt Linc, I don't have to."

"You think I almost passed out because I don't want you to adopt my son?"

"Yeah."

I cupped his face in my hands. "I would be honored for you to be Linc's father. Besides marrying you, nothing would make me happier."

Gabe's face lit up. "Really?"

"Yes, really."

"Even though I don't easily relate to kids and can sometimes be impatient?"

I laughed. "You'll do fine. You have so much love in your heart to give to Linc."

"And to our children."

Sweeping my hand to my forehead, I said, "Whoa now, let's not get too crazy."

"You don't want to have five or six?" Gabe asked teasingly.

"Do you seriously want me to pass out?" I replied.

"All joking aside, Rae, I want us to be a complete family. I want you and Linc to carry my name."

"So do I." I smiled at him. "And I want to give you a baby. Maybe not five, but I want to see you hold a piece of yourself in your arms."

"I'd like that very much."

"Then let's go back to the hotel and start practicing for the day when you get me pregnant."

Gabe laughed. "I like that idea very much."

acknowledgements

Eternal gratitude always to my beta reader/plot adviser extraordinaire , **Kim Bias**.

To my content editor and manuscript magic maker, **Marion Archer**—I always say I can never put out a novel without you, and it's the truth.

Thanks to **Lauren Perry of Perrywinkle Photography** for the wonderful photoshoot of the Chatwin's. It was so fun flying out to Salt Lake to watch the shoot.

Thanks to **Darick and Cara Chatwin** for being my cover couple. It was amazing not only to find twins who fit the descriptions in my mind, but to find they were both married to the female counterparts I needed was truly amazing.

Thanks also to **Lori Jackson** for the beautiful interior design and gorgeous teasers.

And many, many thanks to the readers who loved the Runaway Train series and wanted to see books about Eli and Gabe.

Katie Ashley is a New York Times, USA Today, and Amazon Best-Selling author of both Indie and Traditionally published books. She lives outside of Atlanta, Georgia with her daughter, Olivia, her spoiled mutt, Duke, and her cats Harry and Hermoine. She has a slight obsession with Pinterest, The Golden Girls, Shakespeare, Harry Potter, Star Wars, and Scooby-Doo.

With a BA in English, a BS in Secondary English Education, and a Masters in Adolescent English Education, she spent eleven years teaching both middle and high school English, as well as a few adjunct college English classes. As of January 2013, she became a full-time writer. She loves traveling the country and world meeting readers.

www.katieashleybooks.com
katieashleyromance@gmail.com